# The Reawakening *of* Mage Axum

## TUCKER AXUM

The Reawakening of Mage Axum

Copyright © 2020 by Tucker Axum
www.tuckeraxum.com

First published as an eBook on Memorial Day 2015, aboard the
USNS Mercy (T-AH-19), while docked in Pearl Harbor, Hawaii.

Second Edition, Revised
ISBN 978-0-9979927-3-1 (Paperback)
ISBN 978-0-9979927-0-0 (eBook)

Library of Congress Control Number 2020911665

This is a work of fiction inspired by real events.
The author has taken creative liberty with details to
enhance the reader's experience.

Printed in the United States of America

*To the men and women who served the United States of America during World War II (1939-1945). Your courageous and selfless service contributed to our world's freedom. Thank you.*

# CHAPTER ONE

*November 1944*

THE SOLDIER OPENED his eyes. He felt groggy and his pupils struggled to focus. *Perhaps it was a dream. No,* he figured. *It seemed too real. And my body aches everywhere, like the worst beating of my life.*

The soft voices of nurses filled the air as they attended to at least a dozen men on beds. A small window and a few ceiling bulbs illuminated the cramped area.

"Where am I?" he rasped. His throat burned from dryness. His fading dream and the lyrical murmurings of nurses caring for the wounded soldiers provided his only clues. He groaned out in pain as he strained to pull his weak arms from under the tight bed covers. He touched his face. The stubble indicated he had been there for at least several days.

A young nurse with delicate features and angelic eyes appeared at his side. She spoke in accented English. "Don't move. You must rest." She placed her hand on his forehead. "You have a very high fever."

"Please, ma'am, where am I?"

She put her finger to her lips. "Shh," she whispered. She

grabbed a damp cloth from a nearby tray and wiped away the sweat from his brow and cheeks.

"You must take the pill and drink the water," she said. "It will help you relax and feel better."

"I don't want to relax. I need to know." He was now pleading. "Where am I?"

"Be quiet," she said sternly. "You will disturb the others."

She forced the pill into his mouth, but he jerked his head away and spit it onto the floor.

Another nurse drawn by the commotion ran over to them with a syringe in her hand. She jammed it through the sheet and into his thigh.

"Ah!" he cried out from the impact.

Panic-stricken, his eyes widened like saucers. "Who are you?" he yelled out. "Where am I?"

"Go to sleep," the nurse's voice droned in slow motion. "We'll try this again tomorrow."

The injection proved too strong to resist. He became drowsy and his eyelids fluttered with a heaviness. Then all went dark.

# CHAPTER TWO

THE RESTING SOLDIER trembled from chills. He tightened the blanket over his frail body to harness all the heat he could. As he lay shivering, a hand touched his shoulder. He jolted awake and saw a tall, slender man over him.

This man's concerned look prompted the soldier to blurt out: "God! I must be dead or dying if you're here."

Dressed in an ankle-length robe and a white-cotton collar, the priest leaned in and smiled. "Thank you for the compliment, but I'm not God, and you're not dead. But you will be if you keep fighting the nurses."

His thigh pulsated from pain and he remembered the old nurse stabbing him with the largest needle he had ever seen.

"They were trying to give you this," the priest pinched a white tablet between his thumb and index. "It will stop your fever."

"Who are you?"

"I'm Father Sidney."

"Where am I?"

"You're in a hospital in the allied territory of France."

"France," the soldier repeated. "That explains the accents, but it doesn't explain how I ended up here."

"The good news is you're no longer on the battlefield, but there is one burning question." The priest pointed to the paper bracelet on the soldier's wrist. "UNK" was handwritten in black ink. "What is your name?"

The soldier stared wide-eyed at the priest. A knot formed in the pit of his stomach. "I-I don't know. I can't remember. It's all foggy, like I'm living a bad dream. It must be that medicine the nurse forced in me."

"You're not dreaming, and that shot was to help you calm down. Please take this for your fever."

The soldier tossed the pill in his mouth and took several gulps of water, some spilling onto his chest. He grasped at his neck. "Where are my dog tags? That'll tell you my name."

"You arrived several weeks ago with nothing," the cleric said. "No identifying objects, not even any clothes. To my knowledge, this is the first that you have spoken. Your accent sounds American."

The patient focused on the priest's blond hair and sunken green eyes that communicated a sad humanity. "Yes, I'm American. I'm a soldier. I was in battle. My platoon was ambushed."

The priest leaned in, encouraged by his apparent progress. "What is your name?"

The soldier glanced away, lost in thought. So much was unfamiliar. Even his skin and body felt differently. He felt frustrated. "I'm a grown man and can't even remember my own name."

"Give it time. It'll come to you."

"You keep saying that, but according to you, I've been here for weeks. Is there nobody looking for me?"

"Of course, people are concerned and looking for you, but without knowing who you are, it's like searching for a needle in a haystack."

"Father Sidney, can you please get me a mirror?"

"Good idea." The priest excused himself for a minute while he searched for one. He returned with a pocket mirror. "This is the best I could find."

The soldier looked at the image and almost dropped the mirror. "This ain't me! I may not know my name, but I do know this is *not* my face."

"I realize it's hard to recognize with the swelling and bruising."

With the mirror in his left hand, he used his right to touch his nose, cheeks, lips, and ears. His exploration provided no clues to his identity.

"Your face will continue to heal. Keep the mirror for as long as you need it. I'm sure your name will come to you."

The soldier's face became distressed. "Father, I'm not going crazy. I promise you. I must be suffering from amnesia." The forlorn soldier implored the priest. "You've got to help me."

"I will help you. Give it some time. I've got to make my rounds with the other patients. I promise to come back. In the meantime, here's an English pamphlet to pass the time."

"I don't want to pass the time, Father! And I don't want to read that book. Without my name, I'm nothing but a ghost!" Tears swelled in the soldier's eyes. "Please, help me remember my name."

# CHAPTER THREE

**M**OST MEDICS PATCHED up the injured soldiers in the field and sent them back to the frontlines. The overcrowded hospital in France treated only the most severely wounded patients. So, there were no meaningful conversations with the other patients. The soldier felt hopeless and alone. He grabbed the booklet Father Sidney had given him and started to read it. When he finished, he'd read it again. He stopped only when a nurse brought his food, usually a bowl of soup and bread. He devoured the meals and felt his strength slowly returning.

"Father, in here!" he exclaimed when he saw the priest making his regular rounds. "Please, come over here."

The priest's face lit up. "You are looking much better my friend."

"Yes," the soldier smiled. "Your boss works in mysterious ways."

"That's the rumor," the priest chuckled.

"You gave me this." He held up the booklet. "I've read it several times from cover to cover, and something has been stirring inside me."

The priest appeared pleased. "God's word is alive and active."

"Could I get something to write with?"

The priest found a stub of pencil nearby.

The patient circled the word "image" on the pamphlet cover. "I've been remembering so many names, but none are ringing a bell. Then the word *image* jumped right off the page. That's when things started to make sense."

"Go on. I'm listening," Father Sidney said.

"I'm Mage."

# CHAPTER FOUR

"**O**NE OF MY patients has presented me with an unprecedented challenge," Father Sidney explained to the military official visiting the hospital that dreary afternoon.

"Are you referring to *our* guy? The one who finally woke up?" Lieutenant Blackwell asked.

"Yes," Father Sidney answered.

"I thought he was going to sleep through the whole damn war. Pardon my French, Father."

The lieutenant's sarcasm annoyed the priest. "That this soldier is even alive is a miracle," Father Sidney reminded the young officer.

Like many soldiers, the officer became more jaded each day as the war waged. "Indeed, Father. I guess we should thank God for that."

"Amen," Father Sidney replied. "Perhaps when this war is over, you'll trade that uniform for one like mine."

Lieutenant Blackwell started laughing. "Father, what I've seen while wearing this uniform has scarred me enough that I could never wear your uniform in good conscience. There can't be a God when all this is going on. No offense, Father."

"None taken, although I think it's important to be reminded that people see God in the little things. Your uniform brings people hope, but now that the Americans are here, people *actually* believe this war could end."

Lieutenant Blackwell scoffed and took a drag from his cigarette. "Oh, it'll end one way or another. Whether our souls are intact is a whole other matter."

Father Sidney lazily swatted the cloud of smoke with his hand. "Well, the good news is that his appetite is returning. He's eating well and putting on some weight."

"That is good news. There's no saying how long he was exposed to the elements or having endured starvation. The troops found him in a thicket. He probably crawled there to escape capture. His will to survive is strong. He must have something or someone very dear to him back home."

Father Sidney nodded. He was impressed that at least the military official could recognize that hint of goodness. "He hasn't mentioned anything like that yet, but he is remembering new information every day. Of course, I can't vouch for the accuracy of those memories, especially since the man has settled on the odd name of Mage."

"That is an odd name. I knew a Gage once but never heard of a Mage."

"You think it might be short for major?"

"Negative. We don't have any officers being treated here." The young lieutenant thought it over for a second. "Father, you have a direct line to the Man Upstairs. Have you reached out to Him to see what He thinks?"

Father Sidney smiled. "I hadn't thought of that. I'll give it a try. But in case God is really busy in the meantime, is there any other information about this soldier you can share with me?"

He took another drag of his cigarette. "Nope. That's all I got, Father."

"Well, I shall find my encouragement in the parable of the lost sheep."

"Don't think I know that one," the lieutenant commented.

"Which of you men, if you had one hundred sheep and lost one of them, wouldn't leave the ninety-nine in the wilderness and go after the one that was lost until he found it? When he has found it, he carries it on his shoulders, rejoicing."

"Don't hurt your back carrying him, Father."

Father Sidney turned to walk away.

"Wait a minute, Father. There is one more thing."

Father Sidney stopped mid stride. "Anything could be helpful."

"You can always write to the War Department. They will have more information than me. After all, everything filters through Washington."

"Should I do that before or after I reach out to the Man Upstairs?" Father Sidney jested.

Lieutenant Blackwell laughed. "I enjoy my banters with you."

"And I with you," Father Sidney said.

"I'd first reach out to the War Department. They'll most likely take longer to get back to you."

# CHAPTER FIVE

THE TAXI DRIVER removed his wool gloves and hunter's hat when he sat at the card table in the breakroom. He unscrewed the metal cup from his thermos and filled it with steaming hot coffee. He cradled the cup with both hands to thaw his fingers. "My old bones can't weather the cold like they could when I was still a young man," he said.

"Please don't take your coat off yet, Mr. Percy. I got one more run for you to make."

"My shift ends in ten minutes, boy. Where's the fella wanting to go?"

The *boy* was the owner's eldest son, and was forced to drop out of school and take over the business while his father recovered from a recent stroke.

"There's no fella, Mr. Percy." He held a yellow envelope between his thumb and index.

Mr. Percy recognized the markings. He took one last sip of his black coffee and tightened the lid of the thermos before placing it on the table. "How many more of those am I going to have to deliver before this nightmare is over?"

"Even one's too many," the sixteen-year old said. "I wish I was over there fighting the Nazis instead of being stuck here."

*Only a foolish young'un would wish he was in war*, Mr. Percy thought. "It's best you're here, boy. Your family needs you here running this business while your pa's recovering."

"I'll be seventeen in March. If the war is still going on, I'm going to lie about my age and volunteer for the Marines."

Mr. Percy believed the kid. "Let's hope next year brings some peace to this world, and you're able to celebrate your birthday without the Nazis on your mind." He took the letter and placed it inside his messenger bag and buckled the leather straps.

Mr. Percy often drove slowly, but even more so that day. A few snowflakes tapped his windshield, but not enough for him to need the wipers. He rolled to a stop in front of the house, pressed the clutch and put the shifter in first gear before killing the engine. He blew hot hair onto his hands and rubbed them together while he sat for a moment and watched the small, single-family house. *No more than two bedrooms,* he reckoned. Two women moved about in the living room and kitchen area.

"No sense delaying the inevitable, I guess." He exited the taxi and walked up the gravel driveway toward the front door. Even with a stuffy nose, he smelled the food cooking on the stove. The aroma of roast beef simmering with fresh onions and carrots filled the air. He knew he would be ruining someone's meal. More importantly, he would be ruining someone's life. The thought of leaving entered his mind, but this was part of his job. *There was never a good time to deliver bad news*, he told himself, *but it's my duty.*

He removed his hat and knocked.

A charming lady in her twenties opened the door. She cradled a baby in her arms.

"Hello, may I speak with Mrs. Annie Mae Axum?"

"That's me," she said.

Mr. Percy was caught off guard. She looked younger than he would have imagined. "Is that your baby?"

"Yes, this is our little girl. She's getting bigger each day."

"Don't, uh," he stumbled for the right words. "Don't blink. They grow fast. I have three myself—all grown by now, of course. But they'll always be little to me."

"I know what you mean. She knows how to say 'mommy' and she's learning how to say 'daddy.'"

"Who is it, Annie Mae?" her sister-in-law, Isabel, asked from the kitchen.

"Telegram from Western Union," Mr. Percy answered from the doorway.

The color left Annie Mae's face.

Isabel turned the stove off and moved toward Annie Mae. She reached out and took the baby from her.

"Ma'am," he uttered and extended the envelope to Annie Mae.

She reached for it and tugged, but Mr. Percy held on to it.

"Oh, sorry about that." He released his grip on the crumpled envelope.

Her fingers trembled as she opened the letter and started reading aloud: "The Secretary of War desires to express his deep regret..."

Stunned by the news, her knees buckled and she began to crumble to the floor. Mr. Percy quickly reached out to steady her. "I'm so sorry, ma'am," is all he could manage to say. "I'm so terribly sorry." His voice cracked and his eyes teared up as he walked her to the couch.

He started to say something but instead he turned and trudged back to his cab.

In a mere second, a husband and father were ripped from that beautiful woman and sweet little girl. Their family would never be the same. He wondered if he would.

## CHAPTER SIX

"I'VE BECOME ACCUSTOMED to giving soldiers their Last Rites," Father Sidney lamented, "but with you, I get to celebrate life."

"At least I'm good for something," the soldier quipped. He had never been particularly religious, but he felt a strong bond with the charismatic priest. "Can I tell you a story?"

"Of course," the priest said.

"It's about a dream I keep having. At least I think it's a dream. It feels so real, though." A look of apprehension washed over the soldier's face.

The priest leaned in closer. "It's all right. You can trust me."

The soldier inhaled deeply before speaking. "It's dusk, yet I can see everything clearly. I'm floating in the air over my lifeless body. I see a farmhouse riddled with bullets. An empty German ammo box is tipped over. I feel weightless and free. There's no more fear or pain, and all my senses are heightened."

"Heightened?" Father Sidney said.

"I can hear the blades of grass growing."

Father Sidney hastened to stifle a spontaneous snicker.

"I know it sounds crazy," Mage said.

"No, no," Father Sidney said. "Please continue."

"I could smell sweat, see oxygen molecules in the air, and hear a butterfly flap its wings several yards away."

Father Sidney listened intently and nodded for the soldier to continue.

"A German soldier removed my helmet from my head and started burying me under a thin layer of dirt. When he was done, he placed my helmet, along with his own, on top of my grave."

"What happened next?"

"I woke up in this hospital."

"Wow! That is fascinating. I never remember any of my dreams, even when they wake me up. I used to believe that I was not a dreamer, until a scientist friend told me we all dream, whether we recall them or not. I just hope that if God uses a dream to talk to me, like He did with Joseph, He at least provides me the ability to remember it."

Father Sidney and the patient laughed so heartily that one of the nurses told them to quiet down.

"It's comforting to hear you laugh," Mage said. "You see this depressed environment every day. People are suffering and in pain. It can bring you down if you're not careful. How do you keep such a positive attitude?"

"I celebrate life in all of its aspects. The good and the bad, the sad and the happy. Joy is a choice."

"How can you possibly find any joy in a place like this?"

"It's simple, but not easy. The secret to joy is in the letters. If you want to experience joy, put Jesus first, others second, and yourself third."

Mage nodded as he let the cleric's wisdom sink in.

He raised his finger in the air to emphasize his point. "And, I get my mind off war by thinking of Italy. Rome to be exact. It's the most magical place in the world."

"I've never been," Mage said.

The priest spoke at length about his life in Paris and how he moved to Rome after becoming a priest. "My French family would hear nothing of the sorts, but my heart remained in Rome. The city is timeless. My animated friend, Vincenzo, owned an espresso bar near the Trevi Fountain. Every morning I'd leave my studio apartment near Campo de' Fiori and stroll to Vincenzo's to have one of God's many gifts—an espresso." He smiled. "Then I'd walk past the Trevi Fountain on my way to the Vatican."

"Campo day what?"

"Campo de' Fiori," the priest said in a perfect Italian accent. "It's a little bit of Heaven in the midst of the daily bustle surrounding it. At sunrise farmers would arrive with loads of produce and set up their tables. Before the war, tourists would flock to the square on their way to the Vatican, a short walk to the west, with the historical attractions to the east. At midday, the vendors would pack up, leaving a tidy town square for the rest of the day and night for the enjoyment of natives and tourists attending cafés and bars. The irony is that the idea of rebirth is experienced every day at the Campo de' Fiori, which is appropriate given that *fiori* is the Italian word for flowers."

"I can't understand a lick of it, but it's a pretty language," Mage said.

"*Si*," Father Sidney agreed. "The hope for rebirth that the Campo de' Fiori gave daily remains an ongoing inspiration for me. It's like what I experience at a modest hospital such as this. I feel blessed when I encounter men like you. Just as iron sharpens iron, man sharpens man. One of my favorite Bible verses is from Hebrews. It instructs us not to forget to help strangers, because sometimes we'll be helping angels without knowing it."

"I appreciate the sentiment, Father. But you don't have to worry about me being an angel. If we ever find out who my mother is, she'll confirm it."

The two men laughed together.

"Now that I've told you about a place dear to my heart, please tell me about your home. What did you do before the war?" Father Sidney asked.

The soldier examined his raw and calloused hands. "I imagine I was a farmer."

"What did you grow?"

"Everything from vegetables, cotton, tobacco, to cane syrup. My mouth is watering just thinking about hot biscuits flavored with fresh sugar cane syrup."

Father Sidney smiled. "That does sound delicious. Will you go back to farm work when you leave here?"

"I don't know what I'll do," Mage said with a faraway look in his eyes, "but I can't wait to get back home."

Father Sidney patted him on the shoulder. "For you and many millions of others, the best years are ahead. I'll get you back home."

# CHAPTER SEVEN

FATHER SIDNEY TOOK Lieutenant Blackwell's advice and penned a letter to the American War Department. He told them about the recovering soldier at the French hospital and mentioned the name "Mage."

Three weeks later, the cleric received a letter indicating that official records contained just one American serviceman with that name. The letter noted that Private Mage Axum of the 115th Infantry 29th Division was declared killed-in-action during a ground battle in Germany. The letter went on to say that Private Axum was from Palestine, Texas and that he had been 30 at the time of his death.

*This doesn't make any sense*, Father Sidney thought. "My patient must have served with Mage, and due to all the confusion, must have chosen that name for himself."

It wasn't the first time Father Sidney had talked to a soldier suffering from shell shock. It was not uncommon for soldiers to forget their name or where they came from. Father Sidney refused to give up. He recommitted his limited resources to learn the identity of his new friend.

Father Sidney walked into the soldier's room with a tape measure and notepad. He didn't say a word, instead placing the ruler against Mage's foot. He mentally calculated the conversion from centimeters to inches and scribbled the number 10 on the paper. He then measured from the heel to the soldier's head, and jotted down 71 inches.

Mage opened his eyes and cleared his throat. "Getting the measurements for my casket?"

"Oh no," Father Sidney said. "I'll also need a dental chart. I've arranged for one of the doctors to do it later today. I'm going to send my notes to the War Department. I promised to find out who you are."

"I already know who I am. It's all coming back to me quite quickly."

Father Sidney paused for a moment, encouraged by the revelation. "Who are you?"

"I'm Mage Axum from Texas."

Father Sidney sighed. "Oh no, my son. That's not your name. Mage Axum died on the battlefield. The War Department notified his family."

Mage suddenly went wide-eyed. "What? My family was notified I was killed?"

"Not *your* family. Mage Axum's family."

"That's what I've been trying to tell you. The dream wasn't a dream. I understand it now. God gave me a second chance at life. He said that in the chaos of war I died too early and that I was coming back in another soldier's body."

Father Sidney immediately cupped his hand over Mage's mouth to muffle his words. The priest anxiously scanned the area and leaned in mere inches from the soldier's face. "Don't say another word. This is a recovery hospital. If you tell people you died and came back to earth, they'll send you off to a mental institution. Electric shock treatment and only God knows what else will be your future."

Father Sidney removed his trembling hand from Mage's mouth. Instead, he placed his open palms on the soldier's cheeks. "You are not dead. You are alive, but Mage is not your name."

Mage was terrified. He had never seen the priest so stressed before.

"Do you understand?" Father Sidney asked.

A tear rolled down Mage's cheek as he nodded.

## CHAPTER EIGHT

"GREAT NEWS!" FATHER Sidney exclaimed when he rushed into Mage's room several weeks later, triumphantly holding a sheet of paper high in the air.

The excitement prompted Mage to sit up in bed. He couldn't tell what it said, but it looked official with its typed black ink and rubber-stamped red markings.

"Based on your dental records, an official photograph, and your height and shoe size, we now know exactly who you are."

Mage grinned. "I know who I am. I'm Mage Axum."

Father Sidney's enthusiasm dissipated. "No, you're not. You're an American soldier named James Edward Karl."

Mage collapsed back into the bed. "Who are you saying that I am?"

"James Karl, with a 'K'. You went missing during an intense battle near Gangelt, Germany. You were a war reporter. Your fearless actions on the battlefield put you right in the middle of the chaos. Obviously, your passion for journalism almost cost you your life."

Mage looked straight into Father Sidney's eyes. "Father, it did cost him his life. I ain't John Karl."

"James," the priest corrected him.

"What?"

"Your name is James, not John."

"Plus, I don't know nothin' about journalism or photography," Mage said with an exasperated expression.

Father Sidney continued in a dramatic fashion. "The German Army, overrun by the advancing Americans, unleashed a desperate counter attack. Machine guns, grenades, tank cannons, and mortars. In the fog of that horrible battle, one of the mortars exploded near you and propelled you through the air until you crashed into a tree, and subsequently landed in thick shrubbery. Your platoon wasn't able to find you, so they assumed the Germans had captured you. Thus, James Karl was listed as missing-in-action and the Karl family in Oregon was notified via Western Union."

"You marched in here boasting about great news. Remind me what the great news is, 'cause I ain't heard it yet," Mage groused.

"The War Department has started the process of transferring you back to the United States to be reunited with your family."

"Please, Father. I don't want to sound ungrateful. I appreciate everything you've done for me. I'd be lost without you. You *listen* to me, but you don't *hear* me."

"I promised I'd find your home, and I have," Father Sidney said.

"I am Mage Axum, and the Karls are not my family. You are sending me home to strangers."

# CHAPTER NINE

"KARL RESIDENCE," THE man answered the telephone.

"Hello, my name is Sidney. I'm a Catholic priest serving the Allied Forces at a hospital in France."

"Yes, you're the gentleman I'm told I should be thanking."

"Beg your pardon?"

"My name is Hans Karl. The War Department told me that had it not been for your diligence, my son James may never have been found."

"I only played a small part, but it's very kind of you to say. I'm not sure how much you know about your son's condition, but James has endured quite a traumatic experience. Just to be alive is a miracle."

"His sisters and I thank you, Father Sidney."

"I'm afraid your gratitude is misdirected. It's not me you should be thanking. The glory goes to God and the caring nurses. That being said, I need to speak with you about a sensitive matter."

"A sensitive matter?"

"Ahem," Father Sidney cleared his throat. "I pray you let James proceed at his own pace to refamiliarize himself with you and your family."

"What do you mean refamiliarize?"

"Please be mindful that James was on the verge of death when he was found months ago. He continues to be unsure of who he is and what has happened to him."

"What exactly are you trying to say, Father?"

"Not only has James done battle with the Germans, but he's also battling his own brain. Now I don't want to worry you. This condition is more common than most people realize. I know James's return home is indeed a joyous occasion, but you must temper your expectations of him."

"How long do you think this is going to take?"

"There are no assurances, but I remain hopeful his memory will return sooner once he's back in familiar surroundings."

"It will devastate his sisters if he doesn't remember them. Is there anything we can do to speed up this process?"

"If you'd like to tell me a little about your family, I can start talking to James about it."

"If you think that'll help," Hans said.

"I don't think it could hurt," Father Sidney said.

"Well, my family moved to the United States in the early 1900s. With minimal resources and determination, my mother and father started a successful wheat farm near the town of Hays, Kansas."

"You're a farming family?" Father Sidney asked, thinking back to his patient rubbing his calloused hands together and saying he was a farmer.

"Yes, for a time. Actually, I'm a machinist. In 1931, our family and many others like us were suffering from the three-fold ravages of the stock market crash, the Dust Bowl, and the Great Depression. We were forced to evacuate and head west, where there was more opportunity."

"Ah, so you followed the advice of Mr. Horace Greeley?"

Hans smiled at the priest's knowledge. "I guess, in a roundabout way, some sixty-five years later."

"The West Coast sounds lovely."

"It is lovely," Hans replied. "I found a sleepy little town in Oregon. A few years later, I acquired my own machine shop in the industrial section of Portland. The shop barely produced a living until the outbreak of World War Two. Shortly afterwards, business started to boom. God certainly has a warped sense of humor."

"How do you mean?"

"He boosts my business but nearly takes my son."

"Hmm," Father Sidney muttered. He had learned over the years that sometimes it's wise to listen without the need to comment. But this was not one of those times. "Unlike so many other American families, you're getting your son back. This is incredible news for the Karl family. Until we talk again, may God continue to bless you."

"Thank you, Father Sidney." He placed the phone back on its cradle. *Continue to bless me?* He thought about the last letter he received from his son before he went missing-in-action. James had written about the atrocities and inhumanity of war. He had confided that he no longer believed in God. A loving God would not let this happen.

*Yet*, Hans pondered, *God has not only chosen to save James, but he has introduced my son to a priest whose compassion aided in his recovery and miraculously led him back to me. The irony of life, indeed.*

## CHAPTER TEN

M AGE WAS PACKING the few belongings he
had when Father Sidney greeted him.

"You must be excited to be returning to your
family in America."

"Going back to America, yes. Returning to the Karl family, not so much. Truth is, Father Sidney, I don't know anything about Portland. And the only thing I know about that family is what you've told me."

"Our earthly families can be sources of both joy and sorrow in our lives," Father Sidney spoke with reverence. "In His infinite wisdom, God does not allow us to choose our parents or our siblings. Think of Job in the Old Testament. He loved his children and they were a blessing to him. Yet extreme grief overwhelmed him when they suddenly and tragically died. He called out to the Almighty saying he wished he had never been born."

"I'm not sure what Job has to do with me," Mage said.

"It's better to have loved and lost, than never to have loved in the first place."

"If you say so, but I'm not so sure about that."

"Faith is not about knowing—it's about believing. You have been given a gift. God has graced you with a second chance at life."

"What if I don't recognize my family?"

"They will recognize you. You see, I'm also part of a large family. It's called the priesthood. We don't all know each other, but we're family."

"You feel like my only family, Father Sidney."

A lone tear started to trickle down Father Sidney's cheek as he hugged his friend.

"I'm going to miss you, Father."

"I surely will miss you too, my friend. I will consider our next meeting another blessing from our Heavenly Father. Until then, *carpe diem*."

Hearing that phrase caused goosebumps to spread across Mage's body. "I know that expression."

"I didn't know you spoke Latin," the priest joked.

"It means seize the day," Mage said.

Father Sidney nodded and smiled. "Yes, my friend. Seize this rare opportunity and go forth and do amazing things."

Mage didn't care about setting the world on fire and doing incredible things. *I just want to be with my family. My real family in Texas. Not this second-chance family. I have a family back home waiting for me. I'll find a way to get back home to be with Annie Mae and our precious baby girl.*

Surely they'd be waiting for him, but then his thoughts turned bleak with dread. *Why would they, when the war telegram they received stated that Mage Axum was dead?*

# CHAPTER ELEVEN

I T WAS ANOTHER grey afternoon when the old loco-
motive towing ten cars jostled across the tracks until it
rested at Union Station. As Mage lugged his duffle bag
down the steps, he was only too aware that his "family" would
have to recognize him. Standing among hundreds of people
in the grand lobby, Mage scanned the endless crowd looking
for anyone who could be the Karl family. He knew from a
letter he had received from Hans, that he had two younger
sisters.

About fifty yards away he spotted a lanky older gentleman accompanied by two pretty girls with dark hair not unlike his own. He felt a lump rise in his throat. Grateful to
be concealed by the crowd, he watched as the man and his
daughters searched in vain for James Karl. He saw the desperation in the girls' faces as they clutched at the sleeves of their
father's heavy coat, hoping to see their brother in every face
they looked.

That's when Father Sidney's words struck him like a punch to the gut. "Joy is a choice. Put Jesus first, others second, and yourself third." *I've only been thinking about myself,* he realized. *I haven't even considered the Karl family and the profound impact this return will have on them.* He dreaded having to pretend to be another person, and he was reluctant to reveal himself as Mage Axum. *How can I live a double life without getting caught?* he worried. *More importantly, why live a double life? I'll just run away.*

Father Sidney had once warned him that the War Department would likely start an investigation out of fear a "shell shock" soldier was on the run without a family member or doctor to contain him. Their investigators would find him and send him away for electric shock therapy and medical treatment.

*Nah,* he thought. *There's gotta be a better way. I'll figure it out. Let's hope sooner rather than later.*

As Hans turned in his direction, Mage pensively waved his right hand high above his head. Recognition crept into the old man's face as he locked eyes with his only son. Unashamed, he began to sob. The sisters, shocked at their father's tears, turned in the direction where he was looking. The sight of their big brother standing just footsteps away was more than the distraught girls could bear. Unable to stand, they fell to their knees and covered their faces. As he watched their shoulders heave and tears flow between the fingers of their gloved hands, Mage knew he could not allow their hearts to be broken again. He would have to pretend to be James Karl. He slowly moved through the crowd toward them. He looked into the red tear-stained eyes of his father and smiled. Looking down at his sisters, he gently placed his hands on their shoulders.

"Hello Anna. Hello Agnes."

## CHAPTER TWELVE

THEY ARRIVED AT Hans's modest home in Portland. Mage had said little since his arrival, making their reunion even more awkward. They showed him to his bedroom, which was furnished with unfamiliar items that had no significance to him.

Mage studied the room looking for clues as to who James Karl was and how he should act. There was a single bed with a dresser along the wall. A framed picture of the Karl family sat atop the dresser, along with an expensive-looking camera. He turned to the family. "The train ride exhausted me. Could I have a few minutes alone back in my old room?"

"Of course," Agnes smiled.

"Thanks Agnes," he said, looking down at his short sister.

"Agnes?" Her smile faded and disappointment washed over her face. "You keep calling me that, but you haven't called me by that name since we saw *The Wizard of Oz*."

Mage knew the popular 1939 musical film, but he had no idea what nickname Agnes was referring to.

Hans saw his son's distress. "We can't imagine what you've been through, Son. Take all the time you need." He put his arms around Agnes and Anna and motioned for the girls to follow him downstairs. "We'll get dinner started. We're making your favorite."

*My favorite? What is my favorite? God, this isn't going to work out*, he thought. *I don't know these people. I don't know James Karl.*

He sat at the small wooden desk in the corner and rummaged through the drawers. He came across a few newspaper clippings and several leather-bound journals, which he started reading and then felt guilty for prying into another man's personal thoughts. A black and white photo slipped out of the journal and onto the floor. He bent over to pick it up. It was a picture of James, Anna, and Agnes in front of a downtown theater with the marquis showcasing *Here Comes Mr. Jordan*. He flipped the photo over and saw the handwritten caption. "James, Anna & Munchkin, Broadway Theater, 1941."

*Munchkin! Of course.*

The savory aromas of pot roast and vegetables wafted upstairs. A moment later there was a soft knock on his door.

"Dinner's ready," Agnes said. "We're all downstairs waiting for you. I know it's your home, but you're still the guest of honor."

He smiled shyly. "I'm starving, and the food smells delicious. Lead the way, Munchkin."

She smiled and embraced her brother. "I always knew you'd be back. I never doubted it."

Hans sat at the head of the square table, and Mage at the other end. The sisters sat on the sides, opposite each other. The conversation was almost exclusively one way. Agnes, the more talkative of the sisters, carried on about the demands of her job as an assistant manager at one of the downtown department stores. "Selling things is easy when you have an outstanding product. It's managing people that's a real pain in my side!"

During an awkward lull in the conversation, James glanced at Anna, who had been staring at him. "Tell me about your job," he said.

"Nothing I haven't already told you in the letters I wrote you. Do you still have them?"

James lowered his head.

"Anna!" Agnes scolded her older sister. "Our brother's lucky he's even back, much less still has your letters complaining about your job as a secretary at a steel foundry."

"Nothing interesting ever happens there anyway," Anna said.

"Well, you couldn't tell by all the gossip you put in those letters," Agnes said.

"Will you try to return to your job, Son?" Hans asked, changing the subject before forking a bite of roasted pork into his mouth. "They'll be glad to have you back."

"Glad? They'll be *lucky* to have you back," Agnes complimented her brother.

Mage had no idea what James's prior occupation had been. He was painfully aware that he would display great vulnerability if the others realized how out of touch he was with his pre-war life.

"Well, I reckon," then he paused, realizing he was talking more like Mage. "I'd like to take some time before making any big decisions."

"Of course," Hans said. "Take your time, but don't take too long. The workforce needs men like you."

Agnes reached across and gently patted his shoulder. "Welcome back, James. I wish Mom were here."

"Where is she?" Mage asked.

Agnes teared up and started crying and Anna shot a suspicious glance at the three of them.

Hans was startled. "Son, you do remember that Mom died of leukemia, don't you?"

Mage instantly felt sick to his stomach. His hands tingled and he had trouble breathing. He scanned the room but was getting tunnel-vision. The room was closing in on him. "Where's the bathroom?" he mustered the energy to ask.

Agnes wiped her eyes and pointed.

Mage bolted to the bathroom. His breathing was rapid and he thought he might vomit in the sink. He gripped the counter to steady himself and stared in the mirror. The face looking back at him was flushed. He forced himself to take slow, deep breaths. While doing so, he heard them whispering in the other room.

"That is *not* my brother," Anna said. "He's barely said a word since he's back. He forgot momma died, and he doesn't know where the bathroom is. This is the same house we grew up in."

"With all he's been through," Agnes said, "how dare you say that."

"Quiet down," Hans demanded. He recalled his conversation with Father Sidney. "It's his first day back. He just needs rest."

*How could I have been so stupid to ask that question?* he thought. *I can't be James Karl. I can't do this to them. It's not fair.*

"He'll be his old self again soon," Mage heard Hans tell the girls.

"How can I be my old self again," he heaved, "if I have to keep pretending to be James Karl? This family doesn't deserve this." Mage felt sorry for them. First they had believed they lost a loved one in the war. Then it turned out that he was still alive, except that it isn't the same person.

He splashed cold water on his face and returned to the dinner table. Everyone stared at him.

"I'm really sorry," he said. "Part of my injury, as you can clearly see, has to do with my long-term memory. The medicine the doctors have prescribed me has some side effects. Sometimes I say something without thinking."

"It's okay," Agnes said. "Anna does that all the time."

Nobody laughed at her joke. The situation felt too solemn.

"Doctors told me gradually I'd get much of my memory back, but you can imagine, it's frustrating for me."

"Of course it is," Han said. "I'm sure getting back into a routine with your newspaper job will help your memory."

*Newspaper job*, Mage thought. *What kind of newspaper job? I can't type, and I don't even write well.* He felt his heart starting to race again and he thought about running back to the bathroom. But he forced himself to take a deep breath and slowly exhale. "Please tell me about this newspaper job, so I can start to remember."

Agnes smiled. "You were a reporter at the *Oregon Journal*. You took the job right out of high school, not in the newsroom, but in advertising services." She inhaled deeply, then provided a near recitation of his prior work. "On the morning of December 7, 1941, you had been alone at the newspaper plant, working on ad orders for the next several editions of the daily paper. You suddenly heard a racket from the Associated Press and United Press International wire machines in the adjacent newsrooms. The proximity to breaking news was always part of the allure for you. When you saw the reports from Pearl Harbor and Washington, D.C., you took it upon yourself to become an instant reporter. With pen and notebook in hand, you rushed to the streets of downtown Portland for reactions from passersby. When the *real* reporters started pouring in later that day to produce 'extra' editions about the attack on America, you already had typed up that information and it went into the stories that appeared in the paper."

Hans smiled and interjected. "'Should we give him a byline?' one editor asked. 'The kid works in ad services, after all.'"

"'Why the hell not?' was the answer,'" Agnes said as she enthusiastically retold the story. "'He's got better instincts than most of our regular reporters.' It wasn't long before you were working regular newsroom shifts. When drafted for war duty, your byline was already familiar to *Journal* readers."

Hans's smile showed he was a proud father. "You specialized in human interest stories, many appearing on page one. Then you were called to active duty just before D-Day. You completed basic training and they knew there was something special about you. You could read, write, type, and interview well. You were assigned as a *Stars and Stripes* correspondent in Europe."

Agnes walked over to the cupboard. She stood on her tiptoes and grabbed a photo album. "I've kept all the pictures and clippings you've sent." As she flipped through the pages, one picture stood out. It was of a thirty-year old soldier huddled under an open tent. The soldier was penning a letter home.

He felt those same sensations rushing back that forced him to flee to the bathroom. His heart thumped against his chest and his blood raced through his veins. Emotion overcame him and he blurted out, "That's me!"

"No," she said. "That's *not* you, but you *took* this photo."

"I know that soldier," Mage asserted. He lifted the laminate and peeled the photo from the sheet. He held it with both hands. The soldier's homesick eyes were staring directly into his. He turned the photo over. Handwritten was, "October 17, 1944. Pvt. Mage Axum writing home to Texas."

## CHAPTER THIRTEEN

"I KNOW THAT SOLDIER," Mage reiterated. He had been wondering how he would get back to Texas to finally be reunited with his real family. His golden opportunity presented itself.

"Of course you knew him," Agnes said to comfort him. "You took this photo. You always made an attempt to get to know the people you photographed."

"No. I mean, I *really* know him. Private Mage Axum from Palestine, Texas." His mind drifted back to that cold, wet October evening. Despite the treacherous weather, his platoon was preparing for a night raid into the town of Buscherheide. The civilians had fled, but the German troops hunkered down in the town. The operation was dangerous, and Mage knew his chances of surviving the ambush were slim. So, despite the cold and rain, he had written a letter back home to his wife and daughter. His hand trembled as he wrote:

*"Sweetheart, I had the best dream about you and the baby last night. I only hope God will someday let it come true. I want you to pray for me and every one of us that this war comes to a close. Please don't worry about me as I am okay. Write as soon*

*and often as you can. Take care of yourself and kiss our baby for daddy. I love y'all. I'll see you when I see you."*

Tears streamed down his cheeks like a waterfall as he recalled that event.

Seeing her brother like this prompted Agnes to hug him as tight as she could. Hans followed suit, and eventually Anna did as well.

"Are you okay, Son? I haven't seen you like this since mom's funeral."

"I'll be fine," Mage said, using the crook of his elbow to wipe away his tears. "Seeing this photo reminds me that I made a promise to that soldier. He was eager to win the war and get back to Texas. I know what I need to do now."

"What's that?" Agnes said.

"I'm going to catch a bus to Texas and visit this soldier and his family."

Hans protested. "Son, I don't think it's such a good idea given what you've gone through. I think you need to stay close to home until you're—"

"Sane?"

"Oh, James," Agnes tried to explain. "That isn't what Papa means. It's that we just got you back, and we want to keep you to ourselves for a while. Texas is so far away. And you don't even know where that soldier lives."

"You bet I do! I know a lot about that soldier. More about him than I do myself! I've got to honor my commitments. I need to go to Texas and talk to his family. I'll stay in touch, I promise, but my mind's made up. I have an obligation to fulfill."

## CHAPTER FOURTEEN

MAGE CAUGHT A Greyhound bus from Portland to Los Angeles, and then onto Dallas, before reaching the bus station in downtown Palestine. The multi-day trip would have exhausted anyone else, but the thought of seeing his wife and daughter energized him. He couldn't wait to embrace them. He wondered how Annie Mae would take the extraordinary news that even though he looked differently and spoke with a different voice, he was Mage trapped inside that other person's body.

*She'll think I'm crazy, but I'll prove I'm not,* he thought. *I'll be my stubborn self and give her information that only she would know. Where we first kissed. How we came up with the name for our baby girl.* He was prepared to answer all her questions. He figured the worst that could happen was being arrested and hauled off to a mental institution. *It's worth the risk,* he believed.

He sprinted the four blocks to the tailor shop where Annie Mae worked. He felt like his heart would burst through his chest. He gripped the door handle with a sweaty palm. He took a deep breath and turned the knob. A small bell jingled as he opened the door. He thought he knew practically everyone in this town, but he didn't know the matronly woman behind the counter.

"Hello ma'am. I'm looking for Annie Mae Axum."

"She's not here anymore," the clerk answered.

He glanced at his watch. "She always works this shift."

"No, honey. She hasn't worked here for months. And her name is no longer Axum."

*You gotta be mistaken*, he thought. *Surely Annie Mae would have waited for me.*

"What's the new name?"

"I'm sorry," she said. "I don't know the man. I've only met him once, and he seemed like a distinguished gentleman."

Mage staggered out the door and ran up to a taxi. His anticipation at seeing his wife and daughter after being away for over a year proved unbearable during the ride. He rocked back and forth in his seat.

"Please go faster," he said.

"I can't be getting no ticket now," the driver said.

"Come on, Mr. Percy, you know the sheriff ain't gonna write you a ticket."

The driver looked back at him and squinted his eyes. "I'm sorry, I don't believe I know you. How did you know my name?"

Mage instantly realized there was no way he could stroll through his hometown so carefree. There was too much at stake. He would have to be more careful.

"Ahem," he cleared his throat. "You introduced yourself to me when I got into the cab."

"Maybe my grandkids are right," Mr. Percy said, shaking his head in disbelief. "They say I'm getting forgetful."

"It happens to all of us," Mage said.

Nearing the house, Mage saw a child's tricycle in the gravel driveway. He started looking for his light-haired daughter, but instead saw a wooden stake planted into the lawn. The sign read: "For Sale."

"Wait a gosh-darn minute," Mr. Percy said.

"What?" Mage asked.

"My grandkids might say I can't remember anything, but I do remember this house."

"You do?"

"I'll never forget it."

Mage's nerves fluttered in his stomach. "Why's that?"

"I never forget a telegram delivery. That poor woman. She was holding her baby when I had to deliver the news that her husband was killed in Germany. She couldn't even stand. Feet fell from right under her. She was devastated." Mr. Percy's eyes watered up as he recounted the story. "I'm sorry. It still gets to me when I think about that mother and child. Thinking of that horrible day makes me wish I was more forgetful."

*It's all a misunderstanding*, Mage thought. *But I'll fix it.* He paid the cab fare and approached the front door. He knocked and knocked. He peeked inside the window and noticed the bare living room.

"Looking to move in?" the neighbor's comment startled him.

Mage turned around and immediately recognized her. *Of course*, he thought. *Why would Bertha be any less nosy than she was before I departed for the war?* "I was thinking about it, but I want to talk with the owner first."

"Well, I haven't seen her around in a while. You know, it's very sad what happened to her."

Mage probed for information. "I've heard a few different things. What did you hear?"

"Well, it's not proper for me to be gossiping."

He encouraged Bertha, knowing she was eager to blab. "It's not gossiping if it's the truth."

"The sweet lady who lived here lost her husband over there fighting them Germans. Bless her heart. She got a daughter too. I'm just real glad she found a new husband to take care of her and that precious little girl."

Mage stood stunned. He heard the words, but it felt like someone had just punched him in the stomach. He forced himself to gasp for air. *Surely, Bertha's also mistaken,* he thought. *She's really old. Perhaps suffering from Alzheimer's disease.* "How can I get in touch with her?"

"I'm sorry, honey. I don't know. All I know is that she married a fella by the name of Milton."

"What's his last name?"

"Um." She looked up and strained her eyes to think. "I'm sure they told me."

"Think!" His patience dwindled.

"I can't remember, but it'll come to me at the oddest time. If you leave me your number, I could call you."

"I don't have a number," he said sharply. His anger stirred. A country that had sent him overseas had listed him as dead, and a wife that had promised to wait for him had supposedly remarried. A home that had been full of their precious memories was now for sale.

He hopped back into the taxi. "When does the courthouse close?"

Mr. Percy eyed his watch. "Twenty minutes."

"Get me there in five, and I'll pay you twice the fare."

# CHAPTER FIFTEEN

**M**R. PERCY DROPPED Mage curbside at the Clerk of Court's office, where the county archived all the official marriage licenses. Shuffling through the huge binder of documents, he found the one for him and Annie Mae. He studied the certificate from top to bottom. He smiled as he caressed the paper and saw the signatures of Annie Mae, his brother, his sister-in-law, and his on the dotted lines. He still remembered their wedding like it was yesterday. His mind wandered back to that wonderful occasion when the clerk interrupted him.

"Sir, the courthouse is closing for the day."

"I just need a few more minutes."

"You can come back tomorrow."

"Please," he said. "It's important. I promise. Just five minutes."

She saw the desperation in his eyes. "Okay," she said with a sympathetic smile. "I have to close out some things anyway. That should give you a few extra minutes. But when I come back, you'll have to leave."

"Thank you so much. I really appreciate it," he said and continued flipping through the thick binder. He noticed a substantial spike in marriages right after the war. He continued searching the documents and found the license he was looking for. His hands trembled as he released the paper from the binder. He held proof of what he did not want to believe. As he read the document, teardrops fell onto the paper. It appeared that after the War Department informed Annie Mae that her husband was killed-in-action, she remarried sometime afterward. Her new husband was Milton Glenn.

His blood boiled and his bitterness resurfaced. He answered his country's call for service in a foreign war, and he lost everything precious to him—his wife, his daughter, his home—even his identity. He blamed Adolph Hitler, the Evil Maniac, as he called that monster. It perplexed him how one man's actions far across the globe could have impacted so many lives around the world. The Evil Maniac's grasp had even managed to destroy a family in a rural Texas town 5,219 miles from Berlin.

*I'm back in Texas now. It's my responsibility to be her husband and the father to our child. I'll find Annie Mae and tell her about what happened in the war and how I miraculously survived. We'll be reunited as a family again.*

He hurried out of the courthouse as the janitor locked the doors.

"Sir," a bystander said.

Pressed for time, Mage heard the man speak but didn't process it.

"Sorry to bother you," the bystander said louder, "but I could use your help."

Mage stopped mid stride and faced the man, who was dressed in wrinkled clothes that appeared two sizes too large.

The passerby took a drag off his cigarette. "I'm just blowing through town, and you'd be doing me a favor if you could point me in the direction of the Greyhound station."

"I can do better than point," Mage said to the haggard looking man who could have been anywhere from thirty to fifty years old. "I'm heading that way, but I'm in a hurry. You may follow me if you'd like."

"I'll try my best to keep up." He motioned like an ocean wave with his hand. "Lead the way, sir."

"Where you heading?" Mage asked as they hoofed toward the bus station.

"Seattle. I'm hoping to leave tonight."

"That's a long journey," Mage said. "I just came straight down from Oregon."

"You didn't stop along the way and smell the roses?"

"Nothing rosy about the trip. Heck, I barely even ate. I couldn't wait to get here."

The beleaguered traveler glanced around and scratched his scraggly beard. "Palestine seems like a nice town and all, but not quite a place to be featured in a travel brochure."

Mage cracked a smile. "Well, that may be true, but I've got important family business here."

"There's nothing holding me here," the traveler replied. "I've got a few last things elsewhere to check off the ol' list before I meet my maker."

"I met mine, and it ain't all it's cracked up to be," Mage said. "Believe me."

"Beg your pardon?"

"Nothing. Don't pay me no mind." Mage changed the subject as they arrived at the bustling station. "Here you are."

"Thank you very much," the traveler said. "I've always wanted to visit Venice Beach in California. I imagine I'll be there within two days."

"I hope you like the beach better than I did."

"There's nothing quite like the ocean," the traveler said. "It has a way of erasing all your problems."

Mage scoffed. "It'll take more than a beach to erase my problems." His last beach experience was at Normandy. It would take quite a while before he ever associated the beach with something other than sheer terror and bloodshed.

Mage shook the man's hand and bid him farewell. He walked over to the counter, where a telephone directory was available for transient passengers. He flipped through the pages. He found the "G's" and ran his index finger down the list of names until he found "Glenn." He tore out the page and stuffed it in his shirt pocket. He now had the address and knew what he had to do next.

# CHAPTER SIXTEEN

**M**AGE GAZED OUT the window as the taxi turned down a tree-lined street in an exclusive neighborhood. He had never been to this part of town and now he knew why. These homes had been built for Palestine's elite.

"Here you are, pal." The driver stopped in front of a sprawling two-story Victorian style house. The driver must have noticed Mage's hesitation. "You need me to wait?"

"No. This is fine," Mage answered.

"Are you okay, buddy? You look white as a sheet."

"I've had a bit of a rough day."

"I know what you mean, pal."

*You have no idea what I mean,* Mage thought. He paid the cabbie and as he got out, he noticed two newer model cars parked in the circular driveway. The yard was spacious and the grass was well manicured.

He began to feel uneasy as he walked up the driveway toward the house. *Am I doing the right thing?* he wondered.

The sound of laughter from inside the house caused him to stop short.

*I should have given this more thought.*

Instead of proceeding to the door, Mage moved behind a dogwood tree in the yard. He noticed the curtains of the side-by-side window were open. He saw the three of them in the warmly-lit room. Annie Mae, Sharon and Milton sat at a round oak table. Their laughter continued as they prepared to eat supper.

Mage's chest tightened and it became more difficult to breathe. *Relax!* He admonished himself.

He saw a porch that appeared to wrap around the entire house. The same kind of porch that he and Annie Mae had dreamed of having one day. The porch was decorated with several blooming plants and three Bentwood rocker chairs. His eyes were drawn to a small red tricycle that lay on its side next to a wooden swing that hung by chains from the ceiling. He pictured his little Sharon shouting in delight as she frantically pedaled around the driveway being chased by Annie Mae.

His anger surfaced. *I don't deserve this! Why has my family been ripped away from me? Who is this man who has stolen my wife and daughter? Father Sidney told me I had been blessed with a second chance at life, but what kind of second chance is this?*

His knuckles turned white as he clenched his fists. "This is bullshit!" His attempt to smolder his anger failed and he emerged from his concealed position behind the tree and marched to the front door.

Annie Mae thought she saw a shadow pass across the yard. A sense of melancholy came over her.

"Is everything all right, honey?" Milton asked, surprised by his wife's sudden change in demeanor.

"Smile, mommy. You don't have to eat your *broklee*," Sharon said. "Right, daddy?"

"That's right, pumpkin," Milton answered, smiling at Annie.

Mage felt like he had been kicked by a mule. Hearing his baby girl calling another man daddy was more than he could bear. He watched helplessly as she flung her little arms around his neck and kissed his cheek.

Tears rolled down his face as he backpedaled down the steps. *What the hell was I thinking? No good could possibly come from turning their lives upside down.*

All he wanted was to return home to Annie Mae and Sharon. He loved them more than anything, but in that painful moment he knew in his heart that he had to let them go. God had given them a "second chance" with Milton. They were his family now.

He felt more lost and alone than ever before. As he gulped the toxic cocktail of sorrow and bitterness, he turned his back and sobbed.

## CHAPTER SEVENTEEN

MAGE GAZED SKYWARD as ominous clouds formed when he started his long hike toward downtown. Distant lightning lit up the night sky. "That's just great. Pile it on!" he told God. His entire body shook with frustration. He cried out to God. Not for help, but out of contempt.

"You steal my family! My identity! I've got nothing! What else do you want to take from me?"

The only answer he got was from the rumbles and cracks of thunder. A typical Texas storm was rolling in like a freight train. He started walking faster and faster and before he knew it, he was running to avoid the thunderstorm. He wasn't fast enough, though. The sky opened and rain pelted down so hard it bounced off the streets and turned into mist.

By the time Mage arrived at the Greyhound station, he was completely soaked. His shoes squirted out water and made a whooshing sound with each step. He pulled out a soggy wallet and grabbed a bill that was dripping water.

"Portland. One way," he said.

The clerk hesitated to accept it.

"It's water," Mage said. "It doesn't lose its value just because it's wet."

The clerk reluctantly took the money, and Mage took his seat on the bus. Completely demoralized and feeling hopeless, he leaned forward with his elbows on his thighs and planted his face in his wet hands.

"Didn't expect to see you here."

Mage lifted his head. He recognized the fellow, but didn't know him.

"Going back to Oregon?" the unkempt traveler asked.

"It's the only place I have some semblance of family," Mage replied.

"Some semblance of family is better than none," he remarked. "Mind if I take this seat?"

"It's all yours if you don't mind sitting next to a wet dog."

"Wet or dry, dog is man's best friend." He pulled out a cotton towel from his knapsack and handed it to Mage. "By the way, I'm Andrew."

"Thanks," Mage said as he buried his face in the dry towel.

Andrew stowed his knapsack and took a seat. "I'm heading to Seattle to join a commercial fishing company."

"No offense, but you don't look like a fisherman."

"I'm not," Andrew said as he put his hand to his mouth and coughed several times. "Pardon me." He cleared his throat. "I mean, I'm not a fisherman yet, but that's what I'm most looking forward to. You know, the adventure of it all. You've only got one life to live."

"If you say so," Mage said.

"Beg your pardon?"

"Nothing," Mage replied.

"I can't imagine fishing being all that difficult," Andrew said. He pulled out his last stick of Wrigley's spearmint gum and tore it in half. He offered a piece to Mage. "The way I see it, I got a leg up. My parents named me after Saint Andrew, one of the fishermen who joined Jesus."

"Better than being named Judas, I guess," Mage said.

"Or Nebuchadnezzar," Andrew said. "Imagine having to write that name on everything in school."

Mage laughed.

"It took a while, but I finally got you to laugh," Andrew said.

"Thank you. I needed that."

Two days later, the Greyhound bus pulled into the Los Angeles terminal.

"This is my stop for now," Andrew said. "I'm looking forward to dipping my feet into the water at Venice Beach."

"Sorry if I was a bad travel companion. I know I didn't say much to pass the time."

"Not at all," Andrew said. "If you ever want to try your luck at fishing, look me up in Seattle. This is where I'll be, and they're always looking for able-bodied men. It'll be an adventure for sure." He handed him a piece of paper with an address and the name of a boat.

Mage took the paper. "You've given me a lot to consider."

"You say I've given you a lot to consider, and I don't even know your name."

"My friends call me Mage."

"Mage it is," Andrew said. "Don't lose that paper."

Mage nodded. "I'll see you when I see you."

## CHAPTER EIGHTEEN

AGNES BURST THROUGH the door and ran down the driveway to greet her brother with a bear hug.

Mage couldn't help but smile. "Hello to you, too."

Hans remained on the porch as did Anna, who stood with her arms across her chest.

"How was Texas?" Agnes asked as they approached the house. "Did you see any cowboys and Indians?"

"Yeah, tell us all about it," Anna said with a hint of skepticism.

"There's no place like Texas," Mage said. "That's for sure."

"How was your meeting with the soldier's family?" Anna challenged him. "Did you give him that picture?"

Mage grabbed his wallet and pulled out the photo of him penning a wartime letter back home. Thankfully it had survived the thunderstorm. He stared at the photo. It was in black and white, but he remembered that day in all its color.

"I thought you were going to give it to him?" Anna said, snapping him out of his trance. "You said that was the purpose of your urgent trip."

"Strange thing," Mage said. "Turns out he's not in Texas anymore."

"Where's he supposed to be now?"

"Last I heard, most likely in Seattle."

"Oh, that's not too far from us, James," Agnes said. "Are you going to Seattle? I'll go searching for him with you if you'd like."

"Nah, Munchkin. As much as I would like that, this is something I've got to do on my own."

"You should start back to work at the *Journal* in downtown before you head off on another trip," Hans said.

"I'm not staying here to work at the paper. I'm going to join a commercial fishing company."

The Karls stood in stunned silence.

"Son," Hans finally responded, "what do you know about the commercial fishing business?"

Mage had nothing but respect for Hans and what the family had to endure during their son's absence, but he couldn't disclose the real reason he wanted to leave and get as far away as possible. "Not much, sir. But I'm eager to learn."

"It sounds way too risky." Hans urged him to consider the dangers involved. "I'm sure you are aware that it's one of the most dangerous jobs in the world. Fishermen often get washed overboard and disappear."

"I'll be extra careful, sir. Plus, I'll be fishing with a guy I met named Andrew. We'll take care of each other."

Hans continued. "Every year boats sink at sea. Dangerous squalls form out of nowhere and toss boats around like a pinball. There are no hospitals at sea."

"Yes sir. I don't imagine there are. I understand your concern, but I can't imagine it being more dangerous than war."

Hans sighed. "I guess nothing's riskier than going to war. And you're a grown man. So, I guess if it's really what you want to do, it's best to go and get it out of your system now rather than later."

"Thank you for the support."

"No, I'm not supporting it. I'm just smart enough to know that you're going to do whatever you decide."

Mage nodded in agreement. "I need to do this."

The farther away from Palestine and those painful memories, the better. Bitterness had robbed his joy, and the sea was accustomed to welcoming such broken men.

## CHAPTER NINETEEN

ANDREW DELIVERED ON his promise and gave Mage a chance to earn his seaman's papers. His first trip was north into Alaskan waters, which meant he ended up earning his papers the hard way. The Alaskan waters were icy and unforgiving. They were almost as dangerous as the ship's captain, who always wore a bad-tempered expression. He was a humorless, mostly taciturn man that went by Mack. Mage called him "Captain Ahab" from the classic novel, but his shipmates privately referred to him as a "no good son of a bitch."

Mack cast his nets in even the most turbulent of Alaskan waters. His mission was to deplete the seas of its rich salmon and rockfish. Mack wasn't fond of any man under his command. His crew was a means to an end. That fact was driven home one late autumn afternoon during Mage's first full year at sea. He and his mates were dragging mostly empty nets when Andrew suddenly buckled in excruciating pain. Sweating profusely, he could barely talk. He winced and screamed as he clutched his inflamed gut.

"Let him work it out on his own!" Mack shouted. "We've got nets to pull."

"Dammit!" Mage roared back. "I think it's appendicitis. He'll die if we don't get him into port."

"If it's his appendix," Mack yelled, "we'd never get him to port in time anyway. I'm ordering you to get back on the job or you're gonna be man overboard."

Mage disregarded Mack's order and knelt by his ailing friend, easing him into a more comfortable position. "I'm staying with you, Andy. Try to relax. That heartless bastard can try to throw me in the drink, but I'm not leaving you."

Mack didn't want to take the confrontation any farther. He shouted to the rest of the crewmembers to get back to work and left Mage to stay with the fallen man.

Andrew started coughing up bright, frothy blood.

Mage turned toward Mack, who stood emotionless at the wheelhouse. "We have to get to port, Captain! Andrew needs a doctor!"

"No," Andrew gurgled. "Let it be. It's okay. I've been sick for a long time. Doctors said I ain't getting any better." He took a breath and exhaled. "I wanted to die at sea."

"You're not going to die," Mage said. He took off his coat and wrapped it around Andrew's shivering body. Andrew was frailer than he had been when he first met him in Texas. Mage tried to comfort his dying friend. "My old platoon sergeant used to instruct us to embrace the cold, the pain, and the fear, because he said it meant we were still alive."

The pale fisherman spoke between labored breaths, "It's not about dying. It's about living, and I believe I'm about done with that part."

Mage could tell his friend was fading quickly. "Do you have any family for me to call when we port?"

"We're all family, Mage." He coughed blood in his hand. "I've never been scared of much, but I'm scared of dying."

"You have to trust me, Andy. I speak from more than a little experience. You've got nothing to be afraid of."

Andrew smiled faintly. "This is coming from the man who thinks God hates him." His eyes fluttered closed, and his bearded chin dropped to his chest.

The wind picked up and howled across the deck, whisking the spirit of his friend heavenward. At least that's what Mage hoped.

# CHAPTER TWENTY

THEY ARRIVED AT dawn into the Port of Seattle. Mage made sure that Andrew's body was offloaded with respect. Hat in hand, he followed the two medics in an unlikely funeral procession as they carried Andrew's body on a stretcher along the pier. He watched as they loaded his friend into the back of an ambulance and placed his open palm on the door as it drove off.

Mage arrived at the morgue late afternoon and was met by the coroner who had conducted the autopsy.

"I listed the cause of death as a ruptured appendix, but Andrew's body was riddled with advanced stages of cancer. He had been in bad shape for a while." The coroner grabbed a sealed box off the counter and handed it to Mage.

"What's this, doc?"

"Andrew's paperwork listed you as next of kin."

The gesture surprised Mage. Andrew had told him on more than one occasion: "Sometimes God is gonna hit you hard. You just gotta roll with the punches." Mage knew all too well how hard God hit, but he never imagined receiving his friend's ashes.

He transferred Andy's ashes into an urn he purchased for a few bucks and left the morgue carrying his friend under his left arm. "I carried you the whole trip and I'm still carrying you," Mage joshed. "One thing is for certain, though. I'm never working on another boat with Captain Ahab."

Having earned his seaman's papers during the last voyage afforded him the option to work on any vessel that needed qualified men. That opportunity came a couple of weeks later on a boat that was bound for Ketchikan, Alaska.

Mage worked steadily over the next year on various-sized boats. He accumulated enough money to buy a boat with two other men he had come to trust. They knew the best place to shop for fishing vessels was Seattle.

"What should we name her?" his buddy Jack asked.

"How about Pequod?" Mage offered.

"P-what? Who?" Billy looked at Jack for help.

"He said Pequod," Jack replied.

"What the hell is a Pequod?"

"Billy, my dear unlearned friend, you are a master fisherman, but you are nothing of the sort when it comes to the classics. Pequod is the name of the whaler in the novel *Moby Dick*."

"Well, la di da. Ain't we a Fancy Pants? Are you talking about that book you been reading since I known you?" Billy countered.

The three men eyed each other and laughed.

"I'll tell you this," Jack asserted. "I won't be joining you fellows unless we give her a gal's name. We need to have Lady Luck smiling down on us if we're going to make this deal work. I'm afraid we won't even get a Mona Lisa out of her if we name our boat after a doomed whaler."

"You want to call our boat Mona Lisa?" Billy asked.

Exasperated, Jack shrugged his shoulders and looked at Mage to intervene.

The last year at sea had given Mage a lot of time to consider his reawakening as James Karl. He did not consider living life in another man's body a blessing. He longed for clarity since he departed Palestine, leaving his wife and daughter with another man.

"How about Grace?" Mage suggested. "It's something we all need."

"Grace!" Jack shouted, and then began singing. "Amazing Grace. How sweet that sound."

"Boys," Mage said grinning from ear to ear, "I believe we got us a name."

Pequod still floated in the back of his mind, though. One passage from that famous novel haunted him. Captain Ahab explained that like all men, the whale also wears a mask. Would Mage ever be able to cut through the mask he was wearing and tell people who he really was?

## CHAPTER TWENTY-ONE

T HEY SAILED THE *Grace* up and down the Pacific Coast for three years without experiencing much hardship. The *Grace* was not immune from the normal mishaps that occurred on every sailing vessel, but so far she had kept them safe from any catastrophe. The worst thing that happened was a small cabin fire that Jack had caused when he fell asleep with a lit cigarette.

Mage, Billy and Jack had become more like brothers than business partners. They had made a fair amount of money and discussed selling the *Grace*.

"These old bones ain't what they used to be," Jack complained. "Besides, it's unfair to deprive the eligible females of Seattle the company of one of its finer gentlemen," he said with all the sincerity he could muster.

"Who would that be?" Mage and Billy asked in unison.

"You two are as dumb as stumps!" Jack said.

Billy had gotten married two years before and eight months later his wife, Catherine, had given birth to a son. Mage and Jack teased him about "practicing" before they got married and how they were disappointed that he corrupted such a fine Catholic girl as Catherine.

"You fellows need to know that the first one can come at any time, all the rest take nine months," Billy said. "Catherine's pregnant again and the long trips at sea are taking a toll on me and my wife."

Mage knew it would not be long before the friends dissolved their partnership.

When in port, Mage attempted to make a normal life for himself. He rented an apartment within walking distance from Fisherman's Terminal at the foot of Magnolia Bluff. He kept mostly to himself, venturing out only when Jack or Billy would drag him to a diner or nightclub. His self-imposed isolation forced him to become a voracious reader. He dabbled with a guitar he bought at the local pawn shop and was surprised to find that he had an ear for music.

"Mage, you've got a lot to offer someone," Jack told his friend. "Why do you insist on being such a recluse? You need to enjoy life. You only go around once, you know?"

"I'm not so sure about that," Mage said.

"Huh?"

"I'm working on it," Mage said.

"Well, work harder dammit!" Jack could sound demanding, but he meant well.

Many times Mage had wanted to tell his buddies what happened in Germany and how God had forsaken him, but he remained silent. *Who would believe a story like that? Even Father Sidney didn't believe it.*

The three ate seafood one night at a friendly Creole restaurant near Pioneer Square when Billy made an announcement. "I've taken a job at Boeing."

It should have come as a surprise, but Mage knew the time had been approaching.

"I need to put my family first," Billy stated over the jazz music playing in the background. "A job with Boeing is stable and I won't be risking my life every minute. It's a no brainer."

"Finally you've said something I agree with," Jack said, pounding his fist on the wooden table. "For years I've been telling everyone who'd listen that if you had a brain, you'd be dangerous."

"Piss off, you old barnacle!"

They laughed and slapped each other on their backs.

The Queen City, as Seattle had become known, was the home for Boeing. The growing company employed many people. However, the American aircraft company did not have the same allure for Mage as it did for most. He lived in Seattle, but never considered it home. Texas was the source of his heartache, but he could not rid his desire to return. He missed everything about the South. He missed the down-home hospitality, and he longed to feel the warmth of the sun as he sat on the porch sipping on sweet tea.

"If the truth be told, I'm ready to turn in my rod and reel as well," Jack confided.

Billy laughed.

"What's so funny?" Jack asked.

"Your rod hasn't been working for some time anyway," Billy said.

"Go bugger yourself, you impudent scamp!" Jack tried to sound offended.

Mage would miss the camaraderie of these two fine men. After several beers, they agreed to sell the *Grace*, but not before the three of them would take her out on one last trip.

"Let's make it a trip we'll remember for as long as we live," Jack declared.

"For as long as we live," Billy said and toasted with his beer bottle.

"Beware of what you wish for," Mage said.

## CHAPTER TWENTY-TWO

THE MORNING DAWNED a crimson sky as far as the eye could see. Only the black silhouettes of seabirds dotted the horizon.

"You know what they say," Billy said, "red sky at morning—"

"Sailors take warning," Mage finished the phrase. He took another sip of black coffee from his battered stainless-steel mug. "What's the worst that could happen?"

"We could die," Billy said.

"Nah," Mage replied. "God's enjoying this too much."

"Enjoying what?"

Jack zipped up his weatherproof jacket. "Mage thinks God gets some type of delight out of punishing him. Personally, I think God's got more important things to do than to screw with a half-decent fisherman."

"Like what?" Mage asked.

"Like screw with me!" Jack said. "It's starting to take me longer each morning to get out of bed. My damn bones ache."

"It's growing pains," Mage teased his friend.

"If he's growing," Billy said, "it's width and not length."

The three men laughed.

"If this is gonna be our last voyage together at sea," Jack said, "then let's make it a fun one."

"I'll start the engine," Mage said and headed to the wheel-house. He navigated the *Grace* toward open waters. Next to him was the urn containing Andrew's ashes. He carefully picked up the urn and placed it in the crook of his elbow. He unscrewed the watertight container and looked at his buddy's ashes.

"I wanted to talk to you face to face," Mage said. "The boys and I are goin' out for one last run, and you're coming with us. I'm going to give you a proper burial at sea, my friend."

The crew sailed all day, enjoying each other's company. Their nets had been cast, but this was more of a pleasure cruise among friends than a business run. The temperature had been steadily dropping as the air filled with visible moisture. Off in the distance, Mage eyed a squall line that was forming quickly and appeared to be moving toward them.

"It feels different today," Billy said.

"Today is different," Mage said. "It's bittersweet." He reminisced about how he wouldn't have his seaman's papers or own the *Grace* had it not been for that chance encounter with Andrew on a Greyhound four years ago.

"I'm sure gonna miss this old gal," Jack said, rubbing his hands together to stay warm.

"We had hoped for a memorable last time at sea," Mage said as the thirty-knot winds blew his hair into his face and rocked the boat from side to side. "If we don't start bringing *Grace* back, this trip will end up being one for the books." He pointed toward the thunderstorm and fog that hovered over the waters and seemed to be bearing down on the *Grace*.

"I've got a family I'm responsible to," Billy said. "As far as I'm concerned, this was a great day out with you guys. I vote to bring 'er back to port."

Mage nodded and looked at Jack.

"No argument from me."

Mage chuckled. "That's a first."

"If we hurry back, I might even find a companion for the night," Jack grinned like a Cheshire cat.

Mage continued laughing. "You're right. God is screwing with you if you think tonight's going to be any different than the last few years."

"The hell with you." Jack pretended to be offended. "I'll get us home in record time, and prove you wrong tonight."

The waves crashed over the heel of the boat as Jack headed to the wheelhouse.

"Let's get the nets," Mage yelled out to Billy.

They crouched to steady themselves against the rocking and rolling boat. The rain pelted their faces as they gripped the thick ropes and hand-over-hand pulled in the heavy nets and secured them onto the wooden deck.

The boat's engine whined each time it fought a massive wave. Jack could be heard cursing from the wheelhouse, but Mage knew this was his last chance to honor his friend at sea. He wobbled into the wheelhouse to grab the urn.

"You're crazy!" Jack said, fighting to keep the boat on course. "Wait till we get to port."

"I've gotta do this right," Mage said. He pushed himself against the rain and gusts. The powerful wind howled and saltwater flung over the heel and splashed his rubber boots. Mage leaned against the railing to balance himself and started to unscrew the lid of the urn when a rogue wave shot over the heel, violently dipping the boat and flipping Mage and the urn into the dark waters.

## CHAPTER TWENTY-THREE

BILLY TURNED TOWARD the wheelhouse and cupped his hands around his mouth and screamed to Jack. "Man overboard! Starboard side!"

Billy desperately wanted to rescue his fallen friend, but he could not spot Mage through the dense fog. He sprinted to the side of the boat and yelled out. "Mage! Where are you?" The boat's engine coupled with the blaring gusts of wind muffled any futile shouts for help from Mage.

Jack was still cursing the storm and couldn't hear Billy's cries for help. Billy grabbed the life preserver attached to the side of the *Grace*. He peered into the darkness, but couldn't see anything. His eyes strained to stay open against the cold rain and wind. He calculated that Mage was now behind the fleeing boat. He mustered all the energy he could to hurl the life preserver far into the water. He ran to the wheelhouse shouting all the way. "Man overboard! Man overboard!"

Jack reduced the throttle to idle. "What the hell are you hollering about?"

"Mage fell overboard! Starboard side. He's gotta be behind us by fifty yards now."

"Shit! Why didn't you say something?"

Jack rushed outside with Billy. They frantically scanned the abyss, but couldn't see Mage. They yelled out his name until they strained their voices.

"This ain't working," Jack said. "You've got the better hearing and eyes. Don't stop looking for Mage. I'm gonna radio an SOS."

"Reverse the *Grace*," Billy instructed.

"Too risky," Jack said. "In this fog, we could run right over him. The propeller would slice him in a thousand pieces."

Mage couldn't see the *Grace* or the stars. The fog had completely enveloped him. Every breath was like inhaling smoke. He kicked his feet and waved his arms to stay afloat, but the chilly waters drained his energy. His shouts for help became murmurs. His head bobbed above the waterline and his feet barely kicked. The rhythmic waves raised and lowered his exhausted body. He gasped for air and accidentally swallowed salt water, causing him to gag.

*This is how I die*, he believed. The reality of his current situation and the wasted blessing of his reawakening hit him like never before. He turned to God. "I'm guessing I'll be seeing you face-to-face in a few minutes. I now realize the gift you gave me. In all fairness, you should have known better than to test a C student with a second chance at life. You wasted it on me, and for that, I'm sorry. I'm truly sorry," his whispers trailed off.

He drew one last weak breath and slowly exhaled. He relaxed his entire body and prepared to submerge into the dark, frigid waters forever. Like his friend Andrew, his fate would be death at sea.

Something caught his attention out of the corner of his eye. He glanced over and saw Andrew's urn floating by. He outstretched his arm, catching the urn and pulling it against his chest. He used the watertight urn as a makeshift life preserver. He wrapped both arms around it and rested his limp head on it.

"Thank you, Andy. Thank you, buddy."

He thought he heard his friend reply, "Who's carrying who now?"

A bright yellow light pierced through the fog. Mage couldn't believe it. Jack and Billy were pointing the *Grace's* spotlight at him. His heart jolted with excitement. For the first time since he had fallen in the water, he felt hope. *I might survive this after all.* A shot of adrenaline coursed through his veins and he began kicking his legs again. His spent body continued to shiver, but he didn't feel the cold anymore. He hugged the urn and paddled his feet like a duck, working his way toward the powerful light that beckoned him to the *Grace*.

"There he is!" Billy exclaimed. "Jack, grab the gaff!"

Jack put the radio down and snagged the gaff on his way toward the gunwale. He extended the gaff into the ocean and Mage gripped it with one hand while the other clung to the urn. Billy and Jack pulled their friend over the hull and onto the boat. Mage's entire body trembled and he could barely speak.

"He's hypothermic," Jack said, removing his coat and wrapping Mage with it.

Billy collapsed onto the deck next to Mage. "Oh, thank God you found us."

"Th-th-thank you fo-fo-for shining the spotlight." Mage's teeth chattered. "Oth-otherwise I-I-I would be dead."

Billy looked at Jack, and then back at Mage. "We didn't. That light's been out for days. You know that."

Mage spied the wheelhouse. The spotlight was off. He turned his head side to side, but could not locate the source of the bright light that guided him home. He looked skyward and managed a weak smile. "Thank you," he muttered under his labored breaths. "I won't throw this chance away."

## CHAPTER TWENTY-FOUR

THE *GRACE* PULLED alongside the dock in Seattle. Mage felt much better. His temperature had risen back to a normal level and his strength had returned.

Jack looked at the urn and then at Mage. He placed his hand on Mage's shoulder. "I know you have some unfinished business. Take care of that and leave the *Grace* to me and Billy. We'll tie 'er up."

Mage nodded.

"Wear your life preserver this time," Jack cracked a smile. "You almost gave me a heart attack."

"Are you saying you would have missed me?"

"If so, I'd never admit it." Jack returned to his duties to secure the *Grace*.

Carefully holding Andrew's urn, Mage walked to the stern. The once treacherous storm had gone away and carried the fog with it. The horizon disappeared in the peacefulness of the moon and stars reflecting off the water's calm surface. Mage unscrewed the top and looked into the urn at Andrew's ashes. He pulled out the wartime photo of himself in Europe. He viewed it one last time and placed it among Andrew's ashes.

"Friends being buried together at sea. I wanted to tell you goodbye to your face. Goodbye Andrew. Goodbye Mage. I'm James Karl from here on out."

He raised the urn in the air and turned it over. He watched the light breeze blow the ashes and photo seaward before the water swallowed them.

# CHAPTER TWENTY-FIVE

*OCTOBER 1949*

"I 'M MOVING ON," James told his landlord. "Thanks for keeping an eye on the place when I was gone."

"You were my best tenant," he said.

"Thank you. Would you mind giving this to the postman?" He handed him a letter he had addressed to the Karl family.

"Not a problem. Safe travels," the landlord said.

James loaded all his belongings into the ample trunk of the used 1940 Ford Coupe he'd bought at a bargain. With a full tank of gas and hope in his heart, he departed Seattle on a glorious autumn morning.

He'd taken one of the typical routes toward Portland, east through the Columbia River Gorge, past Boise and into Utah's scenic highway surrounded by red rocks and jagged cliffs. He picked up Route 66 at Gallup, New Mexico. James had seen a number of men and occasionally women seeking lifts at the edges of towns as he drove across the country. As he began the day at yet another gas station, he saw an attractive young woman with strawberry blonde hair. She was looking for a ride.

"Where you heading?"

"As close to New Orleans as I can get. My boyfriend scored a jazz gig at a nightclub on Bourbon Street. I'll even pay for my share of the gas."

"Who could say no to that? Hop in," he said and extended his hand. "James."

"I'm Mary." After brief introductions, she told him how she had gotten tired of her life in the desert and could not afford to fly to Louisiana.

"I'm pleased to have some company," he said a few miles down the road. "Makes the trip go by faster. How come you didn't take a bus, though?"

"If you must know, buses always make me carsick."

James started laughing. "Carsick, huh? Not bus sick?"

"Course not," she said. "Whoever heard of anybody getting bus sick?"

James sensed he'd let himself get stuck in the middle of a comedy routine that befitted a Burns and Allen broadcast.

"How 'bout you, sport?" she asked. "Handsome-lookin' young fella. You oughta be flying in one of those fancy D.C.-3 jobbies."

"Not this trip," he said. "I wanted to be in the driver seat, and this Ford will keep me occupied until the next adventure comes along."

"So, what was the last one then?"

"Well," he sighed, "the latest was deep-sea fishing. Before that, there was the war."

Mary nodded, but said nothing for a while.

"You know," he revealed, "I've always wanted to fly. I'd had half an idea to try for the Air Force when I got my marching orders instead."

"Well, honey, at least you're here. For that we can be grateful, especially me. I'm beholden for the ride."

"You're welcome. Be sure to let me know if you start to feel *bus* sick," he joshed.

"Oh, you'll know," she said. "I'll turn green like one of those aliens that crashed at Roswell. The military is trying to say it was a weather balloon, but I know better."

James averted his gaze from the road to look directly at her. "Did you see it?"

"No, but everybody was talking about it. I heard enough to believe the witnesses and not the Air Force. They're keeping it a secret."

James started laughing.

"What are you laughing at?"

"It's hard to keep soldiers quiet. If some of my war buddies had seen green aliens with big heads and skinny bodies, there's no way the Army could have kept it a secret."

"The Air Force is better at keeping secrets than the Army," she said.

"If you say so."

They spent two nights on the road, treating themselves to hotels—separate rooms, to be sure—one or two notches down from fashionable. During lulls in the conversation or the long stretches of radio broadcasts that constantly faded in and out, James pondered what his new life in Texas was going to be like.

After having breakfast in Paris, Texas, the couple spent their final day driving toward Tyler, where Mary would continue east toward Louisiana and James would drop down along country roads into Palestine. The pair who had engaged in a lot of repartee and even tried to sing radio tunes together suddenly turned serious.

"Let me ask you something," James said. "I'm just wondering. What do you think about reincarnation?"

She paused and then inhaled deeply. "Is that another way of asking me about God?"

"Nah, I believe in God," he said.

"I've never been a churchgoer, but there are strange things I don't understand. Things that go beyond time and distance."

"Like what?"

"I don't tell many people this story. It's sort of my mama's and my little secret. See, we communicate. I mean without paper or pens or phone wires. We've always known it. A few years ago, my family was living in Denver. My mom and dad were traveling to Phoenix to see my grandfather. I got a call the night after they left with the news that Grampy had died. I had absolutely no idea where my folks were, but I had to get hold of them to try to spare them the shock."

"So, what did you do?" he asked.

"It was ten at night. I climbed into bed and laid there, putting my mind as much at ease as possible. Then I concentrated. I trained my thoughts on my mom, repeating to myself: 'Call me, Mom. You gotta call me.' At about ten past midnight my phone rang. It was her. She blurted out: 'I'm at a phone booth. I was supposed to call you. What's happened? Are you okay?'"

"Wow!" James exclaimed.

"So, I guess if I had a religion, it would be one that preached more about practicing my beliefs instead of just believing in them, and not necessarily disbelieving things just because they don't seem to make sense."

"That's profound," James said. "Reminds me of a story when a dear friend gave me a Christian booklet years ago while I was recovering in a hospital in France. One of the articles was about Saint Francis of Assisi. He said, 'Preach the Gospel. Use words if necessary.'"

"Yeah," Mary replied. "Sure would be nice if more people read that quote."

"Even nicer if more people practiced it," he said.

By the time they reached Tyler, Mary had resolved to take a bus the rest of the way to New Orleans. "You're sweet for helping me out." She smiled as she pulled her door handle open and got out at the bus station.

"We'll probably never see each other again," James said.

She paused for a moment and smiled. "We'll always have Paris."

He returned the smile, appreciating her reference to the romantic film. "Yes, we will."

"If I ever find myself in Palestine, I'll look you up," she said.

"I'd be offended if you didn't."

"You're a swell guy." She hugged him and gave him a kiss on his cheek. "By the way, who do you know there?"

He grinned from ear to ear. "All kinds of people."

# CHAPTER TWENTY-SIX

AFTER SAYING GOODBYE to his new friend, James took sleepy farm roads to Palestine. The weathered green sign greeted him as he arrived that afternoon and advertised the population as 32,000.

*Hmm,* he thought. *That's about 5,000 fewer than before the war. They must have picked up and moved to one of the bigger cities.* Perhaps even his own family were among the 5,000 who had moved.

He pulled his Ford into the downtown gas station. The attendant filled the tank and checked what seemed like every aspect of the car.

"How long you visiting, partner?" the friendly young attendant asked as he checked the oil.

"Not quite sure, but I'm looking to settle down somewhere," James replied.

"Our city is slower paced than Dallas or Houston, but folks sure are friendly here," the attendant said.

"I can see that," James said. "You recommend a hotel? Nothing fancy. Downtown is what I'd prefer."

"The O'Neill," he recommended without hesitation. "The hotel is named after the owner's family in Ireland."

The name sounded familiar to James, but he couldn't be sure. He was realizing that his reawakening meant that he couldn't be absolutely sure whether a past experience was being accurately remembered or whether the oddity of his situation made him suggestible to new references.

"Near the theater?" he asked.

The attendant chuckled. "Mister, this is Palestine. Everything's near everything here. We have all the amenities of a city, but with the heart and friendliness of a country town."

"That's why I'm here," James said. He paid the tab and cruised over to the O'Neill, passing the train depot, a few banks, several stores, Joe's barbershop and the newspaper office. He settled into his small room with its basic amenities. The best thing about the place, he decided, was that the room's only window faced the street one floor below. There wasn't a lot of activity that afternoon, but James felt comfortable returning to Palestine.

During his long road trip, he had questioned whether returning to his hometown was the right thing to do. He had decided that he would go nowhere near Annie Mae and Sharon, as much as he longed to see them and know them again. It would be enough for him simply to live once again in close proximity to the life he had enjoyed before.

James lay on his bed in the hotel room contemplating his next move in the town where he had grown up as Mage Axum. He had come to terms with not trying to reconnect in any way with Mage's family and friends, but what if he saw them in public? Odds favored him running into a relative at some point.

"I'll let the predicament play itself out," he said. "I won't seek their company or go out of my way to avoid 'em."

He had accepted being granted this new life and all its peculiar circumstances. The best way to proceed was to allow fate to control everything going forward. But there was at least one glaring imperative that demanded his attention. He needed a job.

He rose from the bed, got cleaned up, and set out to have a stroll around the town. His first stop would be the *Herald*, the main source of news in the county.

# CHAPTER TWENTY-SEVEN

THE *HERALD* HAD been the watchdog and chronicler of the county seat and its surrounding area for decades. James remembered growing up with the comic strips and the sports reports from distant cities up north and back east. One of his childhood memories was of his mother in her bathrobe sitting at the kitchen table. Her glasses balanced on the tip of her nose.

"Well, I guess I'm still alive," Mrs. Axum said as she read the Sunday edition. "I didn't see my name in the obituaries."

His fond childhood memory was pleasantly interrupted when a smiling woman, appearing to be in her late twenties, appeared at the counter near the entry.

*Wow! She's a looker,* he thought.

"Can I help you?" the slender, doe-eyed brunette asked with genuine enthusiasm.

"A-a-actually," he stammered, taken aback by her striking beauty. "I'd like to give you a nickel."

"Usually it's only a penny for my thoughts," she quipped.

He laughed and held up a shiny coin. "If that's what the paper still costs."

"Yes. It's still only a nickel." She took the coin and gave him a copy of that day's modest-sized broadsheet. "It would only be two and a half cents if you subscribed monthly."

He smiled. "I'll keep that savings in mind, but I'm afraid I can't take home delivery until I find myself a home. I'm new in town."

"I gathered that much," she said.

"How's that? Am I that obvious?"

"No, I just know about everybody in town, or at least recognize their face. I think it's wonderful you're here. About all we ever see anymore is people leaving town, not trying to come here and stay."

"Really?" He was surprised, because there was nowhere else he wanted to be. "Why are they leaving?"

"The local joke is we don't need any banks because as soon as someone gets some money, they leave. But the real reason is jobs," she replied.

"Where are they moving to?"

"Up north. Detroit, Chicago, Akron. Car plants, rubber factories and all that. If it keeps up, who knows what this old county will look like in a few more years."

James glanced beyond the charming hostess, at the offices that extended off in several directions then disappeared around a far corner.

"This is your newsroom, then?"

"Oh, no. Up front here is for taking ads, classifieds, mostly. Some customers also like to pay their monthly bill here. Our newsroom is back there, around that corner. Why?"

He smiled. "It's just that I used to work at a newspaper myself."

"I see," she said. "Whereabouts?"

"Portland."

"Wow, Portland, Maine? I've been there. I liked it."

"Nah," he said, feeling embarrassed to correct her. "Oregon."

"Oh, haven't been there. What did you do there?"

"I was a reporter before I left for the war. I guess I must've written about all kinds of things."

"Just guessing? You're not sure?"

"Well, that was before the war."

Her countenance conveyed empathy. "You traveling by yourself?"

"We are," he said.

She looked confused not seeing anyone with him.

"Me, myself, and I," he answered.

"What brings you to our little slice of heaven?"

"I had a war buddy whose family lives around these parts. Actually, out in the countryside. He used to talk about it, and I kind of wanted to see firsthand what he always liked about East Texas."

"What's his name?"

*Dammit! I shouldn't have said anything.* He was getting perilously close to violating his own promise.

"I bet I've heard of him," she said. "Heck, I might even know him."

"Oh, it's okay. I'll find him on my own."

"No, seriously," she pressed him. "What's his name? I know everybody in this town."

James felt a knot forming in the pit of his stomach. He had backed himself into a corner. He didn't know how to change the subject without appearing dodgy.

"Gosh," he finally said. "You sure are nosy."

"I know. It's my job," she said and laughed.

He felt relieved.

"I'm a reporter."

"Well, you certainly are good at your job," he said.

She smiled. "Thank you."

He held up his copy of the paper. "Well, you've been really helpful."

"Helpful is my middle name," she said.

"Now that I know your middle name, will you tell me your first?"

"It's Betsie." She beamed, extending a soft right hand for a quick firm shake. "That's Betsie spelled with an 'ie'."

"James," he replied with a smile. "Common spelling."

She giggled as she held his gaze for another moment. "Blair. Betsie Blair."

"James Karl. Karl with a 'K.' Maybe I'll see you around town, Betsie Blair."

"A girl can dream," she said.

## CHAPTER TWENTY-EIGHT

J AMES CONTINUED HIS stroll through town into the late afternoon, passing several small businesses and well-fortified banks. *Well, the big banks are still here*, he thought, harking back to Betsie Blair's joke.

His stomach growled, which made him realize he hadn't eaten since he was with Mary. He stepped inside a modest café and sat at a window booth.

A waitress poured him a cup of coffee without asking.

"Thank you," he said. "What do you recommend?"

"Everything's good here, and the special of the day is hamburger-steak with all the fixin's."

"How could I say no to that?"

"I reckon you could, but I wouldn't," she said.

"I'll take the special," James said.

"Fine choice," she replied.

While waiting for his order, he perused the newspaper he had purchased from the charming lady at the *Herald*. The main story on page one was about how the mayor had spoken at a Rotary breakfast the morning before, but James couldn't focus on the story. His thoughts were centered around Betsie Blair.

*Wow, she was enchanting. Was she flirting with me? I think so*, he smiled at the thought.

He turned to an inside page of the *Herald* and noted a byline story by Betsie Blair. He excitedly read her story about a fundraising event that was going to take place at the Dogwood Trails.

He put away the newspaper when the waitress returned and laid out his meal. "My goodness, look at this," he said in awe. "I never saw meals like this in the Pacific Northwest. Heck, I never saw meals like this anywhere."

"Well, honey, you're in Texas now. Everything's bigger here."

He devoured the half pound of ground steak, crispy fries, baked beans with onions and molasses, corn on the cob, butter spread on cornbread, and a generous slice of pecan pie for dessert.

The waitress returned to fill his coffee, glanced down at the few cornbread crumbs on his plate. "I'm sorry you didn't like it, sweetie," she teased.

"It was the best meal I can remember eating in a long time." He patted his stomach. "I'm full as a tick."

The waitress placed the bill on the table and he pointed to Betsie's name on the paper. "Do you know this woman?"

"I don't even need to look," she said. "If it's a woman reporter, you're talking about the one and only Betsie Blair."

"She's that popular, huh?"

"She's busy as a cat on a hot tin roof. I reckon a lot of the good ol' boys don't like an ambitious woman working as hard as she does. So, some folks might say she's popular; others might say infamous."

He nodded his head. *The infamous Betsie Blair,* he thought and smiled to himself.

# CHAPTER TWENTY-NINE

J AMES BURST AT the seams from his meal and felt the need to walk it off or risk gaining five pounds. He headed in the direction of the Texas Theater, one of the most famous movie palaces in the state. He remembered the theater well. Virtually everyone in the county knew the place, if only with a sense of pride in the structure as a cultural center in a region otherwise devoid of such amenities.

The marquees advertised the new film, *Twelve O'Clock High*, starring Gregory Peck. "A story of twelve men as their women never knew them," James read aloud from the poster in the theater's ornate display box. He thought back to his wartime experience. *War changes a man*, he thought. *Sometimes for the better; sometimes for the worse.*

He recalled a shared memory with some of his fellow soldiers. They were eating their C-rations during an overnight pause in the fight. One of the soldiers, an eighteen-year-old spoiled kid from Sacramento, was always complaining. It didn't matter what about—the food, their lieutenant, when it rained, and when the sun shined on a clear day.

"You know," he said that night, "if I get through this war, I'll never complain another day in my life."

"You'd complain if the Germans gave up," Mage told him, to the laughter of their platoon buddies."

"No, I'm serious. If I survive this war, and this food, I'll never complain about anything again."

Mage nodded. Strangely, he believed his partner may have really changed. "Well, when we see Hitler, I'll be the first to thank him for changing your view on life. Right before we kill him, of course."

The soldiers laughed some more before they wolfed down their mystery meat.

Unfortunately, that young Californian died several days later in battle, but not first without having been changed by the war.

Back at the Texas Palace, James saw a second poster indicating that the movie would show "real men at war." *How can this be*, he wondered. *The horrors were far too vivid to show an audience on the big screen. One of the reasons I fought overseas was so that Americans wouldn't have to see the truth of that war at home.*

He continued his stroll through downtown and reached a public park and playground. He sat on a bench and opened up the newspaper. He perused the classified ads. There were numerous rooms to rent, which was typical of the postwar era in cities and towns. Families that had lived primarily in urban and rural areas were finding a middle ground that would soon collectively be known as "the suburbs."

He had circled several ads he intended to answer by the time the sun started to set. He walked back to his car and saw from a distance a parking ticket clamped to his windshield. He lifted the windshield wiper and grabbed the ticket.

*Wait a second.* He noticed it was a piece of newsprint-stock paper. He unfolded the paper and read the note. It was written in a bubbly cursive.

"Hey, Mister Portland! Nice wheels!"

"It's not a ticket," he said with relief. "Wait a minute! My Ford's got Washington plates." *The only person I've revealed anything about myself to was that young woman at the Herald. Betsie Blair.* He placed the note in his shirt pocket and smiled.

## CHAPTER THIRTY

THE NOTE WAS still on his mind the next morning when he woke from his best night's sleep for quite some time. He made himself presentable for a stop at the *Herald*. He crossed the street to the newspaper office and noticed a young man clerking the front desk.

"Is Ms. Blair around?"

"She left to cover a story." The clerk must have sensed James's disappointment. "She'll be back later today, though. In the meantime, is there something I can help you with?"

"Do you think the Sunday paper will have the most help-wanted ads?"

"Yessir," he said "Try searching this one. It's from last Sunday."

James took the copy and skimmed the ads. "Well, at the very least, I have the advantage of being a veteran. I see a number of ads encouraging veterans to apply."

"Yessir," the young man agreed. "The lead editorial's headline is: 'Honor Our Veterans.' The piece asks readers to do whatever they can to help returning veterans."

James noticed no name was associated with the opinion piece. "Who wrote this?"

"Newspaper editorials are anonymously written."

"Well, it's particularly timely." James checked his watch. "I'll come back later."

"We're open till five, sir. But many nights we work late."

"Are you part-time?"

"I was for a year while I finished high school, but I've been fulltime for five months now."

"You like the work?"

'Oh, I love it," the clerk said. "I get to read the news before anyone else, with the exception of Ms. Blair, of course."

James nodded and wandered down the street and found a drugstore that had a lunch counter. He had coffee and several refills while the minute hand of his wristwatch crawled toward the hour. He paid the bill and walked back to the *Herald*.

"You're back," the young man smiled and motioned with his hand. "Please have a seat in one of the chairs. Ms. Blair will be with you as soon as she can."

Half an hour later, she appeared from the hallway, stylishly dressed with light makeup and hair fashioned in the mode of the day.

"Ah," she smiled. "Mr. Portland, Oregon!"

He smiled back and pulled her note from his back pocket. "I'm glad it wasn't a parking ticket. That wouldn't have made a good impression on my first week in Palestine."

"Don't worry. The police have more important things to do. Plus, after all you and other vets have done for this country, you ought to be granted free parking for life."

He grinned. "I'll vote for that if you're running."

"I am running…to meet my deadlines. Can we catch up after work?"

He tried to conceal his excitement. He wasn't accustomed to a woman who was so forward, and she must have sensed that because she tried to downplay her invitation.

"Johnny," she pointed to the young man clerking the desk, "told me you were looking at ads in our paper. Since you're new to town, I feel a responsibility to be a good host and steer you in the right direction."

"That's mighty kind of you," he replied. "Or are you just pushing me to get that monthly subscription?"

She smiled. "I'm not worried about that. You're gonna fall in love with Palestine and want to stay."

"I'm already getting that feeling."

"I'd love to chat someplace where the phones aren't ringing nonstop," she said. "How 'bout you come back at five and we'll grab dinner and discuss neighborhoods and jobs."

"Sounds like a da…"

"Business meeting," she finished his sentence.

## CHAPTER THIRTY-ONE

BETSIE CHOSE A restaurant a few blocks from the *Herald*. Bubba's Barbeque would've been the world's best restaurant for blind people, who would swoon over the aromas and not be offended by the aesthetic shortcomings. All the dinner tables were wooden benches draped with red-and-white paper.

"Get the brisket," Betsie suggested as they nestled into one of the booths with its own jukebox selector. "Have the potato salad instead of the slaw."

"Whoa," James said. "Don't I get to make any choices?"

"Sorry. Just trying to make a good first impression about this town of ours."

She slipped a nickel into the juke and punched the number for an Andrews Sisters and Gordon Jenkins ballad titled *I can Dream, Can't I*.

"Seen much of it yet?" she asked.

"I have, actually. I've become friends with the local barber, who seems to know everything about the comings and goings of this county."

She nodded. "Barber Joe has been in business since I was a child."

*Me too,* James thought, remembering his first haircut as a child by Barber Joe.

"He knows everybody," she continued. "Don't tell him a secret, or the entire town will know it by dinner."

"Good advice," he replied.

"I noticed you had your stompers shined while you were there, too."

"I shine my own shoes. I can thank the Army for drilling that habit into me."

They both laughed.

"Joe may have loose lips, but he has steady hands. Got a trim and straight-razor shave. After my new haircut and slick face, I enjoyed a pleasant stroll through Davey Dogwood Park."

"Betcha didn't know the *Herald* was responsible for making Dogwood Park a tourist destination for Palestine?"

"I didn't, but I can see why those gorgeous trees with their white and red blooms are a tourist attraction."

"Yes sir. I wrote a story in the paper suggesting tourists come to Palestine to experience them firsthand, and over twenty-thousand people came to visit!" She smiled. "You didn't know I had this much influence, did you?"

"I guess for a humble, small-town local paper, you don't do too bad." He paused for a moment before smiling. "I'm joshing. I knew how influential you were when you so easily talked me into going out tonight." He smiled wider.

"I didn't even have to twist your arm," she teased.

"I wasn't going to pass up an offer to have dinner with you. You're the prettiest gal I've met in Palestine. Heck, all of Texas for that matter."

She blushed and took a sip of her drink.

"The *Herald* classifieds helped me find a rental. You walk up some outside steps on the side of this old house south of town. It's basically an attic converted into an apartment, but it's got all the essentials."

"Sounds cozy," she said. "Glad my paper could help you out. Some people in this town only get the paper so they can fact-check me."

"They obviously don't have anything better to do."

She shrugged and said, "They keep me honest." Between bites of food, she asked, "Are we anywhere near why a gentleman like you would come to a place like this and be making arrangements to stay here?"

"I reckon that would depend."

She turned her head sideways. "Depend on what?"

"On how this date goes. I mean *business meeting*."

She averted her gaze for just a moment.

"By the way," he said, "my compliments to the fella who wrote that touching editorial about veterans. I appreciated that."

His remark amused Betsie. "I'll be sure to pass that along to him, or to *her*."

James looked up from his barbeque spread. "Don't tell me," he said with an awkward smile.

"Hey," she laughed. "Like you said, we're a small-town paper. Everybody's gotta pitch in."

"Well, it was very thoughtful."

"Thanks, Mr. Portland." She offered a mock theatrical bow. "At the paper we all get to do a little bit of everything.

My father isn't here anymore, so it falls on me to see that things move as smoothly as possible."

"Gee, I'm so sorry to hear about your father."

"He's fine. Harry Truman just needs him."

James seemed confused until Betsie giggled and explained. "My father's in Washington. He's a congressman."

"I know you're not supposed to talk politics at the dinner table, but—"

Her laugh interrupted him. "We're not a normal family."

"Now you've got me wondering," he said. "Democrat or Republican?"

"From Texas?" she asked. "Democrat. How could it be any other way? My father is Mason Blair. He comes from a newspaper-owning family. His brother, my Uncle Jake, owns a daily in Anchorage, Alaska."

"How did your father go from the newspaper business to the people's business?"

She chuckled. "Well, the *Herald* and Congress are both the people's business, right?"

"Seems like a conflict of interest," he remarked. "A politician owning his own newspaper company. He can publish anything he wants to sway the audience one way or another."

"That's why I run the business," she replied. "Congress works for us—the American people, and the *Herald* holds Congress accountable to the American people."

"Have you had to publish anything negative about your father?"

She cracked a smile, appearing amused by his questions. "Not yet, but my father is the most honorable man I know.

His reputation in Anderson County was such that, after his predecessor died in air combat, the governor appointed my father to the vacant seat. He's been re-elected since then and plans to be on the ballot again next year."

James was intrigued, and built up the nerve to ask what had been tugging at him since the day he met her. "There has to be an explanation."

"About what?"

"Why an obviously bright, talented young woman with all your political connections would still be slaving away in Palestine, Texas."

"At least you didn't say *wasting* away. This place has its charms."

"I know," he replied. "Trust me. I know."

"And I'm not as young as I may seem. I buy Avon miracle cream from a sweet lady in Grapeland."

"Well, it's working. Maybe she has some of that miracle cream for men. The war has aged me at least a decade."

"Oh, you look fine, especially with your new haircut and shave. But the next time I talk to Mrs. Chapman, I'll see if she has a soldier special."

He sat back and pointed to himself. "I'm thirty-five."

Betsie mimicked him. "Twenty-nine until November second."

They continued chitchatting and laughing as they enjoyed their meal and time together.

"I'm surprised how much we have in common," James said.

"I know," she said. "Maybe you're not real."

"I'm real," he said and extended his hand across the table. "Pinch me."

She did and he playfully yelped.

The waitress gave James the check and Betsie reached for her purse.

"Oh no," he said and lifted his hand from the table.

"I'm the one who invited you, though," she said.

He smiled. "I insist. Plus, I got the better end of the deal."

"Thank you very much," she said. "This does feel more like a date than a business meeting."

"Good," he said. "It's been so long that I had forgotten what a date feels like."

"A good-looking devil like you? I doubt that."

"It's true," he chuckled.

"Well, the next one will be my treat."

The thought of another date delighted him. "Who said it was over? I may have more questions for you."

"Oh?"

"The night's warm enough, how about we take a stroll along the downtown sidewalks?"

"I thought you'd never ask," she said.

# CHAPTER THIRTY-TWO

D OWNTOWN BUZZED WITH locals window-shopping. Everybody seemed to know everybody. James and Betsie paused and checked out a radio in one of the window displays.

"That's an Arvin 444 radio," he said, pointing to the box radio with two knobs—one for the volume and the other for the station.

"It's nice," she said casually.

"Oh, it's more than nice," he replied, realizing she didn't comprehend its value. "This was gold over there in the war. A soldier in my platoon carried one like this, but this model is obviously newer. We'd huddle around it and listen to BBC news and the Tommy Handley program, *It's That Man Again*."

"I can't imagine life without music," she said. "I'm so glad you had a radio to provide a temporary escape from the war."

"Yes it did. Also kept us informed about the status of the war effort and the important events back home. I often listened to the news and wondered if my family back in America was listening to the same news. The best part was that the radio let me feel connected with my family and friends even though we were on the other side of the world."

"My daddy tells me a similar story," she said. "When he's traveling for work and feels homesick, he tells me he looks at the moon and it brings him comfort to know that it's the same moon I'm looking at."

James felt the goosebumps spread across his arms. "I used to do the same thing. It always worked, even on the worst days."

"I can't even imagine what it was like over there," she said. "How did your family cope?"

"Like any other family, I guess."

"Do you have any brothers or sisters?"

"Two sisters."

"I bet your sisters adore you."

James chuckled. "One for sure. The other doesn't know how to take me."

"What do you mean?"

"She says I'm different since I've come back from the war."

"How are you different?"

"I haven't met a soul who wasn't changed by the war in one way or another. She'll be okay. Like they say, time heals everything."

It was against her nature not to ask questions, but Betsie refrained from pressing him anymore. She figured he'd become more comfortable opening up the more time they spent together.

"What about you?" he asked.

"I'm an only child, but I wish I had a bunch of brothers and sisters."

Their stroll took them as far as the courthouse, where they found a vacant bench to sit a while.

"Isn't this courthouse an architectural achievement?" she commented.

James marveled at its entirety. The three-story brick courthouse with a dome on top took up an entire block. "It looks like a palace," he remarked. "I saw castles in Europe that were much smaller than this."

"You know what they say," she said playfully, "Everything's bigger in Texas. This courthouse serves the entire county. It's a symbol of justice and fairness, but also renewal."

"Renewal?"

"Yes," she answered. "A man lit a fire to the previous one back in 1913 to get out of trouble. He was determined to burn his records."

James was obviously familiar with the story having grown up in Palestine, but he didn't dare stop her. "I take it the sheriff found him anyway?"

"Yeah. They caught the pea-brain, but he had no money to pay for the damage. It hurt us taxpayers. And the historians. All the documents inside were destroyed, and the locals had to come up with two-hundred and fifty thousand dollars to pay for the construction of the new courthouse. This one," she gestured with an open palm," is what we built to show the county that we may get knocked down, but we'll get back up and rebuild."

Her indomitable spirit and pride for everything Texas impressed him. "I'm glad they arrested him and that nobody was hurt. We can always build new buildings."

"Yeah, you're right. I just detest people who do hurtful things without any regard for others."

"I agree," he said. "Heck, that's why I fought in the war."

"The war to end all wars," she muttered. "Hey, this war buddy of yours, you sure you don't want to tell me who it is?"

"No. I don't think so." He smiled, trying to deflect his uncomfortableness.

"I might know him."

"I have my reasons."

"Yeah? What reasons are those?"

"You might go fallin' for him. He's a swell guy."

Betsie laughed.

"Plus, this is our first date. I have to leave some mystery about me for next time."

"That's right," Betsie's voice pitched from excitement. "This *is* our first date."

James smiled. "So, through your paper, you indirectly helped me find a place to live. Now I'm trying to find some work. Know of anything that would be ideal for me?"

"Hmm," she said with mock thoughtfulness. "Work suitable for James Karl, from that faraway metropolis of Portland, Oregon, home of the *Oregon Journal*, the greatest paper west of the *New York Times*."

James laughed. "You're being sarcastic, but I guess I deserved that after calling the *Herald* a small-town paper."

"Water off a duck's back," she replied then quacked like a duck.

James chuckled. "You oughta have your own radio program. Boy, the fellas would have loved listening to you."

"Maybe I will. Or television."

"Even better," he said. "I'd sure tune in every night to watch you."

Betsie smiled and kissed him on the cheek.

They left the courthouse bench and continued their stroll, eventually passing the Texas Theater. Its lobby and outside sidewalk were crowded. The early screening had let out and the late one was about to begin.

"I've been thinking about seeing this one," James said, gesturing to the marquee for *Twelve O'Clock High*.

"Me too. If I could only find a date. Or maybe a second date." She grinned and turned toward him. "Do you like war movies?"

"I guess I'll have to find out. I used to go to the movies a lot, but that was back before they started making pictures featuring *real men* like Van Johnson and Gregory Peck."

"Funny you should bring that up," she said. "I was having this same conversation not long ago with a friend. The war movies were all gung-ho, until the war ended. Now Hollywood's taking a harder look back."

"Somebody oughta write about that in the newspaper," he quipped.

"That *somebody* would benefit if she first went to see the movie in question," and then added with a mock sigh, "but going to the movies alone isn't much fun. Plus, the large popcorn is too big for one person."

James laughed and then offered, "How about tomorrow?"

"Deal, and it's my turn to pay. But that's assuming both of us get off work in time."

"Given my hours," he chuckled, "I'm sure I'll be available."

"Don't be too sure," she replied. "Newspaper work can be pretty demanding."

James raised his eyebrows and looked sideways at her. "Are you offering me a job at the *Herald*?"

# CHAPTER THIRTY-THREE

"YOUR TIMING COULDN'T be better," Betsie said as they walked back toward the *Herald*. Henry, my assistant, recently got hired by one of those big-city rags in Dallas. In some ways I won't miss him. He's this highfalutin private-school chap who liked to remind me that I was a public-school kid who attended UT Austin. It might've occurred to him that my dad and his dad also went to UT, but anyway, I'm rid of him."

"Ahem," James cleared his throat. "So far, this sounds like a self-correcting problem."

"Well, the dilemma is that he did do a lot of work for us."

"How about Johnny?" he offered, trying to deflect what he sensed was coming next. Some would've seen it as an opportunity—the proverbial golden opportunity, but for him, it was a predicament. *There's one major problem*, he worried. *If I accept this job, the chances are overwhelmingly high that I'm gonna be found out nearly immediately by Betsie, the one person I want to get to know better.*

"Johnny is good at what he does, but he's wet behind the ears. I'd be crazy if I didn't offer a job to an experienced war correspondent who walked in off the street."

"Hi-hire me," he stammered. "Just like that?"

"Well, you'd have to give me a contact at the *Journal* so I can make sure you weren't a bank robber or something, but otherwise, why not? I mean, I'm not asking for a career commitment."

He was quiet for a few moments. He wiped his sweaty palms on his pants.

"Golly, Betsie, we've just met. You sure you wanna take a chance on me?" He was reaching for excuses to avoid being found out as an imposter. "The newspaper work I did was when I was younger. Starting right out of high school. There was no time for college."

"Oh, please," she said, dismissing his reluctance. "I grant you that I might be a little presumptuous. It's easy for us who were stateside to figure you vets can come home and start right out with another life as though nothing horrible happened to you. I apologize for being so abrupt, but I think you should join our team. Think back *before* the war, to when you first started at the *Journal*. Remember that first story you wrote for the paper."

"That's impossible," he blurted out.

His reply surprised her. "Impossible? I could never forget my first story."

"You see," his voice conveyed seriousness, "since the war I've lost a lot of my memories." He looked directly into her emerald green eyes. "For argument sake, let's say I did take this job, which I'm not saying I will, what kind of work would you have me do?"

"What I do. A little bit of everything. Ads, circulation and, of course, stories as often as you can."

"Stories?"

"Yes. Stories," she replied. "We're not talking Pulitzer-Prize pieces. Put yourself in the reader's place and think about what would interest you."

"Well," he said with a slight shake of his head, "I'm rusty after years away from it."

"I'm sure it'll come back."

They reached James's black Ford coupe parked in back of the *Herald* building.

"Thanks again for dinner and a pleasant night," she said. "Don't worry about a thing. Get a good night's sleep and I'll see you at eight tomorrow morning."

"Tomorrow morning?" He felt the anxiety swirling inside him. "Don't you need to call the *Journal* first? You know, to make sure I'm not a bank robber?"

"They'll still be there tomorrow afternoon. If I get a bad report, I guess I'll have to fire you on your first day on the job. Or worse, I'll have to make a citizen's arrest and haul you myself to Sheriff Herrington."

# CHAPTER THIRTY-FOUR

JAMES COULD NATURALLY be Mage, but as he stressed about going into work his first morning at the *Herald*, the larger question troubled him: Could James naturally be James?

*At sea, it was easy to be anybody I wanted to be*, he thought. *This job is different. Betsie hired me under the assumption I'm an accomplished journalist. Hopefully, she'll cut me some slack and not expect me to walk right into the newspaper and be the same competent reporter I said I'd been in Portland prior to shipping off to Europe.*

Faced with the greatest challenge of his reawakening, James knew that he needed to walk into the *Herald* and start learning everything he could and pick it all up as quickly as possible.

"Good morning, Johnny," he greeted the clerk who stood at the reception counter.

"Good morning, Mr. James. I'll show you to your desk."

James patted Johnny's shoulder as they walked down the hall.

"I'm glad you're here. We've been needing help for quite some time, but Ms. Blair is particular about whom she hires."

James nodded, but his stomach knotted up. "I hope I don't let anyone down."

An Underwood typewriter, a stack of paper, a notepad, and various pens and pencils tossed in an empty coffee mug rested on his desk. The rotary dial telephone was ringing off the hook.

"Since it's your first day at the *Herald*, I thought it best to get your feet wet by taking calls," Betsie said as she came to say hello. "You know, everything from taking advertising requests, wedding announcements, and death notices. Also, you'll get the inevitable phone calls with complaints about delivery service, editorial content, or lack of coverage at a local event."

"Got it," he said.

"I'm really glad you joined our team. I'll be in my office if you need anything."

He smiled and waved as she walked down the hall.

"You've reached the *Herald*," James answered the telephone, thankful that Betsie had walked away so she wouldn't hear how he handled himself over the phone.

"There's a spelling typo in the caption under Yogi Berra's photo," the caller said matter-of-factly.

"Beg your pardon?"

"Yogi Berra, the New York Yankees' catcher."

"Yes," James said. "I know who Yogi Berra is."

"Under his photo in the World Series story, there's a typo."

"What kind of typo?"

"*You* wrote humility. It was supposed to be humidity. That baseball player said: 'It ain't the heat; it's the humidity.'"

"I'm sorry to hear that," James said. "Seems like an easy mistake to make."

"I'm not paying for mistakes. I'm paying for accuracy, and I'm paying a lot of money each month," the angry man's voice got louder and faster.

*A lot of money?* James figured he was supposed to be more patient, but he couldn't help himself. "You're complaining about spending a nickel for getting the *Herald* every day? Actually, it's only half a nickel for the monthly subscription."

"This type of error is pure carelessness," the complainant continued. "How can I trust the *Herald* to get the major stories right when they can't even get the small stories right?"

"Yogi Berra and the World Series are not a small story," James said.

"I want to speak to the manager," the man said.

"Look sir, if this typo has got you all worked up like this, perhaps you shouldn't be reading the paper. You sound like you're about to have a heart attack over a spelling mistake."

The man huffed and puffed. "I demand to speak to the manager!"

"The manager's busy," James replied. "Today you got me."

A loud click sounded when the frustrated man hung up.

"That was pleasant," James said with sarcasm as he put the handset back on the base unit and leaned back in his chair.

"They threaten to cancel subscriptions." Betsie's voice startled James, and he quickly leaned forward in his chair.

"I didn't realize you had been standing behind me."

"They'll be rude," she continued. "Just be patient. Even if they cancel, they'll be back in a week. Seems arrogant, I know, but one of the first things my father told me about the *Herald* was folks subscribe because they don't have any place else to go for their news."

"That guy was a jerk."

Betsie sighed. "The fact is they need us more than we need them, even though most would never admit it. They're Texans, and Texans are a proud people. To show you how powerful the newspaper is, let me tell you about a paper in Australia. The editors once inadvertently left the daily horoscope feature out of the morning paper and by noon they'd received hundreds of complaint calls. Some of those people said they were afraid to leave home without first reading their horoscopes."

"Imagine that," James said. "People can be so strange."

By closing time, James had faced one challenge after another successfully. He glanced at his wristwatch and felt a huge sigh of relief. *Finally five o'clock and thank God nobody asked me to write any stories.* But he wasn't in the clear yet. He and Betsie had previously planned to go to the cinema tonight. On the one hand, he wasn't sure if he was quite ready for wartime realism on the big screen. On the other hand, it was another opportunity to court Betsie. That trumped everything. *What am I so worried about? She's only the daughter of a popular and influential congressman. She's also the boss's daughter. No, she is the boss.*

# CHAPTER THIRTY-FIVE

"**G**LAD WE GOT out of work early enough for the first showing," Betsie said as they walked side-by-side to the theater. "This is a much-needed break after the hectic day we've had."

"I hear you," James agreed. "I had forgotten how much detail goes into publishing a newspaper."

She giggled.

"Hey, what's so funny?"

"Y'all talk differently up there in Oregon. We call it *printing* a newspaper, not publishing one."

James realized he had to be careful how he spoke if he wanted Betsie to believe he was an award-winning *Stars and Stripes* reporter.

"Please don't tell me you say PEE-CAN pie," she said.

"Of course not," he said. "It's PUH-CON pie."

"Okay." She winked. "We can still go out tonight and not break Pop's heart that I'm dating a Yankee."

*Dating? She said dating.* He smiled. "I'm glad Mr. Blair would approve."

They decided to see *Twelve O'Clock High*, which about American aircrews that flew daylight bombing missions in World War II.

"Let's discuss the movie at a roadhouse just outside Palestine," Betsie suggested as they left the theater. "It's Friday night, and I think we've earned a beer or two."

"A woman after my own heart," James said.

"Maybe so," she said playfully and winked at him. "Let's go, King James."

They sipped their long-neck Lone Stars in silence for a while, keeping peripheral views of the Texas-two-stepping going on nearby on a small dance floor.

"That's Ray Price," Betsie said, using her chin to point to the young man playing the guitar.

James glanced over his shoulder to see the musician.

She continued. "He's been getting a lot of radio exposure from his country music."

James nodded. "I can see why. He strums that guitar well."

"Do you play an instrument?"

"I dabble with the guitar," he said. "Sometimes I'd play at sea while waiting for the fish to bite."

"Did it work?"

"Not really. I think it used to scare them off."

She laughed.

"So, my friend from Oregon, you be the film critic tonight."

"Just don't make me write a review," he joked.

"That's not a bad idea, but I promise not to."

"My impression is that folks in the audience who weren't in the war probably found the first half hard to follow and the second half fascinating. For me, it was the opposite. Those poor guys in the first half were walking dead men. Even if they survived the war, it was hard to see how they could come back home and lead normal lives, not after what they saw and did. Events like that stay with you until you die. You may not talk about them, but you can't help thinking about 'em."

Betsie said nothing.

"Thankfully, it's getting rarer as time passes, but sometimes my body twitches so violently in my sleep that I wake up thinking I'm in battle. I can hear the mortars exploding near me. Although my time on the battlefield was brief compared to many others, it always felt like eternity when the bullets whizzed by my head."

Betsie listened intently.

"And then the actual war scenes. We've all seen dying in the movies, but it's phony and we understand that it's Hollywood. The actors get up when the scene is over and they light up a smoke and go home. Not in this movie. Those men bailing from airplanes and falling from the skies were real men. They had real lives and real aspirations. They had real families waiting back home. No wonder everybody looked sort of stunned coming out of the theater when the movie ended."

He took two quick sips of his beer.

"When I think about it, I can still hear the cries and screams of a lot of my buddies who were fighting alongside me. It's an absolute shame and disgrace to humanity that we ended up with not one world war, but two! I witnessed too many American men with bright futures ahead of them, exhale their last breath on foreign soil."

James looked at Betsie and noticed tears on her cheeks. He grabbed her hand. "I'm sorry. I didn't mean to be so intense. Would you like to dance?"

She nodded yes.

They stood and moved to the dance floor. He took her hand into his and placed his right hand on her lower back.

"By the way," he said as they danced to the slow song, "let's hear your take on the movie."

"Let's just enjoy our first dance together," she said and rested her cheek on his chest.

They ended up dancing to two songs before they returned to the table.

Betsie took a deep breath and exhaled. "Talking about the realism, I guess it didn't hit me until we were leaving the theater. Most of the folks in the crowd were kind of like me, rather stunned by the whole experience. I doubt anybody there tonight envied those pilots and what they had to go through."

James nodded and took another sip of his beer.

"Speaking of what's real, right across the lobby, I recognized a man I interviewed some time ago for a story about a local gentleman who went off to war and disappeared somewhere in Germany. The family had kind of a peculiar last name."

His heart quickened and his body tensed up. James had to stifle himself from blurting out his guess.

"Anyway," she said, "I saw him tonight with his wife. I wonder how he felt about the movie."

"I hope he understood that America didn't have a choice. We had to retaliate after the attacks on Pearl Harbor, and we had to stop Hitler from world domination. If not, you and I wouldn't be sitting here talking about Hollywood movies."

"Tucker!" she blurted out.

A chill shot down James's spine.

"His name was Tucker Axum," she said. "His lovely wife was Isabel. It just came to me."

He realized he had been enjoying himself so much on his date with Betsie that he hadn't paid enough attention to people around him to see his own brother and sister-in-law. He wanted to ask Betsie so many questions about them, but he had to proceed with caution so he did not appear unusually interested.

"Who is this you're talking about?" His cadence was much quicker than usual.

"The man at the movies tonight. I had interviewed him about five years ago. His brother was a local hero who left behind a wife and young daughter to go serve overseas. He was first declared missing-in-action and the War Department couldn't tell the family anything about what happened. Shortly later, they changed his status to killed-in-action. He had a strange name. I can't think of it right now, but it'll come to me."

Betsie noticed James start to tear up. She grabbed a handkerchief and without saying a word passed it to him.

"That's the kind of story that tugs at the heartstrings," he said. "I'd sure like to read that story you wrote about it."

"It's heartbreaking, but I decided not to publish the story because there wasn't enough information. A story like that draws a lot of questions and speculation about what really happened."

"They never found his body?"

"Nope," she said.

"I reckon one day the truth will come out about what happened to that soldier," James said. "I hope it brings the family some comfort then."

"When it does, you'd be the perfect person to write about it," she said.

"Maybe so." James smiled and nodded. "Maybe so."

After dinner, James drove them back to the *Herald*, where a parking spot was reserved for Betsie's 1948 Chevrolet coupe convertible.

"A work bonus from my favorite congressman," she said, stroking the gleaming black finish of the hood.

They yawned simultaneously.

"I guess I'm not eighteen anymore," James joked. "Slaving all day at the *Herald* and then staying up all night can wear out an old man like me."

"My dad is twice your age, and he can stay up all night long drinking with his cronies."

"I will have to meet this man, especially if he's gonna be my representative."

"Does that mean you're thinking about making Texas your home?"

James feigned an exaggerated yawn. "It's getting way past my bedtime. Thank you for a wonderful night."

She smirked.

He opened her door and she sat behind the wheel and rolled down her window.

"The other thing about the movie," he began, "it reminded me of something I've always wanted to do."

"What's that?"

"Learn to fly an airplane."

"Are you fibbing?"

"Not at all," he said.

"Well, honey, you've hit the jackpot this week then. Say when, and I'll take you up in Pop's Cessna. I'm licensed."

James shook his head in surprise. "You can fly?"

"Of course, I can. Women fly, too!" She said a bit defensively.

"I'll hold you to that promise then."

She smiled and rolled up her window. Before she drove off, he motioned for her to roll the window down again. Before she could ask him what he wanted, he leaned in and kissed her gently and quickly on the lips.

"Good night, Betsie Blair," he whispered.

# CHAPTER THIRTY-SIX

J AMES WOKE EARLY and drove to the public library on Saturday, his planned day off. He sat impatiently in the parking lot waiting for the library to open. He listened to his radio, which played the 1949 Burl Ives hit, *Ghost Riders in the Sky*. He wondered if anyone else in the world was living a reawakened life, too.

Five minutes to nine, a truck pulled into the lot and parked. An elderly man got out and walked around to the passenger side. He opened the door and extended his hand to help the lady whose grey hair was pulled in a tight bun. He kissed her and watched her walk to the door of the library while she carried a heavy canvas bag. She unlocked the door and waved goodbye to her husband.

James enjoyed watching the elderly couple whose love for each other over the decades still seemed strong. He walked into the library and approached the lady, who was standing behind a counter and pulling books out of her bag.

"Good morning, ma'am. Could you please direct me to the section for instructional books about journalism?"

She eyed James for a moment. "I guess it's never too late to learn how to write."

Her jab caught James off guard.

She pointed with her hand and answered, "That will be in section zero seven zero."

He walked to that section, but got sidetracked when he saw the massive collection of historical newspapers. He shuffled through the stack until he came across a "Society" story about a dinner party held in *his* honor.

He delicately held the paper up with both hands. "Pvt. Mage Axum of Camp Fannin was honored last Sunday with a dinner party at the home of his sister, Mrs. Estelle Mack. Over 28 guests arrived." The piece brought back fond memories. He remembered that evening well. It was the first time he had returned home wearing his Army uniform. He felt so proud. His mom and dad were there, along with his brothers and sisters and their spouses and children. Annie Mae and baby Sharon were there also. He remembered showing off baby Sharon to some of his family members who hadn't yet had the opportunity to meet her. She had her mother's nose and eyes. She was so beautiful.

James used a handkerchief to dry his eyes and blow his nose. He checked the clock on the wall and realized how time had gotten away from him. He returned to his search for books about journalism, and was disappointed to find only four volumes related to the subject.

Two of the books James had skimmed were more about the history of the press. The third was written in a scholarly, formal textbook fashion, and the fourth was authored by a former world-weary reporter. James concluded it was the jackpot of information for anybody looking for a crash course in journalism. The author had deliberately written in an easy to read style and used his vast experience to share his collection of anecdotes and cautionary tales.

In the Foreword section, the author had written, "The truth is that we're all reporters. Every person who came home one night and told dinner companions about seeing a dog bite a man is a reporter of sorts. If the story proves to be about a man biting a dog, more's the better."

He took the book to the front counter.

"I'd like to check out this one please."

"I'll need to see your library card," the librarian replied, now looking over the spectacles that perched on the bridge of her nose.

"I don't have a card, but here's my driver's license."

"An ORE-ee-GONE driver's license. My oh my. You're a long way from home."

"I've only been here a week, but it feels like I was born and raised here," he smiled.

"I'm sorry, hon. I can't let you check out any books unless you have a Texas driver's license or some proof that you live here. Those are the rules. I'm sure you understand."

"I should be getting my veteran benefits in the mail soon. It might be a few weeks, but I was hoping to read this book this weekend. It's very important."

Her demeanor softened. "I didn't know you were a vet."

"Yes, ma'am. United States Army."

"Bless your heart. Thank you for your service, and for coming back alive. I shouldn't be doing this, but I'm going to let you check out this book. Please don't tell anybody."

James thought it was funny since he didn't see anybody else in the library. "It'll be our secret."

"I'll go ahead and issue you a library card, since you're a veteran, and you look like a responsible young man. As you can see, we're not too busy in here. Ever since Palestine opened up not one, but two outdoor Passion Pits."

"Passion Pits?"

"Movie theaters, sweetie. That's what the youngsters are calling them nowadays. No telling what kind of debauchery is going on there. It seems like everybody is going there for who knows what. All the young kids today are being educated by Hollywood, I tell you!"

"Well, that's one of the things we were fighting for over there. You know, the freedom to make movies and go watch them."

"I don't think they're even watching the movie," she remarked. "But I guess you're right. I just think they should be here reading Dickens and Shakespeare and Twain. You know, the classics."

"Just because you're taught that something's right and everyone believe it's right, it don't make it right," James quoted one of his favorite lines from a novel.

"Oh, heavens!" The librarian was impressed. "Don't tell me you're also a fan of *The Adventures of Huckleberry Finn*."

"Why, yes I am. I picked up a copy at a little thrift store and read it while doing some commercial fishing in Alaska."

"We have lakes and such around here, but nothing like you're probably used to if you were fishing way up there in Alaska."

James smiled. "I'm looking to explore the lakes around these parts. Perhaps next time I'm in here, you can show me the local section."

"I can do even better than that," she said. "My husband knows every fishing hole in the county. I'll have to introduce you to him. He'll be happy to take you out."

"That sounds wonderful," he said.

James hurried back to his place and spent the entire day reading the book. The idea of being a journalist intrigued him. *Could I be a writer?* That question had been gnawing at him. He had marveled at how some of the workers at the *Herald* could rattle off volumes of typed copy effortlessly. *Maybe the better question is: Could I be a typist?*

Early the next morning he headed to the *Herald*. He knew it would be closed on Sunday, but he had been given a key. He figured he'd sit at his desk and start practicing on his Underwood typewriter. He noticed Betsie's black coupe parked in front of the building. He tried the glass door of the office and found it unlocked.

"Betsie," he called out.

A few seconds later she appeared at the rear of the office.

She smiled. "Good grief. Please tell me you've got better things to do on a Sunday afternoon."

*Practicing my typing can wait till another day*, he reasoned. "Well, miss, it's a gorgeous day. I was hoping we could go for a drive, and you could show me around the countryside a bit."

"You're right about that. It sure is beautiful today. I'm finishing up. I'll lock up and we'll go for a spin. I know the perfect place!"

## CHAPTER THIRTY-SEVEN

B ETSIE WORE KHAKI slacks, a black V-neck sweater and a periwinkle scarf. She had no makeup. She didn't need any as far as James was concerned. She was a natural beauty.

"I know it's a tad cool, but I love autumn weather." Her breath formed a misty cloud. "Mind if we ride with the top down?"

"Not at all," he said.

Soon they had left the city behind and cruised along farm roads that hugged trees speckled with yellow, orange, and brown leaves that dropped to the ground.

Betsie surprised James when she tuned the radio to a faint broadcast of the day's World Series game between the Yankees and Dodgers.

"You like baseball?" he asked.

"Well, it's the national pastime, right?"

"Yep," he replied. "It's unpatriotic not to listen."

"Take me out to the ballgame," she began singing. "Buy me some peanuts and cracker jack."

"I never understood that song."

"What do you mean?"

"You're *already* at the ballgame when you sing it," he remarked in good fun.

She nodded. "Hmm. Good point. Take me out to the ballgame," she began singing again, but this time James joined in.

In a bit, she pulled off the road to an airstrip where a twin-engine plane had landed. She drove past the airplanes parked on the tarmac and stopped in front of one of the private hangars.

"Give me a hand, will ya?" she asked and the two slid open the hangar door to reveal a silver Cessna 140 with India-red trim. "She's beautiful, isn't she?"

"Gorgeous," James said, "but looks small enough to fit in the trunk of your car."

"Small but solid," she said. "Two seats, one engine. That's all she needs to get us around."

"I'm ready to go up if you are," he said.

She eyed the distant trees that lined the airport perimeter. "We have blue skies, but today's too windy to fly. It won't make for your best introduction to the Cessna. But we'll fly soon. I promise. Come on, let's walk inside."

An oversized Texas flag hung from the hangar's ceiling. A battered toolbox and several cartons of engine oil stacked on top of each other occupied one of the corners. Along the walls were framed pictures of Betsie and her father on various flying adventures.

He pointed to a picture with coconut trees along a pristine white-sand beach. "Where was this taken?"

"Cozumel. Pop loves going down there. He swears the tequila tastes better in Mexico."

"You flew this cracker box across the Gulf of Mexico?"

"No, along the coastline. That way we always had a beach below us in case we had to land unexpectedly."

"Have you ever had to make an emergency landing?"

"Nope and I hope I never do," she said and knocked on a wooden work bench. "Let me know when you're ready to lock up."

"Whenever you are."

"By the way," she said, during their drive back to town, "I had a brief chat with one of your editors in Portland by the name of Neal Harvey."

"Yeah," James feigned remembering the man. "What'd old Neal have to say about me?"

"That he was disappointed in you."

He felt his stomach tighten up, and he shifted in his seat.

"He said he'd received calls from your father when you got home from the war. Your dad assured him you'd be by once you got settled, but Mr. Harvey said you never showed up. He told me you could have your job back in a minute. He said you have some of the best instincts he's ever seen in a reporter."

James exhaled with relief. He harked back to the book he had checked out from the library. "My rule is to keep it simple. I always try to get the main news value in the lead paragraph, and I make sure to have credible and accurate sources to tell the story to the satisfaction of most readers. I'm certainly no Edward Murrow."

"Maybe not, but I'm getting the feeling the *Herald* is going to be very happy to have you around," she replied.

"The *Herald* huh? What about Miss Betsie Blair? How does she feel about having me around?"

She smiled, but said nothing.

"Keep in mind," he said as they pulled up to the *Herald*, "you were hearing from Mr. Harvey about the James Karl he knew before I went to war. That's the part of me that I have yet to rediscover. Still, a lot of us who were fortunate enough to come home can't possibly be the same people we were before we left. It's like that movie we saw Friday night and what we talked about afterward."

They sat quietly for a moment before James noticed that Betsie's eyes had welled up.

"Sorry," she said meekly. "That movie the other night and all this talk about the war. It had me thinking about Chuck again."

"Chuck?" he asked. "Who's Chuck?"

"My fiancé," she said and let herself out of the car.

## CHAPTER THIRTY-EIGHT

JAMES WOKE THAT Monday morning after having tossed and turned for hours. *Why would she be going out with me if she has a fiancé*, he kept thinking to himself. *Did he leave her and she's not over it? Is she trying to use me to get over their breakup? I thought we had something real.*

He felt conflicted from what otherwise had been a terrific weekend, and he needed to have an answer when he went into work that day.

"Howdy James," Johnny greeted him.

"Morning Johnny," he said as he filed past the reception desk and headed to the back where Betsie's office was.

She stopped typing and looked up at him. "Good morning, James."

"Is it? I thought we had a great weekend, and then out of nowhere you mention this guy Chuck. What's going on?"

Her lips tightened and she nodded, making no eye contact. "I'm very sorry. It wasn't fair to you. I should have said something sooner. You deserved to know. He's gone, obviously."

"What's obvious is that you still love this guy," he said.

She was silent for a moment, then finally took a deep breath, and began. "I genuinely never believed he wouldn't come back from the war. I know that makes me sound unrealistic and maybe like every woman who stood at train stations hugging, crying—in my case sobbing as they said goodbye to their loved ones, vowing that this wouldn't be the end."

James realized she was the embodiment of the collective loss that attends every war. She was the sole survivor of a relationship that no longer could be. He thought of his loved ones for a second, believing that they all shared in this lingering grief that he was witnessing. She dabbed at both eyes with a tissue she grabbed from her desk. "It's been several years now. I've had a lot of time to try to sort out my life."

"I'm sorry to hear about your loss, Betsie. I truly am." He took her hands, lifted her out of the chair and eased her into an embrace.

"I wanted my life to be about the future, not the past, about hope and not tragedy," she said. "I was beginning to believe that would never happen and from out of the blue you showed up in Palestine. You asked me yesterday how Betsie Blair feels about having you around." She looked up into his eyes as mascara streamed down her cheeks. "I never thought I could feel this happy again."

"That makes two of us." He cupped her face in his hands and kissed her.

## CHAPTER THIRTY-NINE

*November 11, 1949*

J AMES SIPPED THE remaining drops of coffee from his battered stainless-steel mug he used while onboard the *Grace*. He saw Johnny twiddling his thumbs between phone calls.

"I'm tired of answering calls all day," James said.

"Mr. James, the phones are always ringing off the hook here. I helped Ms. Blair once over the Easter holiday when a water pipe busted. The phones were even ringing that day!"

"Even on Easter?" he asked in disbelief. "God help us all."

"You should have seen Ms. Blair. She got her Sunday dress all wet. She was madder than a wet hen."

"I wish I could have witnessed that," James laughed at the image. "Anyhow, I'm tired of sitting around listening to people yap. The action is out there," he pointed with his nose at the storefront window that faced downtown. As the words flew from his lips, he knew what to do. It was time to become a reporter. Today was the perfect day to start.

"What are you proposing?"

"I'm heading over to the VFW," James said as he sprung out of his chair.

"Where?"

"The Veteran of Foreign Wars. Today is Veteran's Day, and it's almost five o'clock. There's bound to be some worthy stories among that salty bunch."

"Can I come with you?" Johnny asked.

James thought for a beat. "Why not? But you gotta stay quiet. Speak only when you're spoken to. I need to gain their trust. It might mean sharing some war stories. Experiences that are very difficult to talk about. Stories that you can only tell someone who has been there. You think you can do that?"

"Yessir."

"Okay. If I get a good story and you type it for me, I'll talk to Ms. Blair about adding your name to the byline."

"Honest?"

"You betcha," James replied, knowing he'd need Johnny's help or his typing would take weeks before he completed the first draft.

The VFW building was just outside town. James felt more and more confident his idea was going to work when he saw how many vehicles filled the parking lot. He quit counting after ten.

"First order of business," he told the tattooed bartender, "is let's get a round of drinks for everybody." He slid a crisp bill across the wooden bar. When the bartender grabbed it with his scarred hand, James noticed the bearded man was missing two fingers.

"The boys will appreciate that," the bartender warily replied. "What's the occasion?"

"I'm new in town." He noticed tacked photos and military patches covering the wall. "A soldier always feels at home with his foxhole buddies at the local watering hole."

"You got that right. Name and unit?" he questioned.

"Usually it's name and rank," James replied.

"Rank don't matter here. We're all equal."

"James Karl. *Stars and Stripes* reporter assigned to the 115 Infantry, 29th Division."

"Welcome, James." He extended his mangled hand and the two shook. "They call me Lucky," he said and grinned. "Lucky to be alive."

"I know the feeling," James replied.

Lucky sized up Johnny. "What are you having, kid?"

Johnny looked to James for guidance, prompting him to answer for the late teen. "My pal will have a Jack and coke. Hold the Jack." He winked at the bartender.

James played a round of pool and tossed darts back and forth with a few of the guys while they drank their beers and told war stories.

"How are you putting food on the table nowadays," one of the old timers asked James.

"I was a *Stars and Stripes* reporter in the war," he answered. "Found a job at the *Herald* doing practically the same thing, but without getting shot at."

The men laughed.

"You need to talk to Archie then. He's got one helluva story. He was shot down over yonder and them damn Nazis held him as a POW for over a year."

"That's the type of story I want to highlight," James said. "One of Palestine's own heroes. It'll be my job to make sure this town knows about the men who fought bravely overseas. We should be celebrating people like Archie. Not the people pretending to be a hero on the big screen."

The bar erupted in cheers and applause. "Go get 'em Jimmy!"

*Life's ironic*, he thought as he watched the men inside the clubhouse. He had even gone to school with some of those fellows, but they had no way of knowing the James Karl they were talking to was really Mage Axum. He was Jimmy now. They were brothers-in-arms.

"We got our story," James told Johnny.

"Yessir," Johnny said with excitement. "It'll be a page one lead."

"These are men of remarkable character, Johnny. Most of them wouldn't talk about the war to people who weren't there. It's nothing personal. It's just a hard topic to share. But we're going to share it with the folks of Anderson County."

"That's a great idea, Mr. James."

"Thanks, partner."

"We've been needing someone like you for a while. Thanks for including me on this. I feel like a real reporter now," Johnny said before his countenance turned somber.

"What's wrong?"

"It's just that I know Mr. Archie," Johnny said. "I had no idea he was a hero. I just knew he was in the war."

"There's a lot of unknown heroes who walk amongst us," James noted. "That's why we show respect. We don't know everybody's story."

Johnny nodded. "You're right, Mr. James. Today showed me that."

"Hold the fort," James instructed. "I'm going outside to call the *Herald* and update Betsie on what's going on here."

He dropped a dime in the payphone slot and dialed the number.

"Betsie's not here," Mrs. Rose said anxiously. "She rushed off looking for you. She said something about a psycho being back in town who's looking for trouble."

# CHAPTER FORTY

"HEY, WAR HERO!" the raspy male voice emanated from the darkness.

James turned toward the creepy sound and saw the stranger's silhouette about ten feet away. The man looked as tall and wide as a refrigerator. "Do I know you?"

"Not personally, but by reputation."

"You're going to have to be more specific than that," James said.

"Tom Bannon."

"Who?"

"Tom Bannon," he repeated. "You got my job. And my girl. I heard she hired you because you got shot up over there. Is that what happened?"

James took two steps toward the man, but stopped when he saw the gun. He wasn't sure how to respond, but he knew one thing for sure. He'd spent enough time in hospitals and he didn't want to take any chances now with a lunatic gripping a six-shot revolver.

"I'm just a G.I. trying to fit in somewhere. You a vet, too?"

Bannon wrinkled his face and shook his head. "Nah, some of us had to stay back and see to it that Betsie got taken care of."

"From what I've seen, Betsie can take care of herself." James was getting angry and it showed in his voice. "Perhaps you were interested in being more than a caregiver."

The revolver made a distinctive click sound when Bannon pulled the hammer back. James was familiar with that sound, and death usually followed it.

"What would you know about that?" Bannon asked. "Did she tell you about us?"

"Only about a guy named Chuck."

"Chuck's a nobody!" he yelled out as a black '48 Chevrolet coupe came barreling around the corner, inadvertently shining its bright headlights on the confrontation.

James recognized Betsie's car and tried to wave her off. "Keep driving!" he yelled.

Bannon pulled the trigger. A flame lit up the parking lot as the sound of a single bullet pierced the air.

James rushed toward Bannon, but he had disappeared into the darkness. He ran back to check on Betsie. She threw both arms around him. "Are you okay? Were you shot?"

"I'm fine." His breathing was rapid but controlled. "Your headlights must have blinded him. He panicked and fled. He's gone now."

"He's never really gone," she lamented. "Thank God you're okay," she sighed with relief. "I'm glad I wasn't a second later. I raced over here to tell you about him."

"Who is he?"

"Tom Bannon?"

"Who the hell is Tom Bannon and why did he try to kill me?"

"Because he's crazy. His problems started when he tried to join the Marine Corps. He was found unfit for emotional reasons. He was sent back wearing a light-blue uniform."

James nodded. "Baby Blue Marine. I'm familiar with these types of men who were kicked out of boot camp, but had no civilian clothes. The Corps would give them a light-blue uniform to get back home."

"Yeah, well, Bannon was humiliated by the experience."

"What's that gotta do with you?" he asked.

"In time he earned a degree in journalism and I hired him last year. I was so consumed with running the family business and I needed the help. But hiring that giant idiot was a disaster. He thought the sun came up to hear him crow. He told everyone he had a bigger and better job offer in Dallas and I told him not to let the door hit his backside on the way out. He was so arrogant and delusional that I guess he never expected me to say that," she reflected.

"It's not your fault," he tried to comfort her.

"It gets scarier, though," she said. "The Dallas editor told me Tom had contacted him several times, and lately he's been saying that if they hired him, he'd bring along the woman he's engaged to."

James's eyebrows raised.

"That's right. Yours truly."

"Whoever said small towns were boring were flat-out wrong. This has been a fun-filled first two weeks in sleepy little Palestine," he replied.

"I'll call the sheriff," she said.

She, James, and Johnny waited inside the VFW with the other patrons while the sheriff's department conducted an unsuccessful search for Bannon.

"We'll find him," the sheriff promised. "In the meantime, get a gun and keep your head on a swivel."

"This is Texas," Betsie said and chuckled. "My daddy has plenty. I'll make sure James gets one." She turned toward James. "Maybe we'll see that skunk scurrying around somewhere."

"Bannon will be better off if the sheriff finds him before I do," James warned.

## CHAPTER FORTY-ONE

AS PROMISED, BETSIE picked James up at eight, and they drove to the airport diner to eat breakfast before flying.

"Eat light," she recommended with a tinge of humor. "I don't want you throwing up on me while we're in the air. If you throw up, then I'm gonna throw up."

He pressed his back against the chair, pushed out his stomach and patted it. "Don't worry. This is an iron stomach."

He noticed pilots coming and going as they enjoyed their meals. "I feel like we're part of an exclusive club," he said with excitement.

"Yes," she smiled. "An exclusive club of adventurers."

"I'm looking forward to joining this club."

She was cheerful as they walked across the airfield to the hangar.

"How long have you been a pilot?"

"I've been flying with my dad since I was knee high to a grasshopper."

"So, you've got a lot of hours then?"

"I have around one hundred," she said.

She was all business while going over the preflight inspection. She checked the tire tread, examined the prop for nicks, and the fuel to make sure they had plenty. Once she completed her preflight routine, they boarded. Betsie sat on the left side, James on the right. She flipped a switch and the engine roared to life. The propeller started spinning, becoming seemingly invisible. She reviewed her checklist and referenced every instrument one by one to make sure it was functioning properly.

"Are you ready to soar with the birds?"

"I was born ready," he said, beaming from ear to ear.

She taxied the short distance to the runway, and pushed the throttle all the way forward. The Cessna raced down the runway. When the plane reached sixty miles per hour, she pulled back on the yoke and they climbed into the clear blue sky.

"Everything okay, Mr. Charles Lindbergh?" she asked with a grin.

"More than okay, Miss Amelia Earhart. It's magical."

They'd been up for about an hour enjoying the gorgeous panoramas of green pastures and ponds. Seeing the matchbox-size cars and how tiny people looked below gave James a different perspective on life. *The Great State of Texas, and life, for that matter, had once seemed daunting and complicated, but from several thousand feet above it all, it seems small, manageable, and much easier to navigate*, he thought.

"You want to see my favorite place to fish?"

"Only if you take me fishing there one day," he said.

She banked the plane toward a lake and descended to a few feet over the water. "That's Old Man Lane in the canoe." She pointed the plane right at him.

James squirmed in his seat. "That's kind of close, ain't it!"

She pulled up at the last minute to buzz over the fisherman casting his bait.

"He likes when I give him a li'l scare. Keeps his heart young."

James turned his head and saw the red-faced fisherman waving with one finger.

"Yeah? He looked like he really enjoyed that," James chuckled.

She banked back southeast toward the airport. She brought the steady Cessna down to the tarmac and finished with a smooth landing that only made a "chirp" sound.

"That was even better than I expected!"

"Thank you, sir. I'm glad you enjoyed it so much," and tipped an imaginary cap.

"This flight was the most fun I've had in a while. I'll never look at earth the same way again."

"It's sweet you called me Miss Earhart," she said as they climbed out and commenced the post-flight routine. "She was my role model as a teenager. My mother told me all about her. The world needs more daring females."

"I agree. Have you ever thought of flight instructing? More women would probably fly if more instructors were women."

"I can't seem to find the time anymore with Pop working in Washington and my managing the *Herald*."

"So, you wouldn't teach me?"

She thought a moment and smiled. "I'd be too distracted to teach you."

"I'd be too distracted to learn," he said with a smile.

Driving back to town, they were quiet for a while, content just to be with one another.

"I was wondering," James said.

"Wondering about what?"

"I've heard you talk about your father, but nothing about your mother."

She didn't answer right away, and James worried he might have overstepped his bounds.

"Leukemia," she said barely audibly. She shook her air-blown brown hair back into place. "1935. I was sixteen years old. Daddy and I buried momma at St. Joseph's."

James took several slow breaths before responding. "I'm very sorry," he whispered.

"Thank you. She was a real go-getter. She liked to be in charge behind the scenes. She's the one who talked my father and uncle into getting into the news business. If she were still alive, my daddy would probably be the Texas governor… maybe even president."

"She must be very proud of you," James said.

"I hope so." Her tone changed. "Speaking of parents, the congressman will be in town this week. In fact, I have to rush off after I get you back and start straightening the house so it will pass his inspection."

"I assume you Blairs live close to town."

"We live in one of those haunted-looking mansions built for families with ten kids, and me an only child."

"Your folks were obviously going for quality instead of quantity."

"If that's supposed to be a facetious statement," she said as she dropped him off, "it's most welcomed. I could never spend a lot of time with a man who had been born without a sense of humor. I think it's the most charming of qualities."

James got out of the car and waved back at her. She rolled her window down and gave him an animated pouting expression.

He made an exaggerated show of hustling around to her open window and kissing her.

"Oh, by the way," she began, "the congressman loves to visit with war veterans. He especially enjoys having them over for dinner. I hope six o'clock works for you."

She drove off before he could answer.

## CHAPTER FORTY-TWO

THE PROSPECT OF meeting Congressman Mason Blair intimidated James. He was such an important person in Palestine, but more to the point, he was also the father of the woman James was in love with.

Betsie tried to put him at ease prior to the dinner party at the Blair house, but comically, almost everything she said made the occasion seem more stressful.

"Oh, you'll love Pop. He's regular folks, same as Lyndon."

James had lived outside Texas too long to pick up on the reference.

"Lyndon?"

"Lyndon Baines Johnson. He's our new junior senator. He and Pop are flying down together. Then Lyndon's going ahead to do some weekend business in Austin, but not before he has dinner with us. He even requested the fried chicken I made for them when he and Pop were in the House of Representatives together. You'll love him. He eats like a horse. Or a pig. But don't tell him I said that." She laughed at the image.

James hopped in his Ford and drove to the Blair house, navigating by using a pad of paper with scribbled directions.

Peering out the windshield as he turned down a tree-lined street with Victorian-style houses, he immediately recognized the exclusive neighborhood.

He pressed the brakes and stared through the passenger window at the sprawling two-story house with the circular driveway. He felt his chest tighten and his breathing slow. The dogwood tree was still there, but had grown quite a bit over four years. The curtains were open and he could see through the side-by-side dining room window. Annie Mae, Sharon, and Milton were eating together, just like he last saw them. They still appeared very happy together, and Sharon grew at least two feet. He wasn't sure how long he stayed there in the street, but it felt like forever. He wiped away a tear, and removed his foot from the brake and slowly pressed on the accelerator.

A three-story house sat at the end of the cul-de-sac. Three fancy cars lined the stone-paved circular driveway and a man wearing a hat stood alongside one of them.

"Good evening, sir. Are you here for the party?"

"Yes," James answered the uniformed man and extended his hand. "James Karl."

"Clifford Green, Mr. Johnson's driver. It should be a good time tonight," he said with a devilish smile and pointed to a bay window on the ground floor. "Mr. Blair and Mr. Johnson have already gotten into the whiskey in the private study."

James could see two men standing in the room and carrying on in animated fashion. "Are you driving Mr. Johnson all the way to Austin tonight?"

"It's an easy drive with this new Lincoln Cosmopolitan. Plus, Mr. Johnson will be passed out in the back, so I can concentrate only on driving."

"Be safe tonight, Mr. Green," James said and walked up to the oversized wooden door with stained-glass windows. He knocked with a closed fist.

A few moments later, Betsie opened the door and greeted him with a hug.

"The guest of honor is here," she said.

"I thought that was Mr. Johnson."

"Ha! We'll let him think that."

Shortly afterward, the congressmen joined Betsie and James in the parlor next to the dining room, where Betsie had set a festive table for four. Congressman Blair gave James a firm handshake while taking his forearm in his left hand. Johnson held back for a moment, then boomed with laughter.

"Mason, my friend, that's unmistakably a campaign-style handshake, and unless I just awakened from a bout of amnesia, this ain't no election year."

"You would know, you ol' baby-kissing coot," Mason replied.

The two statesmen laughed.

Johnson faced James. He towered over James by almost half a foot. He gave him precisely the same handshake. "Mister, you've done a honorable service to your country, and it's a blessing you're here with us tonight. I've known this young woman here for a long time and I'm real pleased that she's included you in our little get-together."

"I was going to tell you the same thing, sir," James replied.

Lyndon paused and then burst out laughing. He looked at Betsie and winked. "I like this fella already."

"What can I get you to drink?" Mason asked.

"Whatever you and Senator Johnson are drinking."

"Please, call me Lyndon. Or LBJ," he said in a friendly tone.

Mason handed James a tumbler and raised his chest level. "A toast. Here's to you, James, for making it out of the war alive."

"And," Lyndon interjected, "for choosing the great state of Texas for your new home."

"I'll drink to that," James announced as the three lowball glasses clinked together.

Betsie walked in with a plate full of chopped spicy deer sausage and a pack of toothpicks. "Your favorite to snack on until dinner's ready."

"Your daughter is something else," LBJ said as he discarded the toothpicks and grabbed a handful of venison.

Johnson charmed them over dinner with light-hearted stories from his service during the war. The man who would be president 14 years later had been stationed stateside until President Franklin Roosevelt directed the Undersecretary of the Navy to transfer Johnson to an assignment gathering information in the South Pacific.

"And James," Johnson said as he buttered another biscuit and picked up a piece of corn on the cob, "you'll never guess who he had me directly reporting to."

James smiled broadly and said, "You don't mean God himself, do you?"

"General Doug MacArthur is great in my book, and even greater in his."

The four of them joined in a hearty laugh.

Later that night, after Johnson's had departed, James helped Betsie straighten up the kitchen.

"A man of enormous appetites, was I right?" she commented. "I'm always surprised when I see them together that he's more than a decade younger than Pop, but he looks much older."

"Maybe he had a much rougher paper route as a child," James joked.

She giggled.

"You kiddos are having too much fun," Mason said as he walked into the kitchen with an ear-to-ear grin. "I thought I'd join y'all."

"No, no, no," Betsie shooed him away. "The constituents don't want to see dark circles under your eyes tomorrow. Get some rest."

"Hey," he protested. "How else will they be able to see how hard I've been working for them?" He turned toward James. "My daughter tells me you survived a perilous air adventure with her the other day."

"Enjoyed it thoroughly, sir. I'm hoping to become a pilot myself."

"That so? Then don't get my Betsie here for an instructor. She's far too demanding. And it takes twice as long to get a license when you're learning from a pretty teacher."

James smiled in her direction. "So, who would you recommend?"

"Frank Rogers is the fella I'd recommend. He never flew military planes, but for small aircraft, there's nobody better. He saved this county when the grasshoppers were destroying everybody's crops. He flew day and night to get rid of those pests and keep money in the farmers' pockets. Look him up, and give him my regards."

"I will. Thank you, sir."

Before heading off to his bedroom suite, he turned and said, "Oh, heads up. Frank Rogers is quite the character, but don't let that scare you off."

He climbed two steps and turned around. "And please call me Mason."

"Will do," James replied. "Good night, sir. It was a pleasure meeting you."

After her father had turned in for the night, Betsie squeezed James's hand and walked him into the parlor. They sat side by side on the sofa in dim light and kissed. James abruptly stopped when he glimpsed Mr. Blair out of the corner of his eye.

"Oh," a startled James quickly sat upright.

"What's wrong?" Betsie asked.

"Jeez!" James drew a breath and slowly exhaled. He motioned with his chin at the portrait that hung on the wall.

Betsie burst out laughing.

"Shh!" he tried to quiet her.

"Don't worry," she said. "Daddy sleeps like the dead. Especially after drinks, dinner, and more drinks with Lyndon."

James embraced her and leaned in for another kiss.

Mr. Blair smiled and tiptoed up the stairs, happy that his daughter had found someone to make her happy again.

# CHAPTER FORTY-THREE

*DECEMBER 25, 1949*

JAMES CELEBRATED CHRISTMAS at the Blair residence. It was the perfect place to be for that special holiday. Red and green lights adorned the exterior of the house and an enormous tree that reached to the ceiling stood center stage in their grand room. He hoisted Betsie up so she could place the angel on top.

"You men catch up," she told James and Mason with a smile. "I'm gonna check on the turkey."

"It smells great," James said. "I can't wait to eat."

James and Mason stood by the fireplace, not too far from where Mr. Blair's life-size portrait hung.

"The decorations look nice," James remarked. "I liked the manger scene in the front yard."

"That's all Betsie's doing," Mason replied. "Dotty, her mother, loved decorating for the holidays. This place would look like Santa's village." He smiled at the memory.

James nodded. "Thank you for letting me celebrate Christmas at your home."

"It's a pleasure to have you here. Thanks for bringing the eggnog."

"Do you like it?"

"I love it. It's rich, but light and creamy. Is it a family recipe?" He took another sip and used his pocket handkerchief to wipe off the excess on his upper lip.

James finished a gingerbread cookie and smiled. "I guess you could say that. It was a favorite of an old fisherman I used to be in partnership with."

"Where's this old fisherman now?"

"Not exactly sure where ol' Jack is. If he had his way, he'd be in the arms of a beautiful woman. Or at least in his own mind."

"Well," Mason chuckled, "let's hope he has some company. The holidays aren't as special without friends and family. Dotty passed fourteen years ago, and my only brother is far away running a newspaper in Alaska. Betsie's my only child. Because I'm gone all the time, I appreciate the friendship you and she have developed."

"Me too, sir. She's my best friend." James cleared his throat. "That's what I wanted to talk to you about, sir. I can't imagine my life without her. She's loyal, caring, funny, and I admire her sense of adventure, which she undoubtedly gets from you."

"Who's running for office? You or me?" Mason laughed.

James nervously placed his cup on the mantel.

"Is there a question somewhere in your flattery?" Mason asked

"Betsie thinks the world of you, and I think the world of her. I'd like to have your permission to marry her?"

"To be frank, ever since you came around, she's been like her old self—before Chuck was killed-in-action. She beams like the sun now. Both of you have so much in common with your journalism, aviation, and you're tough enough to put up with her strong will. It's a relationship made in heaven."

"Is that a yes?"

"Yes, you have my permission."

James extended his hand, but Mason swatted it away and leaned in for a hug. "When do you plan to pop the question?"

"It's a surprise," James answered.

"She doesn't like surprises," Mason smirked.

"I know," James grinned.

"Dinner's ready," Betsie said when she entered the living room. She saw the men standing oddly close to each other. She turned her head sideways and cracked an awkward smile. "Am I interrupting?"

The men abruptly created space.

"Not at all," Mason said. "I was telling James about how you always go above and beyond with the Christmas decorations. It makes me never want to leave Palestine and head back to Washington."

The three enjoyed a dinner of stuffed turkey, green bean casserole, and mashed potatoes with gravy. For dessert, they had their choice of sweet potato pie or coconut cake. James had a slice of each.

"I'm so full I'm about to pop," Mason said and stood up. He grabbed a present from under the Christmas tree. "Let's open some gifts before I take a nap." He handed James an ornately-wrapped box.

"Impressive wrapping," James noted. "Did you do this?"

Mason chuckled and looked at Betsie.

She smiled. "I do all the wrapping around here. Otherwise Pops would use newspaper and rubber bands."

"That way you can catch up on the news as you unwrap your gift," Mason joked.

James opened the box and pulled out a silk scarf and logbook. "Woah. These are perfect. They'll come in handy when I start flying lessons next week."

"That's great to hear," Mason said. "Who did you end up choosing for an instructor?"

"The crop duster you recommended."

"Frank Rogers?" Mason chuckled. "God help you."

James handed Mason a bottle of twenty-year old single malt Scotch. "Merry Christmas, sir."

"Thank you," Mason said. "I'll have to hide it from Lyndon, or he'll drink it like iced water on a summer day."

James handed Betsie a box. "I confess. I'm like your father when it comes to wrapping gifts."

"It looks fine," she said, slowly unraveling the paper. "Who did this for you then?"

"I bribed Mrs. Rose at the office."

Betsie giggled. "Yeah, Mrs. Rose is a grandmother. So she's had lots of practice over the years." Betsie continued opening her box. "Oh, I love it, James," she exclaimed and held the pearl necklace in the air to show it off.

"Beautiful," Mason said.

"Wait," James said. "There's another gift in there."

"What? There is? She removed all the tissue paper and noticed a bottle of perfume. She placed it to her nose and inhaled. "Mmm, it smells wonderful," she said and smiled. "Thank you very much."

"He's a fisherman after all," Mason said. "He knows the right bait to use," he chuckled.

She shot a glare at her father. "Did you just refer to me as a fish?"

"Metaphorically," he smiled.

She turned her attention back to James. "Now open mine," she said and handed him a large box with a peppermint pattern and oversized gold bow.

He opened it and discovered there was another box in it. He opened that box and discovered there was yet another box. The three of them laughed as he opened at least four boxes until he discovered the gift inside.

"Oh, gosh! You remembered," he said as he admired the Arvin 444 radio.

"Of course, I did," she replied. "It was our first date. And how could I forget that story you told about being in the war listening to an Arvin radio to make you feel closer to home?"

He nodded, not wanting to speak for fear of his emotions getting the best of him.

"Now you'll never feel homesick again," she said.

# CHAPTER FORTY-FOUR

"SO YOU KNOW Mason Blair," Frank Rogers stated when James reached him by telephone to discuss flight training. "Tell me how that old tax-and-spend rascal is giving away my money back in Washington these days."

"I have no idea, but I'll sure pass along your concern to him."

The outspoken crop duster started laughing. "If he ran his business like he runs Congress, the *Herald* would be bankrupt."

"Well," James said, "it's only Betsie and me running the *Herald* nowadays."

His gruff voice softened. "I've known Betsie since she was a pup. I've always liked her. She's sweet as a summer peach." He cleared the phlegm in his throat. "Meet me at the airport at noon and we'll see if we can make a pilot out of you."

James rolled up to the airport and saw a man tinkering with an airplane by the fuel pumps. James couldn't tell if he was a mechanic or a pilot, only that it was freezing outside and the man was wearing a button down short-sleeve shirt and cursing. James saw no other pilots, so he approached the stranger.

"Are you Mr. Rogers?" he asked.

"It's just Frank. Mr. Rogers died a decade ago. I buried him myself."

"I'm James."

"I figured," Frank said. He used a dirty rag to dry his hands before shaking James's hand.

"Do you have a jacket?" James asked.

"Yeah," he coughed. "It's colder than a well digger's ass, but I get hot. Doctors say it's my thyroid, but what do they know?"

He lit up a cigarette.

"Why do you want to learn how to fly?"

"The feeling of freedom. When Betsie took me flying, it was revelatory."

"It was what?"

"Revelatory," James repeated.

"Don't be using them five-dollar words. I ain't a journalist. I'm a crop duster."

James grinned. "Flying changed my perspective. I saw the world and my place in it differently. It's also a challenge, and an opportunity. I can hop in my car and drive for days, or I can hop in an airplane and be there in hours."

He sucked air through his teeth and spit out a piece of tobacco. Seemingly satisfied with James's response, he nodded. "Amigo, this ain't like your jalopy, where you can pull over and fix any problems. Any pilot worth his salt first has to learn how to aviate on the ground. I'm gonna teach you how to aviate, navigate, and communicate," he exhaled a chain of smoke rings.

It occurred to James that Frank's name might more appropriately be "Joe Camel." It seemed as though a cigarette was one of his appendages. Coffee and tobacco had stained brown what James imagined was once a white mustache. He also found it distracting that Frank would hold one between his thumb and pointer finger or have one dangling from his lips.

"Amigo, I must've been thirty the first time I saw one of these winged contraptions fly over," he recalled. "It was 1928. By then, it seemed everybody was flying because Lindbergh had crossed the Atlantic. You'd thought the whole world had changed. I reckon it sorta did."

"For the better," James offered.

"Yeah, after Lindbergh got back from France, dozens, maybe hundreds of cocky pilots tried to fly the Atlantic. I like to fly where there's land below. Ol' Frank never learned to swim." He lit another cigarette from the one he was smoking.

"Or had to buy more than one box of matches," James mused.

Rogers started laughing, but James wasn't quite sure how to take him yet. *Maybe he had inhaled too many of the chemicals he had been spraying over the fields*, James thought. *An occupational hazard.*

"Well, we've done enough yakking." Frank ogled his faded red taildragger with adoration. "How about seeing if she'll fly?"

"Sounds more like a question than a statement," James replied, now feeling much more appreciative of how well-maintained Betsie's pristine Cessna was.

Once they climbed into the plane, James grabbed the pilot's operating handbook to reference the checklist, as he had seen Betsie do whenever they flew together.

"This ain't the library, amigo. If you wanna read a book, you can go there after this lesson. At this moment in time, you are in the presence of a flying machine. You think Orville and Wilbur had a book?"

"I don't think they even had a pilot's license."

"Exactly!" Frank said. "You pilot this by feeling it with your hands on the stick and your butt on the seat. Hell, your Ford has more instruments and gauges than this thing. Visualize what you want to do, and then do it."

James soon discovered that Frank was an incredibly talented aviator and an outstanding flight instructor. He could be brash when he spoke, but he was always calm and collected when he was flying.

"You make it look so easy," James said after watching Frank demonstrate a takeoff and a few turns.

"Anybody can learn it, amigo. I could teach a monkey how to fly this thing. Now, landing it would be a different story. Speaking of landing, let's head on back to the field. I'm gonna let you land this one," he told James as they approached the runway.

"You sure about that? This will be my first landing. Ever."

"The sword is forged in the fire," Frank replied.

"Let's hope I can land this contraption better than a monkey can," James joked.

"That goes for both of us," he said as he exhaled a plume of smoke. "Pull the throttle to idle," he instructed. "Pick a spot on the runway and glide us all the way down."

James felt a rush of adrenaline course through his veins as he piloted the plane toward the ground. He did as Frank had told him and right before landing, he pulled back on the stick for the tires to make contact with the asphalt.

"You landed that like a duck with hemorrhoids," Frank said. "You keep flying like this, and I'll feel comfortable letting you fly my kids around."

"You have kids?" James asked incredulously.

"I'm sure I do. Somewhere."

## CHAPTER FORTY-FIVE

"**I**'M GLAD YOU started taking flying lessons," Betsie told James one morning at the *Herald*.

He could tell in Betsie's voice that she was plotting something.

"Why's that?"

"I've been thinking about expanding our business to serve folks in the countryside who don't make it into the city as often as they'd like."

James stopped chewing his sausage biscuit to listen more intently.

"We have the Cessna sitting in the hangar, and we can help the folks in Frankston, Montalba, Slocum, and Elkhart get the news. We could call it the 'Plane Paper' subscription, and we'll only charge a fraction more for it than our regular edition."

He smiled and pointed both hands toward his chest. "And you're looking for a pilot?"

"You can build your hours while flying with Frank."

"That's true," he agreed.

"You can work on your pilot's license while helping the community at the same time. I already have several confirmed subscriptions."

"You sold me on the idea," he said.

"Good, because we need to start tomorrow."

"For someone who doesn't like surprises, you're full of 'em. I'll call Frank right now," he said and picked up the phone.

"That's a terrific idea, amigo. We can kill two birds with one stone," Frank said. "On second thought, let's hope we don't kill any birds. It does make for exciting landings, though."

"Okay, Frank. I'll grab the newspapers first thing in the morning and see you at the airfield at eight."

"Don't forget your logbook," Frank said before hanging up.

## CHAPTER FORTY-SIX

THE IDEA OF flying over Anderson County to deliver newspapers like Santa Claus on Christmas morning excited James. He skipped breakfast and drove straight to the *Herald* to pick up a stack of papers and a map that Betsie had marked for him.

Frank was enjoying a cup of coffee at the airport diner with the sheriff when James arrived.

"Morning Sheriff," James greeted the uniformed lawman who wore a white Stetson. "Did you ever find Tom Bannon?"

He shook his head. "Not yet, Mr. Karl. There's an active warrant out. If somebody comes across him, we'll book him. We always find our man one way or another. He'll make a mistake."

"Hopefully that mistake doesn't cost someone's life next time."

"Amigo," Frank interrupted, "go preflight the plane while I finish telling the sheriff how to clean up this county."

"You clean the county by taking out the trash," James said before heading outside.

While James was checking the fuel and oil, Frank started marching toward him. James could tell that Frank was eager to depart.

"Sheriff said there's a boy in Elkhart who got bitten by a rabid fox," Frank said as they climbed into the cockpit. "They got a search team looking for that beast right now. We might even fly over 'em and get a cash reward if we hit the fox with one of our newspaper bombs," he laughed.

James made a smooth takeoff and turned southeast toward downtown. After soaring over Main Street and the *Herald* building for fun, they followed the railroad tracks to Elkhart and an area known by the locals as "Scrounge-out."

Using Betsie's map for guidance, Frank piloted while James threw the paper bundles out of the plane from a few hundred feet off the ground. After about the tenth and final airdrop, James took the controls and started flying them back to Palestine.

James and Frank were discussing the lost boy when their engine suddenly lost power and quit. The cockpit became eerily quiet.

Frank, completely calm, remarked, "This is a perfect teaching opportunity and proves one of my points. This airplane is basically a glider with an engine that works most of the time. Landing this glider requires following the ABCs."

"'A' is for airspeed," Frank continued. "Let's make our emergency glide speed at 55 knots. That will give us our greatest glide distance. 'B' is for best landing spot. That open field over there looks like the best place to set 'er down. And 'C' stands for cockpit checks. Carb heat is on, mixture is rich, and ignition is on. Check your seatbelt."

"Mine is on," James replied as he pulled his tight.

"They don't really matter in a plane anyway," Frank chortled. "I'm going to unlatch the door in case we have to get out quickly when we land. You know, in case there's a fire."

"Okay," James said as he focused all his energy on the emergency landing.

Frank, out of seemingly nowhere, filled their silent descent with, "*In der Not frisst der Teufel Fliegen.*"

"My German is bad," James said as his breathing increased. "Mind telling me what the hell you just said?"

"That's what my instructor told me when I experienced my first engine failure. I'm passing his pearls of wisdom onto you. You never know when it might come in handy. It's Kraut for 'In times of need, even the Devil eats flies.' Beggars can't be choosy. We'd all like to have a ten thousand-foot runway to land on, but today it's a farmer's field with trees and barb-wire fences. We gotta do what we gotta do to survive until another day. Ol' Frank Rogers ain't going out in a plane crash. That'd be a mark on my record."

"A mark on your record," James said as he glanced at the airspeed indicator that was pointing at 63 miles per hour. "That would be the *end* of your record!"

Frank calmly lit a cigarette he had retrieved from his shirt pocket.

"How can you even think about smoking at a time like this?" James asked. "You're not nervous?"

"I am, but smoking calms me."

James wiped the beading sweat from his forehead and gave himself some positive affirmation. *You can do this. You can land this plane.* Then it dawned on him. He recognized the farm. "We can't land here!" he protested.

"Amigo, if you have a better option, I'm all ears. But we're descending at five hundred feet per minute. I'm no mathematician, but if I were a betting man, and ol' Frank Rogers is, I'd estimate that rubber will kiss the grass in less than thirty seconds."

*I'm landing in John Robert Axum's field, my dad's farm!*

## CHAPTER FORTY-SEVEN

FRANK GAVE JAMES some very last-second advice before landing.

"The grass creates a lot of drag. Make sure to land tail low to keep the propeller higher than the grass. This farmer ain't paying us to mow the yard."

James's novice landing made a thumping sound and they continued hopping across the field until the airplane came to a rolling stop.

"Not too shabby, amigo," Frank said as they exited the plane.

A hulking German Shepherd came running toward them. His canines protruded and his barks grew louder as the animal closed the distance. An old farmer in overalls hastened to catch up.

The dog jumped on James.

"Good boy! Good boy!" James repeated as he petted the dog.

"Hold it right there!" The farmer's command boomed in the countryside. In true Texas fashion, John Robert Axum greeted Frank and James with a double-barrel shotgun pointed straight at their chests. "What in tarnation are you fellas doing landing that contraption on my property?"

The dog remained on two feet, its tail wagging in circles as he licked James's face.

"Easy, Ace," James said. "Come on, boy. Get down. You're slobbering all over me."

"How'd you know my dog's name is Ace?" the farmer asked.

"Uh-uh," James stammered. "He looks like an Ace to me."

"Get over here, Ace!" The farmer demanded, but his dog didn't listen. "I can't understand this. Ace don't like nobody but family."

"Ace is a good judge of character," James replied. "He knows we mean no harm. We're just delivering the *Palestine Herald*."

"We don't subscribe," the farmer said.

"Neither do I," Frank remarked.

"Well, it's your lucky day," James said. "Here's your complimentary copy. Hand delivered. As a matter of fact, here's a few copies. Would you mind passing them out?"

"If you don't read the paper," Frank said, "you can use it as kindling to stay warm on a cold night."

John Robert laughed and lowered his shotgun.

Frank lit up a cigarette and began inspecting the fuselage for damage. He carefully slid his hand across the red-colored fabric that showed its age. "Ginger, we've survived another one unscathed." He smiled and puffed out a white cloud of cigarette smoke. "We'll fix you up and be back in the air."

"My dog sure has taken a liking to you," the farmer noticed. "Can I give you some help with your broken plane?"

"You know how to fix airplanes?" Frank asked with skepticism.

"Never tinkered with an airplane before, but I'm pretty mechanical. One of my sons drives a school bus that's always breaking down. His brother used to help him with the maintenance, but after he died in the war, I'm the one who helps him keep the engine running. I'm actually the one who taught my sons how to work on equipment. We have to be self-sufficient out in the country."

"Frank," James said looking at his instructor, "why don't you enjoy your smoke? This kind gentleman and I will get your plane running again."

"Nobody works on Ginger but me," Frank said.

"Well, why don't you tell us what to do and we'll do it. Consider it part of my lesson."

Frank nodded and inspected his dirty fingernails. "That'll work. I won't have to get these mitts any dirtier. I can supervise."

James opened the cowling, which revealed the plane's engine and components.

"I'm sorry to hear about your son," James said as he and John Robert stood shoulder to shoulder peering into the guts of the plane.

"Preciate it," he said. "You got kids?"

"No sir," James answered. He removed the scarf Mason gave him and wrapped it around his forehead to keep the sweat from dripping into his eyes.

"You never get over the loss of one. It's odd. I've known you for five minutes, but in some ways, you remind me of him."

"Yeah? How's that?"

"Nothing ever rattled him. You crashed this plane into my field and you haven't shown any fear. He was like that when he got drafted into the Army. He never showed any fear. You didn't show any when Ace charged at you, or even when I pointed my shotgun at you. You didn't even flinch."

"I knew you weren't gonna pull the trigger," James said.

"How did you reckon?"

"I just knew," he said.

"This engine ain't much different than a tractor or a bus engine," John Robert noted.

James smiled. "No hill for a mountain climber," he quipped.

A strange feeling washed over John Robert, almost spiritual. He felt goosebumps on his arms and the hair on the back of his neck stood up. "I used to say that to my sons."

"My dad used to tell me the same thing."

"Have we met before?"

"It certainly feels like it, doesn't it?" James answered. "The French call it *déjà vu*."

"I don't know what them Frenchies call it," John Robert said. "But I feel like I know you."

James fought back tears and used his scarf to wipe his face. He knew he was about to breakdown and had to change the subject quickly.

"Looks like it was the carburetor that had iced up," he said as he pointed to the part.

"Wouldn't be the first time," Frank said. "Probably from the constant changes in airspeed coupled with the high humidity this region is so well known for."

"Are you sure we haven't met before?" John Robert pressed the issue. "My name is John Robert Axum. My friends call me J.R."

James's legs trembled from the emotions of seeing his father for the first time in five years. "I'm sure I'd never forget someone like you," he said.

Frank spoke up. "This here Yankee moved here from ORE-ee-GONE a couple months ago. Found work at the *Herald* and now he's trying to impress Betsie Blair by getting his pilot's license."

"Hmm," John Robert scoffed. He cracked a smile and nodded his head. "Sounds like something my son would do to impress a girl, especially one as fetching as that newspaper gal. Boys will be boys, I guess."

James laughed. "Sounds like he and I could have been best friends." He suddenly hugged his father. "Thank you."

"For what?"

"For everything," James replied. "For everything."

Surprised, John Robert hugged him back and held on.

"I hate to break this up," Frank coughed. "But we still got trainin' to do."

James waved goodbye to his father as the taildragger climbed over the trees and headed back to Palestine.

"Give me your logbook," Frank said after James landed in Palestine. Frank tossed on a pair of flimsy glasses and opened the small book to one of the first few pages. He scribbled on one of the many lines: "1.2 hours. Off-airport landing successfully demonstrated. Avoided being shot."

He handed the logbook back to James. "I'm proud of you. You kept your cool today when everything should have been telling your mind to panic. You're a real aviator in the making."

James couldn't help but smile from the compliments. "Thank you, amigo."

## CHAPTER FORTY-EIGHT

J AMES CONTINUED HIS flight lessons with Frank Rogers for a few months.

"Taxi us to the ramp," Frank said one afternoon after James had demonstrated three perfect takeoffs and landings. "Keep the engine running. I'm going to grab a coffee. You want anything?"

"No, thank you," James answered. "I'm not quite ready to fly *and* drink coffee at the same time."

"No, but you are ready to fly Ginger by yourself. Go have some fun and I'll see you back in an hour."

Frank shut the door, turned his back toward James and casually headed toward the diner. He lifted his hand for a lazy goodbye.

Any feelings of nervousness quickly dissipated when James realized he was once again in control of his destiny. He hummed with jubilation all the way to the runway. He advanced the throttle and soared over his natal homeland and marveled at the countryside. It was springtime and green pastures and flowers appeared to cover the entire earth. He felt free as a bird and grateful God had saved him in Europe, and at sea. After flying what seemed like hours, he searched the landscape for the white-water tower and navigated back to Palestine.

Frank had trained him so well that he made his first landing completely by himself without any complications. Pure joy poured out of him as he rolled to a stop near the diner and cut off the engine. A crowd of well-wishers surrounded the airplane to congratulate him, but one person stood out.

"Oh, James," Betsie exclaimed. "I'm so proud of you! This calls for a celebration."

"Hold your horses," Frank demanded. "Get over here, amigo. Turn around. We have to stick to tradition."

He drew an airplane landing on the back of James's shirt with the inscription: "James Karl – Solo 04/08/1950 – Palestine, Texas." He pulled out a folding pocket knife and cut that part of the shirt off and hung it on the wall of the airport diner. Next to it were the other shirts from student pilots who had successfully piloted an airplane for their first time.

Betsie explained the history of cutting the shirttail after a first solo flight. "The old training planes were designed where the instructor sat behind the student. There were no headphones, so the instructor had to tug on the back of the student's shirt to get his attention. Cutting the shirttail symbolized that the student no longer needed the help."

James looked at the tacked shirttails on the wall and noticed one missing.

"Where is yours?"

Betsie laughed and did her best impression of Frank Rogers. "Amiga, I would cut your shirt, but I don't think the conservative folks around these parts are ready for you to be running around here like a Juarez street walker. That would be a mark on my record."

"He's a helluva character," James said as they enjoyed pie and coffee. "He taught you and me how to be a pilot." He leaned back in his chair and smiled with pride as the words sunk in. "I'm a pilot now, a bona fide aviator."

"You certainly are," she said.

"With your encouragement, I accomplished one of my dreams."

"Just *one* of your dreams?" she asked.

"Well, I have a few more on my list," he said.

# CHAPTER FORTY-NINE

"WE NEED A break from the *Herald* for a few days," James suggested. "This work never stops."

"That's the news for you," Betsie replied. "It's a good thing. Otherwise, we'd be out of work."

"How about we fly to Cozumel?"

"That would be wonderful," she said. "Pops and I have vacationed there several times, and it's such a special place to us."

"I know," he replied. *I hope to make it a special place for us, too.*

The Cessna picked up radio stations and they sang along to the tunes. It made the journey fly by. Betsie was a much better singer than James, and she seemed to enjoy the lime-light—even if it was just an audience of one.

They landed in Cozumel and caught the ferry to Playa del Carmen. The town was as colorful as the iguanas that lounged in the lush foliage. Betsie loved the fresh seafood, which had been swimming in the shallow bay hours earlier, but she couldn't conquer her fear of the iguanas. She shrieked each time one crossed her path, but James secretly liked them because their presence threw Betsie into his arms for protection.

"This is so wonderful," Betsie said while sunbathing a few feet from the crystal clear waters.

James nodded. "You and your dad are right. This place is paradise."

He put down his novel. "How about a dip in the water? My friend Andy used to say that the ocean erases all problems."

"Problems? We don't have no stinking problems," she said in her best Mexican accent.

He laughed. "You're right. We don't." He grabbed her hand and gently pulled her into the warm ocean water.

They spent the next two days relaxing and enjoying each other's company. On the third night, as they sipped chilled margaritas sitting on the warm sand, James reached into his pocket.

"You're not gonna believe this, sweetheart. I forgot to tell you that I found this on the beach earlier today. It might be something you'd be interested in seeing."

It was a wooden box no bigger than a lady's compact and wrapped with a single strand of gold ribbon. She held it for what seemed like a minute. She was expressionless.

"Well, aren't you gonna open it?"

She smiled. Her eyes dotted back and forth to the box and James. "So, you're saying you found this on the beach, and it was wrapped this nicely and everything?"

"Well," he relented, "I made up parts of this story."

Her fingers trembled as she untied the gold ribbon and unlatched the box. The inside revealed a yellow gold band with an ornate setting and a sparkling diamond.

"Oh, James. It's gorgeous."

James knelt one knee onto the sand and took her hand in his. "I never knew in this lifetime that someone like you could make me this happy. I'm the happiest man on earth when I'm with you. Will you marry me?"

"Yes! The answer is yes."

He placed the ring on her finger, and she hugged him tighter than ever.

"You had this planned the whole time, didn't you?"

"Guilty as charged."

"You rascal." She laughed while wiping away tears.

She couldn't keep her eyes off the diamond ring, and James couldn't keep his eyes off her. They held hands and walked barefoot on the sandy beach. Not only had his life been a reawakening, but his heart as well. He was completely in love again.

# CHAPTER FIFTY

*JULY 4, 1950*

BETSIE DIDN'T WANT her wedding to become a political event even though she shared the day with the nation's birthday. So, she and James planned a simple ceremony with a Justice of the Peace, who was a dear family friend. Mr. Mason Blair graciously hosted the private wedding reception at his estate. Employees from the *Herald* and a few of Betsie's childhood friends attended the reception.

"Daddy, this is all so wonderful," she expressed as she and James walked through the door and gazed upon the living room and dining room that were tastefully decorated in red, white, and blue décor. A two-tiered wedding cake surrounded by flowers sat in the middle of the long dining table.

"Well, if you didn't let me throw you a lavish wedding, this is the least I could do. Your momma would have been disappointed if you didn't have a wedding cake and flowers," Mason said.

"I love it! Thank you." She hugged him and kissed him on the cheek. "You did great!"

"*You* did great," he replied. "You found a good man and I'm happy for the both of you. Your momma would be so proud. She's watching you from above right now."

"Don't make me cry on my wedding day," she said.

"I thought that's what fathers of the bride were supposed to do," he joked.

"I think you got that backward, Daddy."

The wedding took place in their backyard. Betsie and James stood inside a gazebo decorated with sprays of red and white flowers, while their guests watched from chairs set up in four rows on the manicured grass. Betsie's pearl necklace perfectly accented her elegant satin-white A-line dress. James wore a tailored grey suit.

"We are here to celebrate the marriage vows between James Karl and Betsie Blair," the Justice of the Peace announced. "A marriage ceremony represents one of life's greatest commitments and is also a public expression of love."

He looked at the groom. "Do you, James, take Betsie, to be your wife, to have and to hold from this day forward; for better, for worse, for richer, for poorer; in sickness and in health; to love, to honor, and to cherish till death do you part?"

"Yes, I do," he affirmed with a dazzling smile.

"Do you, Betsie, take James, to be your husband, to have and to hold from this day forward; for better, for worse, for richer, for poorer: in sickness and in health; to love, to honor, and to cherish till death do you part?"

She gazed into James's brown eyes. "I do," she said.

"May the circle of your wedding rings remind you of your unending commitment to love and respect each other. By the authority vested in me by the State of Texas, I now pronounce you husband and wife."

James dipped Betsie backward and kissed her, to the applause of the onlookers.

While the guests enjoyed barbeque, lemonade, and cake, Betsie regaled them with the story of how she and James met and about the surprise proposal in Mexico.

Mason pulled James aside and escorted him to the private study.

He cracked open the bottle of Scotch that James had given him for Christmas. "I've been waiting for the right time to let this breathe. I'm delighted you two found each other. It's a joy seeing my little Betsie so happy."

"I feel the same way, sir," James said.

"I've got something for you," Mason said and reached into his gun display case. He grabbed an ornate, intricately carved 1925 Ithaca model double-barreled shotgun.

"This beauty was given to me by my father, and now. I want you to have it."

"Mr. Blair, there's no way I can accept this. It's your family heirloom."

"Exactly right. Son, you are family. Now, go on and take it." He smiled and hugged James.

Lyndon Johnson navigated his way to Mason's study to help himself to a drink much stronger than the provided lemonade and was pleased to find Mason and James.

"What's a fella gotta do to get a decent drink around this joint? It figures you two would beat me to the whiskey."

"Try this," Mason said and poured him some of what he and James had been drinking.

Lyndon took a gulp.

"Mason, you've been holding out on me."

"It's a gift from my son-in-law."

"Well, I should be drinking with him then," Lyndon said and smiled. He turned toward James. "Lady Bird and I couldn't be happier for the two of you today. Our wedding gifts aren't nearly as fancy as that there scattergun, but they're practical." He pointed to a wrapped box in the corner of the room. "I'm not much for surprises. They're matching Lucchese western boots. Custom-made for both of you."

"How did you know my size?" James asked.

Lyndon took another swig. "I didn't. If they're too big, wear an extra pair of socks."

When the last of the guests departed, James and Betsie collapsed onto a comfortable couch.

"This was such an amazing day," James said.

"Yes, it was," Betsie agreed. "I wished Uncle Jacob could have made it. It's not like him to miss such an important event in my life. I'm concerned about his health. I had also hoped your family could have attended."

"They would have loved to be here," James said, knowing he had not told them until last-minute, "but Portland is so far away and we threw this wedding together in record time."

"Record time?" she scoffed. "It's not like we eloped. Well, that settles it then. If they can't visit us in Texas, we'll go to Portland and see them."

"What?" James felt the buzz of an exciting day start to wear off. "We gotta stay here and run the *Herald*."

"It can be our honeymoon," she said.

"My God! There are better places to spend a honeymoon than in Portland."

"We could leave in late summer. The weather should be pleasant. Johnny can run the *Herald*. We'll only be gone a week. It'll be good for him to get that kind of experience."

James knew she wouldn't let it rest until she got her way. He kissed her on the forehead.

"Okay. I'll make some calls and check the airline schedules."

She giggled. "Airlines? We both have our pilots' licenses now. We'll take the, or should I say, *our* Cessna."

*A flight across the country with us at the controls. What a grand adventure.*

"You're right," he said with a new perspective. "I better let the Karls know we're coming."

*That's so odd,* she thought. *Why does he refer to his family as the Karls?*

## CHAPTER FIFTY-ONE

JAMES AND BETSIE sat side-by-side in the Cessna's cockpit.

"We'll fly west to California, then north to Oregon," James said as he dragged his finger across the brand-new aeronautical chart. "If we're lucky, we'll be in Portland by nightfall."

"We'll be lucky," Betsie said with a smile. "After all, it's our honeymoon."

He grinned and kissed her.

"I'm going to have to add that to my preflight checklist," she said and smiled.

"Only if I'm flying with you."

He started the Cessna and the plane shuddered to life. He advanced the throttle and soon they were climbing into the sky.

"Off into the wild blue yonder," they sang.

He leveled the plane at 4,500 feet. They soared over mostly flat, barren landscape as they traversed West Texas.

"Imagine visiting each of the forty-eight states during a single barnstorming event."

"Sounds like a grand adventure," she replied. "America is trying to expand its national roads. We could do a news story on it. Our theme could be that more and more Americans have access to better roads, more reliable cars, and more money to travel."

"Exactly!" he said. "Our theme could be the ultimate visit to each of the states, but by personal airplane."

After flying all day, they landed at an airstrip outside Portland. It was one of the few places in the region where the fledgling car-rental business had taken hold. They had arranged to pick up and drive a new Chevy coupe for a few days, so that they wouldn't burden the Karls.

"By the way, what's the most fun thing to do here?" Betsie asked.

"Portland's a neat town. There are plenty of things to do, I suppose."

"You suppose?" she asked.

"Well," James struggled to come up with a quick answer, not knowing anything about his *hometown*. "Ahem," he cleared his throat. "Remember, I haven't been here in several years."

"In that case, show me some of the places you liked as a kid," she insisted.

"This old city has changed a lot," he remarked, feeling the stress building up inside him as they checked into The Benson Hotel.

"Here's your key," the clerk said. "You'll be staying with us in the penthouse. The bellhop will take your luggage."

"I'll catch up," he told Betsie. "I'm going to talk with the concierge first."

"Okay," she said. "I need to freshen up before dinner anyway."

Clocks depicting the current time of major international cities lined the wall of the concierge. A balding man in a three-piece suit stood watch at the desk. James was about to ask the employee for sightseeing ideas and recommended restaurants when he heard commotion from across the lobby. He turned to the sound.

"James!"

*No need to be concerned about how we spend our time,* he realized. Hans, Anna, and Agnes ran toward him, and they had already planned every detail of the trip.

## CHAPTER FIFTY-TWO

"ONE OF MY fondest memories as a father," Hans began as they crossed the Steel Bridge over the Willamette River, "is when I took James to see Harry Houdini drop from this very bridge, sealed in a trunk. He managed to escape even though he was bound and shackled! That was November 1924. My, how time gets away."

"Dad, you always tell that story when we cross this bridge," Agnes said.

"Well, it's a good story," Hans replied, to the laughter of everyone. "My James has always loved magic."

Betsie looked at James. "I didn't know that about you."

He winked at her. "That makes two of us."

Hans insisted they dine at an elegant steakhouse to commemorate the occasion. He held a glass of red wine in the air and offered a toast.

"I'll never forget that call from Father Sidney." His voice started to crack. Agnes and Anna each reached out and touched him for support. "That my son was not only found, but that he was alive." He fought through the words. "In many ways, my James came back a different man. But I've never seen him as happy as he is with you, Betsie."

Betsie smiled.

James raised his glass and spoke. "Fate delivered me from the battlefield and led me to Betsie." He turned to his beautiful wife. "I've never been more in love. There isn't a day that passes where I'm not thankful to be alive. God has blessed me."

"That's so sweet," Agnes said.

"Yes, it is," Anna said, wiping away a tear.

"Are you crying?" James asked Anna.

"It's the pregnancy," she said. "I'm more emotional now."

He nodded in surprise.

"To new beginnings," Hans toasted.

"To new beginnings," they repeated.

They raised their glasses and took a drink.

Sometime after dinner but before dessert, Anna struck up a conversation with Betsie.

"I'm amazed at the effect you've had on our brother. He's a different person around you."

"I had always hoped he would find someone in Portland," Agnes said. "Not such a distant place like Texas where we'd never see him. But after seeing how happy he is, I'm just glad both of you found each other."

Betsie smiled. "Me too. It's like he fell out of the sky."

As the night ended late and everyone was saying goodbye, Betsie hugged Hans and the sisters. "I already feel like a member of the Karl family."

With a slight smile, James thought to himself, *Yes, and so do I.*

James and Betsie's honeymoon to Portland passed quickly. As they flew back to Texas, Betsie commented about how well the trip had gone.

"That was such a wonderful visit with your family. I'm so glad I finally got to meet them. I wish I had sisters like them growing up."

James nodded. *If ever a man had to be adopted by a family,* he had thought many times, *I could have done much worse than the Karls.*

# CHAPTER FIFTY-THREE

J ACOB BLAIR, BETSIE'S only uncle, had experienced a precipitous decline in health. Diabetes weakened him, and the rigors of running a large daily newspaper in Anchorage was also taking its toll.

Mason, the elder brother, had always been more of a father figure for Jacob. Knowing that Jacob likely had limited time for anything resembling a normal life, Mason freed his calendar for two weeks for a visit to Alaska.

It was still midday and Mason suggested that the brothers stop for lunch at the Milky Way Café, a popular diner on the main drag in Anchorage.

"Same menu, I'm happy to see," Mason smiled as he considered his options. "I'm sticking with the triple-hit breakfast, same as I had last time."

"You could always eat breakfast no matter the time," Jacob said.

"It's the most important meal of the day, regardless the time you eat it," Mason said.

Jacob ordered a much lighter meal, no doubt due to his diminishing health.

At the Milky Way, Jacob apprised Mason of the ongoing problems faced by the *Midnight Sun*.

"I can't tell you, Mace, how much I wished I'd married and had a daughter like Betsie so that I'd have the help I need to keep things moving at the paper. Wouldn't want to lend her to me, would you?"

"I wish I could," he said. "She's got plenty on her plate as it is, running the *Herald* and being a wife."

He shook his head in disbelief. "Married...I still think of her as a little girl."

"She'll always be my little sunflower," Mason said.

"I'm sorry I couldn't make the wedding. I would have loved to."

"I know," Mason said. "We missed you, but we understood."

They enjoyed catching up while eating their meal. When they finished, they drove to Jacob's cabin.

"I see you haven't cleaned the cabin since you built it," Mason said. "When are you going to get rid of all this junk lying around?"

"Junk? These are memories," he declared. "One man's junk is another man's treasure."

"Yeah, yeah. More like what's cow dung to a farmer is a banquet to a fly."

"Hey buddy. I know where everything is. It might be a mess to you, but it's an organized mess. Music records over there, newspaper articles there, pictures on the floor in the corner there. My manuscript over there."

"Oh, you finally finished it?"

"How can I finish it when I'm still a work in progress?" Jacob chuckled. "Someday I'll get around to finishing it."

"Someday ain't on the calendar," Mason wisecracked.

"In all this mess, I still have something I want to show you." He rummaged through some files on his desk and pulled out a faded newspaper article. He blew the dust off and showed it to his brother. Mason smiled at the photo of his younger self taking the oath to become a congressman.

"I was so proud of you that day. I wish Mom and Dad could have been there to see it," Jacob reflected nostalgically.

They talked all through the night and the following morning, Jacob brewed some strong coffee, before they sat on the porch to watch the sunrise.

"The weather's going to be great today, and I'm taking you to see one of my favorites."

"They're all your favorites," Mason said.

"Yeah, but this one is majestic. I'm flying you to Portage Glacier."

"Flying? Don't tell me you're still flying. Driving with you is scary enough."

"I'm not dead yet," Jacob chuckled. "I still fly my float-plane. I've been flying it a lot lately. Trying to preserve my memories of this great land one last time."

"How long of a flight will this be?"

"It'll be a quick flight. It's only about fifty miles south of Anchorage."

They climbed into the truck and started the short trip to the airport. They drove directly into the sun's beam. Its rays reflected like a mirror off the hood and through the windshield.

Jacob drove with squinted eyes. "Can't believe I forgot my sunglasses. I must have left them on the counter by the door."

Mason removed his and extended his arm toward Jacob. "Here. Use mine."

Jacob turned his head to the right to grab the sunglasses.

"Jesus! Watch out!" Mason exclaimed and reached for the steering wheel.

# CHAPTER FIFTY-FOUR

THE ONE-WOMAN SWITCHBOARD at the *Herald* put the call through to the cramped editor's office where Betsie spent much of her time.

"This is Betsie," she answered cheerfully, taking a break from proofreading the next day's edition.

"This is Champ Albright," the high-pitched voice came through on the static-filled line. "I'm the Alaskan bureau chief for Reuters."

His "chief" title being something of an exaggeration given that the "bureau" was his one-room apartment in a neighborhood a few blocks west of downtown Anchorage. Champ, so nicknamed for having won an amateur sled dog race in Anchorage one year, had allowed the victory to change him for the worse.

Betsie's cheerfulness faded as soon as he identified himself as representing an Alaskan reporter. She instinctively knew the news was going to be about Congressman Blair.

"I have no comment about my father's official or personal business in Alaska," she said.

Champ Albright asked point blank, "Can I have a reaction from you about the car crash this morning?"

"What car crash?" she asked.

"Oh," he said with excitement, eager to be the first to report the breaking news. "I see you haven't been told yet."

Her heart sank. Rather than answering him, she hung up and ran to the room where the Associated Press and United Press International printers had set off loud bells, signifying a breaking story was moving across the wire services.

Dateline Anchorage: "United States Congressman Mason Blair and his brother Jacob, owner-publisher of the *Midnight Sun*, perished this morning along with the driver of a truck in a head-on collision near Anchorage. Details TK."

She hoped the story was wrong, but she knew better. TK was newspaper-speak for "to come." She didn't wait for the TK. She ran across the newsroom and found James typing in his office.

He glanced up and immediately noticed her face was ashen. He stood and she grabbed and embraced him. Unable to speak, she started heaving and sobbing.

"Sweetheart, what is it?"

Barely able to get the words out, she stammered, "Pop and Uncle Jake are dead."

He felt a lump the size of a bowling ball form in his throat. "What?"

"They're dead, James."

He held her tightly.

Johnny walked into the office.

"Senator Johnson is on the line," he said in almost a whisper.

"I'll take it," James said.

"No," Betsie said. "I've gotta take this." She paused for a second before picking up the handset and gently placing it against her ear.

"I'm so sorry, Betsie. Lady Bird and I feel so awful about what happened to Mason and Jacob. You are not grieving alone. Your father was like a brother to me, and he was a great advocate for Texas. The whole country is grieving with you today. The flag at our nation's Capitol is flying half-mast in honor of your daddy. If you need anything, darling, you please let me know. If you and James need to get away for a bit, feel free to go out to our ranch. It's always available for you."

"Thank you for calling, Lyndon," she said. His words renewed her energy. She grabbed a piece of newsprint paper from James's desk and dabbed her watery eyes.

"Right now we need to put together what will be the most regrettable page one of my lifetime."

"Please," James begged. "The rest of us can put this one together. Let me take you home."

"The *Herald* is home for me," she said.

James nodded. "Well, if you're going to stay, let's assemble the staff. We'll address them together. Like you said, the *Herald* is home, and we're all a family here."

# CHAPTER FIFTY-FIVE

JAMES PUT HIS arm around Betsie and escorted her to the breakroom, where all the employees had gathered for the urgent announcement that was spreading across the wire services. He drew a breath and summoned the strength to honor Betsie's wish.

"Betsie wants us," he solemnly addressed the team, "to be the professionals Mason and Jacob would expect us to be. We've lost a titan of a man and a dear friend. So has everybody else in this region. Mason was a patriot and dedicated his life to the service of others. You are the ones who make the *Herald* what it is."

Mrs. Rose started sobbing.

James walked over to her and placed his hand on her shoulder. "It's going to be okay," he said.

"I've worked here over twenty-five years," she said. "Mr. Blair hired me."

"I know," James said, looking at the crowd. "He hired many of you. Even for those who came after he left for Washington, please know that he loved each of you, and he loved the *Herald*. That's why we have to get to work and put together the story that the Blair brothers would expect of us."

The employees wiped their tears away and Johnny started clapping, which prompted the other employees to join in the applause.

James nodded in appreciation.

"On behalf of the entire family, thank you. We're going to get through this. Now let's honor Mr. Mason and Mr. Jacob."

Within the hour, part-time employees and even a couple, who had long since retired from the *Herald*, came into the office and joined the effort to cover the story. Many made phone calls while others hit the streets and asked random residents for comments.

The next morning, the *Herald* featured a photo on page one that took up most of the space above the fold. It showed the Blair brothers, arms over one another's shoulders on the occasion of a hiking trip to the peak of Flattop Mountain several years earlier.

The headline that led to several news and reaction stories simply stated: "He was the most wonderful man." The writer, of course, was Betsie.

# CHAPTER FIFTY-SIX

MASON BLAIR'S LAST Will and Testament requested a private ceremony only attended by his close friends and family, but the Speaker of the House would not entertain any of that.

"Mason Blair died while serving in his official capacity as a congressman," the Speaker declared. "He's afforded the honor of being buried in Arlington National Cemetery."

"That's very thoughtful of you, Mr. Speaker. But I know my dad, and his wishes were specific. He wants to be buried at St. Joseph's next to his wife, my mother. He even purchased the plot in 1935."

"In your grief, I don't believe you're thinking through this clearly," he replied. "We're talking about the death of a United States Congressman!"

Betsie's reply matched his tone. "I don't believe *you're* thinking through this clearly. He was my father, and his wishes will be honored!"

"Have it your way, Missy," he huffed before hanging up.

Betsie turned to James. "The gall of some of these politicians who want to use my daddy's funeral as a way for them to grandstand."

James nodded. "Mason was more than a father. He was a compassionate man and well-regarded leader to Texas. We can still honor him with a private ceremony at St. Joseph's, but we shouldn't deprive folks of the opportunity to pay their last respects."

"You're right," she concluded.

"I'll call the Speaker of the House," James said.

# CHAPTER FIFTY-SEVEN

"**G**OD'S SHEDDING TEARS for your father," James told Betsie that late morning as they sat under a tent at St. Joseph's Cemetery for Mason's funeral. The rain slid off the fabric and onto the ground, where the thick grass quickly absorbed the water.

The six-member uniformed honor guard marched three-by-three on each side of the lone black horse that pulled Mason's body down the path. An American flag draped his wooden casket. The procession halted at the gravesite. The guests jolted with each shot as seven riflemen fired three times into the air. Among the tombstones, approximately thirty yards away, a lone bugler began playing *Taps*. The solemn sound filled the air and reminded James of his service to the country. It also reminded him of Mason's service to the United States.

The honor guard reverently removed the American flag and folded it into a triangle. They presented it to the military officer, who clamped it with his white-gloved hands. He marched toward Betsie and knelt in front of her.

"On behalf of the President of the United States, the United States Congress, and a grateful nation, please accept this flag as a symbol of our appreciation for your father's honorable and faithful service."

"Thank you," Betsie whispered as she accepted the flag. Her shoulders quivered as she wept behind her black veil. James understood her devastation and put his arm around her.

The elderly priest clutched a worn-out Bible as he walked toward Mason's coffin. He placed his free hand on the casket and cleared his throat before addressing the audience.

"Thank you to everyone who has come today to celebrate the life of Mason Blair and the legacy he has left. Mason was a humble man despite all of his success. He would not want me to speak of his success, so I'll be brief.

"Because of my unique position, sometimes it is difficult to form a close friendship with others. However, it brings me pleasure to say that it was never the case with Mason. I cherished his friendship and respected him greatly. I believe he cherished my friendship as well. He was a wise man and a great judge of character. He was a generous man, having often invited many people to eat at his house. I've been fortunate to be a guest at Mason and Betsie's beautiful home many times, which is why I'd like to read from John 14. If you've seen Mason's house, you can imagine he was especially fond of this particular passage. He'd quip that he was just trying to be like God," the priest smiled.

Soft laughter trickled throughout the crowd.

The priest opened his Bible.

"I recite this holy verse in honor of our friend Mason, who had a great sense of humor and a heart of service. 'My

Father's house has many rooms; if that were not so, would I have told you that I am going there to prepare a place for you? And if I go and prepare a place for you, I will come back and take you to be with Me so that you also may be where I am.'"

The priest closed his Bible and bowed his head.

"Rest in eternal peace, our dear Mason. We love you. Amen."

They carefully lowered Mason's coffin into the ground.

After everyone had left, Betsie scooped a piece of dirt and tossed it on the casket.

"Goodbye, Pops. I love you. Tell Momma I said hello, and give her a kiss for me."

## CHAPTER FIFTY-EIGHT

THE MEDIA SURROUNDED Betsie and James as they neared the parking lot.

"Mrs. Blair," one correspondent from Dallas shouted. "Rumor is you're talking to Congress about trying to slide into your dad's position. Is that true? Are you moving to politics?"

"This is not the time or the place," James admonished the man as he cleared a path for him and Betsie to walk to their car.

Raindrops struck the windshield of their new Ford Tudor, but it was all a blur. Betsie said nothing during the drive.

At the house, the phone rang incessantly.

"It's better to get this over with now," she said and answered the phone.

"Mrs. Blair, or should I say Congresswoman Blair?"

"It's Mrs. Karl," she corrected the man with a high-pitched voice.

"You didn't answer my question, ma'am. Is politics in your future? Do you think you deserve to win because of your father?"

"Not a single person has broached the subject with me about running for office. But I would be less than candid if I didn't admit that the thought of running for office has crossed my mind. I've been part of public life since I was old enough to go into the *Herald* as a little girl and help my father any way I could. I wrote my first editorial when I was still in high school. I'm certainly capable of rising to a political position as my father was." She paused for a moment. With a faraway look in her eyes, she said, "I could envision my winning a write-in campaign and becoming Congresswoman Karl."

"So, it's true then?" he asked.

She sighed. "What is true is that my husband and I now own two newspapers in places thousands of miles apart. My father and Uncle Jacob loved their papers, and I will not let them perish on my watch."

"How do you plan to do that?"

"With the help of my husband, we will be looking after Uncle Jacob's beloved *Midnight Sun* in Alaska. James and I are very much up to that challenge."

James looked up from reading his magazine, and stared wide-eyed at Betsie. "I suppose I'll need a parka."

"Mrs. Blair?" the reporter said.

She placed her hand over the phone. "Is that okay with you? I realize I just threw that out there to shut this jerk up."

James smiled. "I've fished in Alaska many times. Never imagined I'd be living there. I guess we're heeding the call of the wild."

"Mrs. Blair, Mrs. Blair," the reporter repeated over the phone. "So, you're coming to Alaska? In that case, I look forward to seeing you."

"Who is this?" she asked.

"They call me Champ Albright. You and I spoke before."

## CHAPTER FIFTY-NINE

"UNCLE JAKE'S PAPER is like a boat adrift without a rudder," Betsie said several weeks after the tragic accident. "We need to get there sooner than I had imagined, and we've got more luggage than our Cessna will hold."

"It's not a problem," James said, trying to ease her concerns. "I knew we weren't *vacationing* in Alaska; we are *moving* to Alaska. So, I booked a commercial flight for us."

She sighed with relief. "Good. Transportation is one less thing we have to worry about."

"There's a silver lining in all this."

"Let's hear it, because I could sure use one," she said.

"There's no direct flight from Dallas to Alaska. So, we'll have an overnight in my old stomping grounds."

"I haven't seen you quite this excited in some time. I think you're looking forward to this crazy move more than I am."

"Alaska is our trip of a lifetime! We're trading the hustle and bustle for bears, whales, and glaciers."

She smiled. "Somehow I imagine several trips of our lifetime with you."

They landed into SEATAC airport, which was about 14 miles from downtown Seattle. A misty chill greeted them as they exited the commercial plane.

"It's just like I remember it," James said.

She scanned the area before replying, "Grey, cloudy, and wet?"

"No. Shitty," he smirked.

"Wait a sec. You told me you loved it here."

"I do miss the fifty days of summer, though," he chuckled.

After the taxi had dropped them off at their hotel, they walked to Pike's Place Market.

Seagulls cawing provided background noise as they walked alongside the tables of fresh produce and local vendors. Ice-packed buckets of fish were on display and for sale.

"Even smells like I remember it," he said, harking back to his years as a commercial fisherman. "Betsie, take a look at the size of these fish. We shed a lot of blood, sweat and tears battling those monsters. There wasn't an ounce of quit in them or us." He paused and gazed out over the bay. "Lots of great memories...sometimes you don't realize it in the moment."

"Where's your boat?" she asked.

"Hopefully *Grace* is at sea, where she preferred to be."

He looked out at Elliott Bay. His gaze transfixed on a floatplane that skidded across the water until it climbed into the signature grey overcast and disappeared. He looked back at Betsie and saw a weathered man in rubber boots and a reflective slicker. The man moved like every bone ached.

"I'll be damned!" he said as he moved toward the familiar fisherman.

"Jack Young?"

"You can drop the young part," he said. His straight face turned into disbelief, then a smile formed as he recognized his fishing partner. "Not even a postcard? I haven't heard from you in a year!"

"Forget about a postcard. I'm here in the flesh." James hugged his friend. "It's so good to see you."

"I figured I'd never see you again after you hit the road for Texas," Jack said.

"We're passing through on our way to Alaska."

Jack turned to Betsie.

"Oh, I'm sorry," James said. "Where are my manners? This is my beautiful wife, Betsie."

"How did a good-looking gal like you end up with this barnacle?"

Betsie blushed. "Just lucky, I guess."

"Speaking of luck, did he ever tell you about our last voyage?"

"No. He didn't."

"Hold on there, bucket mouth. Don't be talking out of school," James warned.

"No. I want to hear about it. Please go on," she said.

"He's the luckiest guy I know. This clumsy fool fell off the *Grace* in one of the worst thunderstorms I've ever been in. He swore that *Grace's* spotlight guided him back to us. The only problem with that is the light hadn't worked for days."

"I got goosebumps," Betsie said.

"A light may have saved him," Jack continued, "but it didn't come from our boat. I know that for a fact because I had to fix it before we sold the boat."

"I never heard that story," Betsie said. "Is that true?"

James nodded. "I'll never forget that day. I didn't deserve it, but God saved my life. Twice, actually. Once in the war and then at sea."

"Well, I'm glad He did," Betsie smiled.

"Me too," James smiled and looked at Jack. "My God, you doing electrical work? I'm surprised you didn't shock yourself into a heart attack."

"I never said I didn't," he grinned. "Good to give the old ticker a jolt every now and then."

James laughed. "You were always Billy's favorite storyteller. You'd lie when the truth would work better. How is our old partner?"

"Cathy's got him wrapped around her little finger. You know how women are once they get their hooks into you. No offense, ma'am."

"None taken," she replied and held her fingers in the form of a hook and waved it at James.

"If the truth be told," Jack continued, "I've never seen Billy happier. He dotes on junior and their baby girl."

"No woman has sunk her hooks into you yet?" Betsie teased.

"Not yet, Missy," he chuckled.

"How are you getting along?" James asked. "I thought you were going to hang it up?"

"Still fishing every day, but you knew it was never really about the fish."

"Sometimes I miss it," James said. "A bad day fishing is still better than a good day in the office."

"You work in an office now?" he laughed. "Marriage has domesticated you!"

The deafening blast of a nearby ship's horn echoed through the seaport and bounced off the downtown buildings. Everyone turned their attention to the cruise ship transiting the harbor.

"Look there!" James pointed. "It looks like the Grey Ghost cutting through the mist."

"Now he's seeing ghosts?" Jack joked.

"That's what we affectionately called the *Queen Mary*," he answered. "It was a magnificent ship—a true beauty. She ferried me and thousands of other soldiers from New York to England on August twentieth, 1944. I remember that six-day voyage like it was yesterday." He seemed frozen in thought.

"I've gotta hear this tale," Jack said.

Betsie smiled at Jack. "I always love his stories."

"Me, too," Jack said and winked at Betsie. "Half are lies and the other half are B.S."

"I was standing on the top deck, marveling at how bright the stars were over the Atlantic—away from all the city lights of the Big Apple. I had never been away from Texas before."

"Texas?" Betsie asked.

"I mean Oregon," James quickly corrected.

She gave him a quizzical look and then turned to Jack. He shrugged his shoulders.

"Anyway," James continued, "there I was on a grand ship steaming across the ocean to join the war in Europe. Normally I'd be excited, but I was scared. My stomach felt queasy, so I stood near the rail in case I needed to throw up when, from out of the darkness, the ship's captain walked up to me. He was immaculately dressed, with a trimmed white beard, and a chewed-up smoking pipe that had been his companion for at least thirty years."

"Enjoying the night air, soldier?"

"I snapped to attention. 'Yes, sir.'"

"You're not playing poker downstairs with the fellas from the Nineteenth Tank Battalion?"

"Cards are the last thing on my mind, sir."

"The captain nodded. He had looked at me with such intensity that it was as if he were looking straight through me. 'You know, I've been making this trip back and forth with thousands of soldiers. They come from all over America, but they're all worried about the same thing…staying alive, getting back home to their families, and regretting the things they didn't say or do before they shipped off.'"

"I'll never forget what the captain said next."

Betsie and Jack drew closer to James.

"Have you ever heard the Latin expression *carpe diem*?"

Betsie shook her head no.

"Fish of the day?" Jack said.

James started laughing.

"I hadn't ever heard the phrase either. The captain raised a clenched fist into the air and said it meant to seize the day. Relish the present and live as if it were your last day on earth."

"Come on, Jack!" a crewmember yelled from one of the nearby boats. "We're kicking off with or without you."

"Yeah, yeah!" Jack shouted back and turned to James and Betsie. "I'm the best fisherman they got on that rust bucket. They won't catch anything without me."

"Then you better go save the day," Betsie said with a smile.

"I suppose so, Missy." He shook Betsie's hand and embraced James, holding it for a second longer. "It was good to see you, mate. I'm glad life's smiling on you."

"Thank you, buddy. Take care of yourself, Jack."

Betsie and James continued their stroll along the waterfront.

"I'm glad you got to meet ol' Jack," James said.

"Too bad we're only here for one night," she said. "I reckon he's got a lot more stories about you."

"Thank God we're only here for one night. I can't have Jack telling you all my secrets."

"I'll figure them out on my own," she chuckled. "Now let's take that ship captain's advice and see about seizing this night."

James smiled. "Aye, aye, captain!"

## CHAPTER SIXTY

THE AGING, OVERWEIGHT man used a cane to steady himself as he waited inside the Anchorage terminal. He smiled at Betsie.

"Recognized you from your photos. The name's Murlin Spencer. I've been second-in-command to Jacob for more than a year."

"It's a pleasure," she said. "Thank you for helping Uncle Jake. It's been a whirlwind for us."

"I can only imagine," said the former war correspondent. "How was your flight?"

"Slow moving," James answered as they walked past a stuffed moose on display in the terminal.

"Life's pace is a tad slower here," he said. "I'm just thankful you arrived today and not tomorrow. First major snowfall of the extended cold-weather season is supposed to hit tomorrow. Let's grab your luggage and go, shall we?"

"Thank God you have a large car," James said as they hauled multiple suitcases through the parking lot.

"This is my tank," he said with laughter as he struggled to slide behind the steering wheel. He cranked the car and handed Betsie a manila envelope. "Some legal documents. Jacob's wishes were easily settled because of an orderly will. The estate was to go to Mason, but since he also perished in the accident, you inherit the entirety of Jacob's property, which also includes a single-engine airplane. I imagine you'll want to sell it, or get your pilot's license. Alaska has six times more pilots per capita than the Lower Forty-Eight."

"We'll keep it," Betsie said. "James and I are both pilots."

"Oh," Murlin said with surprise. "Forgive me for my assumptions, and for forgetting my manners. I should have first said how sorry I am to hear about your father and Jacob."

"Thank you," Betsie said.

"The accident shocked our city. People talked about it for weeks," Murlin noted.

"I figured as much," Betsie replied flatly, thinking back to how she learned the tragic news.

"Jacob was a workaholic," Murlin said and his demeanor seemed to take on a more ominous tone. "Despite being married to the job, the *Midnight Sun* has been losing circulation for several years."

"That's what we've heard," James said. "We plan to turn that around."

"The enterprise is the proverbial revolving door for reporters, editors, and advertising staff," Murlin began. "New hires are always needed. Those who show up for job interviews are mostly men. These persons invariably are in Alaska because in various ways they've failed elsewhere, either in the U.S. or Canada. Even those men with good skills are drifters, many of them drunks or criminals escaping north to The Last Frontier."

Murlin finally pulled up to a waterfront cabin that overlooked Cook Inlet.

"We're here. This was Jacob's home. Now it belongs to you," Murlin said as the car rolled to a stop. "Jacob, even though he wasn't feeling well, would still walk the shoreline twice a day—once in the morning and once at night."

"Until recently, Uncle Jake was always in great shape. He had intended to be a physician in Palestine. Did you know that?"

Murlin nodded his head and chuckled. "Oh, yes. He often told us that story, too. He was smitten with the Great Land after a visit with some medical missionaries who were seeking to help members of the Alaska native population. I thank God. Otherwise, I'd never have met your wonderful uncle."

James and Betsie got out of the car and started unloading the luggage.

"Here's the key," Murlin said as he handed it to Betsie through the passenger-side window. "Forgive me for not getting out. My ailing leg is troubling me today."

"Don't give it a second thought," Betsie said. "We understand. Thanks for the lift and the background. Sounds like it's going to be an uphill battle for a while."

"Alaska's always an uphill battle," he smirked. "Like I said earlier, snow's coming tomorrow. So, I'll pick you up at eight." He honked the horn in two quick successions as he reversed to leave. "Welcome to Seward's Folly."

James waved goodbye, then turned his attention to the cabin. He reached down and grabbed two oversized suitcases and lugged them up the steps.

"Yep, let's hope it doesn't become the Karl's folly."

## CHAPTER SIXTY-ONE

"WHEW," BETSIE EXHALED as she walked inside the log cabin. "Uncle Jake's place is a tad musty." She fanned the air in front of her face.

"And in need of a lot of maintenance," James said, as he leaned his body against the warped door to close it. "Good grief!" he exclaimed as he saw the hundreds of books and newspaper clippings that covered the floor, and the various trophy animals that hung on the wall.

Betsie sneezed as she trudged through the maze of dusty cardboard boxes and forced open the living-room window. The cool, crisp air blew into the cabin.

James took a deep breath and smiled. "Fresh Alaskan air. There's nothing like it."

"This is going to take a lot longer than I had imagined," Betsie sighed.

"It's like eating an elephant," James remarked.

Betsie giggled. "Why would you want to eat an elephant?"

"I wouldn't, but if I had to, it would be one bite at a time."

She laughed. "Okay, you start over there and I'll start in this corner."

"And remember," he reminded her, "we don't have to finish this in one day."

About an hour later, James called out to Betsie who was tidying in the kitchen.

"Hey, sweetheart, Uncle Jake has an amazing collection of music. He's got records from my favorites. Frankie Laine, Dinah Shore, Nat King Cole, The Les Paul Trio."

"Uncle Jake always had great taste in music," she noted. "Why don't you put a record on?"

James sifted through the pile and found a 1939 Bluebird Records original by the Pine Ridge Boys. He blew off the dust and gently placed it on the record player. The sweet lyrics from *You are my Sunshine* filled the room.

"Makes the place feel homey," she smiled, now having joined him in the living room.

James extended an open palm. "May I have this dance?"

"Promise me," she said as they slow danced, "If the Alaskan winter ever gets us down, let's dance to this song."

"Deal," he replied. "It'll take more than an Alaskan winter to get me down, though." He kissed her softly. "Because you are my sunshine."

## CHAPTER SIXTY-TWO

"JAMES! WAKE UP!" Betsie elbowed her husband who slept like the dead.

"What's wrong?" he groaned and sat up.

"Look outside!"

He used his fingertips to rub his eyes. The sky's soft glow cast just enough light to illuminate the cabin's quaint room.

"It's magical," she said. "I've never seen anything like this."

"It's the Northern Lights," he said and pulled back the blanket.

They shuffled toward the window. They stood with their forearms resting on the windowsill. They pressed their foreheads against the cold glass and stared into the heavens. Shades of green, red, and blue danced across the sky. The celestial light backlit the pine trees and several feet of fresh snow.

"The stars are so bright that it looks like I could count each one," she said. "Ah, I could look at this for the rest of my life."

He smiled and put his arm around her. "Me too, as long as you were next to me."

She smiled and kissed him. "We're going to have so much fun in Alaska."

# CHAPTER SIXTY-THREE

MURLIN SPENCER PULLED into the driveway at exactly eight o'clock. James and Betsie hopped into his tank.

"Good morning. How did you sleep?"

"I'm so glad we didn't," she said. "You should have seen the Northern Lights. They were unbelievable."

"One of the many highlights of living here," Murlin replied. "They're quite spiritual to see, some even think they're romantic. According to Japanese mythology, a child conceived under the Aurora Borealis will be blessed by the Gods."

"We'll keep that in mind, right Betsie?" James said.

She blushed.

"It's freezing in here," she said.

"Sorry about that," Murlin said. "The heater doesn't work. Stopped working last year and I haven't gotten around to it yet. You know what they say, it's hard to find a good mechanic."

"Mr. Murlin, I'll fix that for you," James said. "But in the meantime, once we get to the office, please rally the troops. Betsie and I would like to address our team."

"All fifty something employees?" he asked, surprised at the request.

"If we're going to turn this ship around, we need to have all hands on deck."

"Yes sir," he replied. "You're the boss."

"Betsie and I may be in charge, but we're all in this endeavor together."

Several hours later Murlin had accomplished the task.

"My Uncle Jacob was an amazing man with a generous heart. His passion was journalism," Betsie said in her charming Texas accent.

A couple of workers bowed their heads as though praying at the mention of Jacob's name.

"Our intention is to see that the *Midnight Sun* not only survives, but thrives in these tough times. My husband James and I will stay as long as necessary to see to it my uncle's dreams are honored."

"But Mrs. Karl," came the interruption by a loudly-voiced man in the rear of the newsroom. "What do you say about the *Sun* being a failing paper that can't survive much longer, the way advertising is dropping?"

His question both startled and challenged Betsie. She paused for a moment. "And with whom am I speaking?"

Everyone else in the room seemed to know only too well since there was a collective quiet moan.

"They call me Champ," the fellow shouted. "From Reuters. You and I spoke."

Betsie sighed. "Ah, yes. I recall. Thank you, Mr. Albright, for being the first to tell me my father had died. I hope the long-distance call didn't set you back too much money."

Champ smiled broadly. "Reuters is flush. They pay expenses, unlike some news outlets where I've worked. Why did you hang up on me? A pro like yourself oughta be more considerate with your peers."

Betsie's face flushed, but she managed to smile and answer. "I usually decide who my peers are on a case-by-case basis. By the way, I'm not sure why you feel you can attend our staff meeting."

"Just doing my job."

A number of employees seemed eminently uncomfortable with his intrusion.

"Champ," Murlin Spencer spoke up. "You'd still be welcomed here if you drank your drinks on your own time. Beyond that, this isn't a public meeting. It's private."

"Thanks, Murlin," Betsie said. "I doubt whether Reuters can use any of this discussion, but since this may be the last time we'll see their stringer—"

"Correspondent," Champ interrupted. "Correspondent Albright."

"Sorry. I mean the Reuters *correspondent*," she emphasized. "My answer is we're prepared to meet all challenges that arise. Feel free to quote me. I assume Reuters will want this information out right away for all the readers in Africa and South America, not to mention Antarctica and even the moon who are dying to know what's going on with a newspaper in Anchorage." Her sarcasm brought smirks and a few chuckles from the staff members.

"Fact is," Champ replied, not finished with the banter, "Miss Blair here—or is it Mrs. Karl?"

"It's Mrs. Karl," James stated.

"Mrs. Karl can be a real witch when she wants to be one," Champ continued. "I heard that from a buddy of mine who worked in Dallas. He said she's a stuck-up, spoiled rich kid who always made everybody know how important her father was."

"Watch your mouth! That's my wife you're talking about." James stepped forward and grabbed Champ by the scruff of the neck, knocking his felt hat to the ground.

The staff applauded as James escorted Champ out of the building.

"I guess it shouldn't surprise me that weasels like you and Tom Bannon would know each other," James said as he tossed Champ against the brick wall.

Champ gulped for air. "Newspaper people looking for jobs know that an easy way to get connected is to contact other reporters and editors. That's what led Tom to me."

"Go on!" James said, inches from Champ's reddish face.

"After his departure from Texas, Tom found work in Washington. Evidently he identified me as a likely Anchorage contact after I reported on the deaths of the Blair brothers. He traveled here on a one-way ticket. Your paper rejected him for a job and he was too broke to afford anything. He slept on the floor at my apartment for a while."

"Where's he at now?" James demanded.

"I don't know," Champ replied.

James clenched his fist and reared it back, ready to launch across Champ's face.

"I swear! I don't know. He found some work and moved on."

"I don't trust you!" James saw Champ and Bannon as kindred spirits, with plenty in common for their objects of jealousy and hatred.

"I know one thing," Champ said. "He hates you. He blames you for stealing Betsie."

"I didn't steal anybody. Now get the hell out of here and don't come back. I better not see you or Tom Bannon again."

James walked back into the business and saw Betsie smiling. She beamed at the sight of her husband.

"On that note," she said, "are there any other questions?"

Heads shook "no" in the crowd.

"Okay then. We look forward to working with you and making our beloved paper even better," she said before James and she headed to Jacob's glassed-in office.

"What do you think?" she asked.

"I don't think we've heard the last of Champ or Tom Bannon for that matter."

# CHAPTER SIXTY-FOUR

*SUMMER OF 1953*

JAMES AND BETSIE rocked back and forth on wooden chairs as they watched the pink sky from their cabin's patio.

"Sweetheart, life sure has been good to us these last three years here."

She sipped her tea and smiled at him. "Yes, it has, but despite all of Alaska's wonders, I still yearn for our lives back in Texas."

"Me too. I get nostalgic on evenings like this," he said, rocking back and forth.

"I don't want Alaska to be our home for many untold years to come."

"We did what we came to do," he said. "Under our leadership, the *Midnight Sun's* prestige for reliable news has grown throughout Anchorage and even to the remote villages."

"Well, that was because you befriended some bush pilots and recruited them to supply the outposts with our paper as they flew their normal routes to drop off food and medical supplies."

"I can't take all the credit. You were the original genius behind the 'Plane Paper' subscription."

"That was a good idea, if I say so myself," she said.

"Since we're on the same page, no pun intended," he laughed, "I'll keep my eye open for the right opportunity to get us back to Texas."

"You do that," she said. "In the meantime, our three-year anniversary is coming up. Do you have any plans or should I be making some?"

He smiled. "You thought I had forgotten, huh?"

"You? Never."

"Don't worry," he said. "I've arranged for Murlin to watch the office for a few days so we can get away. I have something extra romantic planned for us."

## CHAPTER SIXTY-FIVE

*July 8, 1953*

J AMES AND BETSIE crammed a tent, two sleeping
bags, and five days of supplies into Uncle Jacob's float-
plane.

"Is this what you had in mind when you said you had
something *romantic* planned for us?"

"Trust me. This is going to be fantastic." He shoved the
last piece of equipment into the cargo space and started looking around. "Betsie, where's your new camera?"

"Oh, good grief. Hold on," she said as she ran back to
the truck.

They departed eastbound along the shoreline toward
Prince William Sound. Betsie cranked the gear on their new-
ly-purchased 8mm movie camera as they soared over white
and blue glaciers and dense forests.

"It's so untouched," she said with awe. "There's no roads.
No people."

"I told you I had something romantic planned. You have
your own personal aerial safari."

He smiled and descended the airplane to one hundred feet above the terrain. They watched caribou and mountain goats graze before he landed at Lost Lake in Chugach National Forest.

He anchored the airplane to a stake by rope at the edge of the lake and set up the tent that would be their home for the next few days.

American bald eagles flapped their wings overhead as James and Betsie stood knee deep in the crystal-clear water and cast their fishing lines.

"You don't realize how busy Anchorage is until you come to a serene place like this," he said after they had been fishing for hours.

"It feels like we're the only people within a hundred miles," she said.

"Yep, it's just us and the grizzly bears and timber wolves."

"I'm not worried," she said. "Nothing's gonna sneak up on me. It's practically twenty-four hour daylight. That's what I love about the Alaskan summers. Plus, I've always got you to protect me."

"That's right," he said. "You keep fishing if you'd like. I'll start a campfire for us."

He grabbed a hatchet from his backpack and started chopping wood when she screamed out.

"I've got one!" She bent her knees to lower her center of balance and started reeling in the fishing line. "Oh, it's a big one."

James tossed the wood into a pile and ran into the lake. He reached into the water and pulled out a three-foot salmon.

"Great catch! This fella's gotta weigh ten pounds."

Betsie smiled from ear to ear. "I told you a country girl can survive anywhere."

"Yes, I believe you're right. We can eat now."

They sat on a log next to the fire and enjoyed their fresh catch. When they finished, they roasted s'mores for dessert.

He checked his watch. "Time has a way of becoming irrelevant out here. It's three o'clock in the morning and it's still light out."

"I don't want it to ever end," she said, extending her hands to feel the warmth of the crackling fire. "This is such a wonderful trip. Thank you, Mr. Karl."

"It's my pleasure, Mrs. Karl."

They nuzzled and chatted by the fire until they nestled into their tent around four in the morning.

An hour later thunder boomed across the cloudless sky and echoed between the mountains. James and Betsie shot up.

"What the heck was that?" she asked. "That sounded like dynamite."

He unzipped the tent and crawled out to scan the entire valley.

A grey ash cloud billowed into the stratosphere.

"Mt. Spurr is erupting!" James exclaimed.

Another blast of volcanic ash exploded into the air.

"Let's get out of here," he said. "We'll fly as far east as we can."

She reached over and grabbed her 8mm video camera. "You fly and I'll record."

"What?" he asked.

"We've been waiting for a moment like this. This is exactly what the *Midnight Sun* needs."

James thought for a brief moment. "It's way too dangerous."

"Let's leave everything here," she suggested. "We can come back for it later, but we can't miss this opportunity."

He knew she was too stubborn to try to persuade. He pulled the stake out of the ground and pushed the airplane back into the water and turned it around. He cranked the ignition and they skidded across the water and clawed for altitude to 12,000 feet.

James flew straight to the smoke and circled the volcano as it spewed black ash and red lava into the air. The heat pressed against the airplane and the thin air was already difficult to breath without the smoke.

"Eww," she said. "It smells like rotten eggs."

He closed the vents. "It's the sulfur. Get the footage you need because we can't stay up here much longer."

She continued filming from her passenger window and captured the avalanche of lava flowing down the mountain. "We got it!" she exclaimed and kissed him on the cheek. "We can head back now."

Powdered ash sprayed the entire windshield.

"I can't see!" He turned his attention to the instruments in the cockpit. The turbulence bounced them around and made it difficult to read the circular dials and gauges.

James applied full power for the propeller to blow the ash off the windshield.

"It's not working," she fretted. "Look! The ash is melting the plexiglass."

Their single-engine plane coughed and sputtered to a stop.

"We've become a glider," he said and abruptly banked the airplane away from the spewing volcano. "We have to get away from the ash and lava or we'll be cooked alive." He pushed the nose down to gain airspeed and pointed the plane southeast toward Anchorage.

"MAYDAY! MAYDAY!" she broadcasted over the radio. "Cessna two-one-six declaring an emergency. Engine failure and obstructed view."

"Cessna two-one-six, this is Anchorage air traffic control. State location and souls on board."

"Two souls on board. We are over Beluga. Descending at seven-hundred feet per minute. We'll land at Lake Hood."

"All airports are closed because of the volcano eruption. Emergency services are not available. I repeat, emergency services are not available. Land at your own risk."

James tried to restart the engine but nothing worked. The ash continued to burn through the plexiglass and smoke filled the cabin.

"My lungs are burning," Betsie said between labored coughs.

"Wrap your scarf around your face," he instructed as he also began to cough.

"I can't breathe!" she said as she started to hyperventilate. She looked at James with sheer terror. Her face turned pale and her lips became blueish.

"Stay with me, babe. I'm trying my best to get us down, but everything is going to shit!"

She clutched her chest as her eyes rolled back and her head went limp. Her entire body slumped forward.

"Son of a bitch!" he exclaimed. He started to panic until he heard Frank Roger's voice clear as day. *In der Not frisst der Teufel Fliegen.*

He grabbed her scarf and loosely wrapped his knuckles before launching his fist through her window. The impact shattered the plexiglass, sending shards through the air. He unlatched his door and used his foot to prop it open against the seventy mile-per-hour wind caused by the rapid descent. With all his might, he extended his knee and broke the door off its hinges. The aluminum door tumbled awkwardly out of the sky. The smoke funneled outside the plane and provided instant relief.

"Come on, baby. Wake up!" He jostled her body.

She started coughing.

"Thank God!" he said as tears streamed down his face.

She appeared disoriented. "Where are we?"

He peeked his head outside and recognized the water below. "There's Cook Inlet," he declared. "We'll follow the shoreline." He didn't have to yell because the engine was dead. Only the rush of air flowed over the wings as the ground rose to meet them.

His emergency dive cooled the ash and extinguished the ambers from burning further through the plexiglass. He removed the scarf from his knuckles and began to wipe away the ash from the exterior of the windshield. The clearing provided a small circle from which he could see forward.

They glided back with barely enough altitude to land on the water at Lake Hood. The floats touched and brought the plane to a quick stop.

"Like a duck with hemorrhoids," she said.

He smiled and turned to Betsie. The color in her face began to return. He hugged her tightly. "I thought I had lost you up there."

"I'll never leave you," she said.

"Is that a promise?"

She nodded. "That was impressive flying, James! Anyone else at the controls and we'd be dead. I can't wait to tell Mr. Frank how you saved my life."

"Make sure to tell him that the Devil ate flies today."

"What?"

"I'll explain later. In the meantime, let's get you to a doctor so they can check you out."

"I'm fine...thanks to you. Let's get this film developed. It's going to be incredible."

"I hope it's not damaged," James said. "This airplane sure is."

They rushed to their office downtown as darkness started to engulf the entire city of Anchorage.

"Please process this immediately," Betsie instructed Murlin.

"Yes ma'am," Murlin said and wrapped a paper bag over the film and secured it in his briefcase.

"I'm still shaking from the excitement," Betsie told James as they washed the smoke and ash off their bodies and threw on a fresh pair of clothes.

Murlin returned several hours later, caked in ash. He coughed a few times and then smiled. "You guys did it! Nobody has ever filmed anything like this before. The outlets are offering to pay big bucks for it and they want to air it nationally—maybe even internationally."

"It was Betsie's idea."

"It might have been my idea, but I couldn't have done it without you."

"I'm thankful we had Uncle Jake's plane and Betsie's camera," James told Murlin.

"You're either the bravest or the craziest couple I know. One thing is for sure. Your coverage today has undoubtedly saved this company. Jacob would be mighty proud of you two."

James looked at Betsie and shook his head. "Yeah. Well, he almost got the chance to thank us in person."

# CHAPTER SIXTY-SIX

*OCTOBER OF 1954*

JAMES AND BETSIE were at the office discussing the next morning's front-page headline when a phone call came through on Murlin Spencer's office number.

"Betsie," Murlin interrupted them. "There's a call from Dallas. The man says it's important and he'll only speak to you."

"Well, I guess I'll take it then. Which line?"

"Oddly, he called my line. I'll stay with James if you'd like to take the call in my office."

She looked at James and smiled. "He doesn't need any help, but I'm sure he'll appreciate the company."

She walked to Murlin's messy office and took the call.

"Hello, this is Betsie."

"The name's Max Schumacher. I'm a television station producer in Dallas and wanted to arrange a meeting with you. Could you come to Dallas? At the station's expense, of course."

"I'm sorry," she replied, "but I'm not sure I understand. You want me to come to Dallas and meet you?"

"Yes. You first popped up on my radar in 1950. Your editorial piece on going to Alaska and keeping your uncle's newspaper running was a class-act move. Then you popped up on practically everyone's radar when we saw your film of Mt. Spurr's eruption. I had never seen anything like that before. That was incredible footage and such daring instincts."

"Thank you," she said. "Since you called me, I'm sure you realize we're still in Alaska."

"I know, and I think you're doing great work there. My contacts tell me you and your husband have turned the *Midnight Sun* around, but I have a ground-breaking opportunity for you in Texas." He spoke with confidence and encouragement.

"And for what exactly?"

"Television," he said. "You've been a pioneer in newspapers and have managed two companies. Now you could be a pioneer in television. It's going to change our entire world."

Betsie's stomach fluttered with excitement. "I've always wanted to be a television reporter, before I even knew what a television was. I even started—"

"There's no need to sell yourself to me. I recommended you!"

"Oh my gosh," she said.

"Fly out to Dallas for the formal interview and show the bigwigs what you got."

"Oh my gosh. This is so exciting. But I'll have to talk to my husband first."

"I understand. But an opportunity like this won't last long," he said. "If you want the job, you'll need to be here to interview in two days."

"I'll be there," she blurted out. After she hung up the phone, she ran through the newsroom where she found James and Murlin. "You mind giving us a moment?"

"Sure thing," Murlin said and hobbled back to his office.

She rushed up to James and grinned from ear to ear. "I'm trying to stay calm, but they want me to go to Dallas for a job interview."

"Who? What kind of job interview?"

"To be a television reporter!"

He wrapped his arms around her. "That's fantastic news! It's what you've always wanted. When do you go for the interview?"

"They want me to leave tomorrow, if that's alright with you."

He returned the smile and matched her excitement. "Well, let's get you home and start packing."

## CHAPTER SIXTY-SEVEN

"I'VE BEEN WAITING for your call," James said.

"I just got settled," she replied. "Max reserved me a room on the twenty-ninth floor of the Magnolia Hotel."

"The one with the rotating neon Pegasus on the roof?"

"Yes," she answered. "I think it's still the tallest building in all of Texas. I can see out for what seems like fifty miles."

"Stop," he joked. "You're making me homesick."

"I'm sorry."

"So, how did the interview go?"

"It's been a very, very, *very* strange day. Max is the NBC television affiliate at KDAL. Within minutes of my arrival, Max and another producer had given me a cursory tour of the KDAL layout, then walked me to an office by the station's main studio, where the stage was set up for a live cooking program. I have to tell you darlin', I thought they were going to put an apron on me and have me audition for that show."

"Go on," he said.

"They had me talk and interview in front of the cameras."

"And?" he drug out the word.

"Max said if I wanted to become the first female reporter at the station, the job was all mine!"

"Obviously, he saw in you what I saw the first time I met you. You're pretty terrific-looking."

"Max used the term 'telegenic.' Now that's a new word to describe me."

James started laughing. "What does that mean?"

"Means that I look okay on television...and that my voice is pleasant."

"Except when you're talking with your mouth full," he teased.

"Max was very candid with me. He noted that television is so new that nobody knows where it will go, but he believes it will spread like a wildfire."

"Innovation is one of your strengths," James said.

She smiled. "What we really need to discuss is whether we could make this offer work. We'd have to move back to Texas."

"That's not a problem. We miss the warmer weather and Southern food."

"Frankly," she continued a bit apprehensively, "I could take this job and fall flat on my face."

"I doubt that, sweetheart. But if you did, don't worry. I'd hire you back at the *Herald* and give you Johnny's job."

"Now, dammit, James, be serious. This is something I think I want to try. What do *you* want me to do?"

He thought for a beat. "Life throws fastballs and curve-balls, but I'd rather be at the plate than in the stands. Let's swing the bat. If we strike out, at least we will have swung the bat."

She looked outside her hotel-room window. "I'm so glad you said that, because I told them yes."

"Congratulations!" James exclaimed. "I'm so happy for you."

"I told them I would accept, but only under one condition."

"Huh?" James braced himself for what followed. "What was that one condition?"

"I'd only work for them if they hired you, too!"

# CHAPTER SIXTY-EIGHT

**M**IDNIGHT SUN'S PRESTIGE for reliable news grew throughout Anchorage and even to the remote villages. Despite the company's profits, James and Betsie made the bittersweet decision to sell the *Midnight Sun* to concentrate on their new career. The contract stipulated that the transfer of ownership would take place in February of 1955, which gave them three months to prepare the staff for the transition.

One Friday night in mid-December, James and Betsie decided to join a bunch of their employees for beer and snacks at Parallel 60, a dive bar a few blocks from the office. Pool, shuffleboard, and darts were the main attractions, along with a jukebox filled with pop tunes of the era. The owner gussied up the place with tacky trappings for the yuletide season. At one point, a regular played Bing Crosby crooning *White Christmas*.

"You lose again," Betsie mused after beating James for the third time in a row at a game of eight ball.

"But have I really lost?" he chuckled and embraced her. He kissed the top of her head.

Betsie squeezed James tighter as a gust of icy air whipped through the bar from the open door as two patrons stumbled over the threshold. Even from a distance it seemed clear that Parallel 60 hadn't been their first stop that night.

"Looks like we aren't the only ones having a good time tonight," Betsie said. "They're blitzed."

James smiled. "One more game before we call it a night?"

"Sure, as long as…," she gasped, "Oh, no!"

James turned to see the two men with their hoods now pulled back. A scruffy Tom Bannon and Champ Albright glared through bloodshot eyes. They approached James and Betsie.

## CHAPTER SIXTY-NINE

"WE FINALLY CAUGHT up to the little princess," Tom Bannon taunted Betsie.

James turned to his wife, who had quickly moved to his side. "Stay behind me until we see what's coming."

"You have a lot of nerve coming in here," James told Bannon.

"I'm not afraid of you," Bannon slurred.

"Fear ain't got nothing to do with it," James replied. "This time you aren't getting away."

"This time I ain't missing," he said and reached his hand into his coat pocket.

James tightened his grip on his pool cue as he saw a shiny revolver coming out of Bannon's pocket, rising toward his chest. James reacted without hesitation. He swung the pool cue across Bannon's face.

A loud bang sounded from the pistol as Bannon stumbled backward and fell to the floor.

Several patrons screamed and a crowd of bystanders dropped to the floor. Others rushed toward the exit. The jukebox stuttered to a stop when one burly man knocked it over as he fled outside.

The odor of gunpowder filled the air and overshadowed the smell of beer and cigarettes.

James scooped up Betsie and carried her across the bar. "Stay here!"

"I'm going to kill you!" Bannon shouted as he rolled over and coughed out two bloody teeth. He reached for his pistol.

Champ Albright stumbled forward, lost his balance and collapsed onto Bannon.

"I got him!" Champ said with pride.

A second shot rang as Bannon and Champ wrestled for control of the pistol.

"I've been shot!" Champ yelled. "He shot me!"

"Call the police!" James shouted to the bartender as he charged through the clutter of chairs, tables, and beer bottles on the floor.

"Help me, Karl!" Champ exclaimed with a red, sweaty face.

James realized that Champ was still trying to pry the weapon out of Bannon's hand. Bannon squeezed so hard on the grip that his fingers turned white from the pressure.

James threw himself onto Bannon and used both hands to pin Bannon's massive wrist to the floor.

"He's too strong!" Champ yelled.

Bannon roared and summoned raw strength despite his drunkenness. His hand lifted from the floor and he twisted his wrist, angling the pistol toward James's head.

Betsie appeared seemingly out of nowhere and smashed a beer bottle over Bannon's head. The brute went limp as blood streamed down his brow. His eyes rolled back in his head and he fell unconscious.

James took the pistol and looked at Betsie.

"For once, I'm glad you didn't listen to me."

She smiled for a brief moment. "I'll grab some ice from the bartender and wrap it in a towel."

"Thank you, but I'm okay."

"It's for me," Champ said.

"It ain't for you!" she replied.

Gasping for breath, Champ lifted himself off Bannon's unconscious body. He felt for the wound on his shoulder. "He shot me. Oh my God! I'm bleeding. That son of a bitch shot me! I'm going to die." His voice became panicked. "Is it cold in here?"

"Yeah, it's cold," James said. "Your friend shot out the window."

James grabbed Champ's hand and moved it from his shoulder. A slight trickle of blood appeared from the abrasion.

"All you have is a little scratch. You're gonna feel a helluva lot worse when I get done with you."

"Karl, please! Wait! You gotta believe me. I had no idea he had a gun. I swear. Hey, I'm the one who got shot here! I'm the hero in all this. I stopped a bullet for you!"

Two police officers barged through the doors with their pistols drawn.

"You're late to the party, fellas," Champ said. "I already did your job. That's the culprit over there."

The police questioned Betsie, James, and several witnesses. After learning what happened, the officers handcuffed Tom Bannon for attempted murder and hauled him away. He was still unconscious.

"As if we needed any confirmation," Betsie said, "this crazy night reassures me we're making the right move to leave Alaska."

"You guys are running away?" Champ asked.

"Not running away," James replied.

"Then what?"

"You're the ace reporter. You'll figure it out. Rest assured, Mr. Albright, you haven't seen the last of us," she smiled.

# CHAPTER SEVENTY

NOT LONG AFTER Max Schumacher had hired James and Betsie, he treated them to lunch in Dallas. He chose a fancy restaurant near the television studio.

The former war correspondent who wore suspenders and a bowtie, handed his fedora to the host before they sat.

"That surname of yours, Karl," Max said cordially, "Do I detect something of the Old Country?"

"My family shortened it from Karlsruhe," James answered. "Probably for the best. I can imagine having to always correct people who would say Karls-ROO-hee."

Max laughed. "My moniker's odyssey has been slightly different. I was born about the time my immigrant parents changed the family name from 'Schumacher' to 'Shoemaker.' When I got older, after my dad passed away, I asked my mother about the Anglicizing of our name. She said, 'Your father thought it would be easier for all concerned.' So, I was Max Shoemaker until the 1930s, during the rise of Hitler.

"A lot of Americans were wary of German-sounding names. Assumptions are still made today about names that 'sound' German or 'sound' Jewish. Anyway, after I established myself professionally as Max Shoemaker, I deliberately changed my name back and urged my kids to do the same."

Betsie and James sat spellbound by his lengthy explanation.

Then Max divulged, "I changed my name back to the German because it was my way of showing solidarity. Not for Hitler and the Reich, of course. It was to make a statement that not all Germans were complicit in what Hitler and the Nazis did. And with that, I'll conclude by thanking you for your military service, James. It's truly fortunate that we didn't lose you over there."

James reached his arm across the table and squeezed Betsie's hand.

"It's a blessing. I could have died on that battlefield and never gotten to meet my soulmate."

"This calls for a drink," Max said and snapped his fingers in the air. A waiter clad in a tuxedo appeared at their table. "I'll have a Tom Collins."

"Please make that two," Betsie said and looked at James.

"Why not? As a show of unity, make that three," he said while holding up three fingers.

"Certainly, sir," the waiter answered.

They enjoyed several rounds of drinks and the alcohol lent itself to a more relaxed conversation.

"I have to warn you about how demanding this job is," Max said. "I've missed birthdays, anniversaries and family reunions. It's going to be difficult and very stressful raising your children in this line of work."

"Betsie would make an incredible mother," James said and smiled at her. "But it's not in the cards for us."

"My doctor says I can't have children," she said.

Max nodded. "Pardon me for prying. I'm sorry I brought it up."

"It's okay," she said. "James and I are family, and we couldn't be happier."

"Oh, I can see that even without my glasses."

Max finished off another Tom Collins, and continued to delight Betsie and James with some of his milder war stories from his early career.

"I'm sure you two are aware that you're both pilots, at least partly, because of that great aviator known as Charles Augustus Lindbergh."

They smiled and nodded in agreement.

"The 1927 parade in New York was about a month after Lucky Lindy landed in Paris," Schumacher noted. "I had this skeptical editor at my newspaper who was certain all the hubbub about the Atlantic crossing was dying down and that the parade wouldn't amount to much. He told me to try to find people on the street who were going about their business and ignoring all the hoopla. Fat chance of that. Everybody from New York City and Northern New Jersey was on the streets that day. Ticker tape fell like a snowstorm. It was so loud that, even when I found a pay phone to call my rewrite man, I couldn't hear myself talk, much less him."

Betsie marveled. "What did you do? You had to get the story, right?"

"We got the story, all right. So did every other rag in New York. Whether any of us got accurate details is still a matter of opinion. In those days, 'reporters' were the ones who were out where news was being made. Keep in mind there were fewer women in the field then. The rewrite guys were the maestros, the artists, and on many occasions, the fiction writers. The scribes phoned in the details and the rewrites created the news stories based on the info we gave them. While it was the best day ever for New York newspaper street sales, the irony was that everything you read about the Lindbergh parade was basically fabricated by the rewrite Shakespeares back at the office. I gotta say, I was still picking ticker tape out of my pockets three days after that parade. Those were the days!"

"Yes, those were the days," James agreed. "But these are also the days as well. We're living in exciting times. We have the strongest military, our economy is booming, and color television is expanding."

"I reckon you're right," Max said. "You and Betsie are the new breed of reporter. Y'all are going to do great things, and I can brag about being the recruiter."

# CHAPTER SEVENTY-ONE

*MARCH 1961*

"I 'VE HAD THIS idea for a long time," James told the NBC executive. "Imagine Betsie and me exploring America by private plane and having a camera crew follow us. Our country is beaming with patriotism right now. Let's also give the people a renewed sense of adventure."

"It's brilliant," the executive said. "Your careers are already soaring, both literally and figuratively. Let's showcase this great land of ours."

"We'll tie it into the construction of the interstate highway system. It'll be like a modern-day Lewis and Clark expedition," James continued his sales pitch. "Betsie and I will take off and land in forty-eight states in forty-eight days."

"We don't think in terms of states," the executive clarified. "To us, there's only one demographic designation. It's the television market. The plan will be to have our publicists stay well ahead of your comings and goings. An on-air talent from a local NBC-TV station will greet you when you land. If we can grab viewers first thing in the morning, then we'll be the station playing when they flip on the tube to watch the evening news."

"It'll be one hell of a publicity stunt," James asserted and looked over at Betsie. He smiled and put his arm around her. "Many will view you as something of a latter-day Amelia Earhart and a modern inspiration for all the women who are pushing for more equal rights. And it certainly doesn't hurt that you're very telegenic."

"Yes," Max said. "There is definitely that."

She smiled. "I love the idea, but—"

"Uh oh, she's about to rain on my parade."

"I'm worried it's too ambitious. We can't control the weather, local camera crews, or mechanical issues with our plane. How about we take eighty days, like the popular book and movie, *Around the World in 80 Days?*"

"Ah," the executive smiled and nodded. "Even better, since we can capitalize on the marketing of an established fan base. When would you want to start this ratings venture?"

James and Betsie looked at each other.

"There's no time like the present," they said in unison.

# CHAPTER SEVENTY-TWO

THE SKY OVER Love Field in Dallas cleared after the morning drizzle had stopped. James and Betsie departed soon after and made their first stop in Oklahoma before heading to an Air Force base in Arkansas.

"What is unique about Little Rock?" Betsie asked upon landing. "I might need a quick answer if the reporter asks me what we're looking most forward to."

"They invented the toothbrush," he replied.

"Oh," she said surprised. "I guess it's true what they say: 'you learn something new every day.'"

"Yep, because if another state had invented it, it would be called the teethbrush."

They laughed until a military official marshalled them toward a prearranged photo-opportunity spot. He directed the flying duo to park their Cessna next to a giant Boeing B-47 Stratojet.

"Time to get serious," Betsie said and dabbed her cheeks.

"That is one sleek-looking plane," James noted.

"Is that six engines on that bird?" she asked.

"Yep, a direct result of the Cold War. It's job is to fly high and fast and drop the bomb when needed."

"That's a dreadful thought," she said. "Now I understand why our publicists wanted us to land here. To remind people of the men and women defending against any possible future attacks."

A military band played the Air Force's official song as they exited their plane. Alongside the NBC reporter was also a *Stars and Stripes* reporter.

"Service members thank you for flying here," the military reporter told James, "and for highlighting the important work our men do every day to keep Americans safe. I know y'all are doing this for work, but does it feel like work?"

"Piloting a small airplane across this vast country requires a lot of preparation, but it's important to make sure it's also fun. We've allotted enough time to make it challenging, yet relaxing enough to visit with folks without feeling rushed."

"Where will you and Mrs. Karl be flying to next?" the *Stripes* reporter asked.

"We'll be staying here tonight," Betsie answered. "We're attending a formal event with the Tactical Reconnaissance Group. I asked them what they do, but they told me it's classified. They could tell me, but then they'd half to kill me."

The group of reporters and bystanders laughed.

"We certainly wouldn't want that, Mrs. Karl," the *Stripes* reporter said.

"No, we wouldn't," James said.

# CHAPTER SEVENTY-THREE

**T**HEY MET WITH station talent in Louisiana, Mississippi, and Alabama over the next four days. At each stop, the local TV workers graciously greeted them and asked what seemed to be endlessly repetitive, but never monotonous questions. Indeed, through all the travel and travails they experienced, they never tired of meeting people.

"An afternoon thunderstorm is popping up on our path," James told Betsie as the turbulence bounced them around at 8,000 feet. He struggled to keep the single-engine aircraft straight and level against the wind shear. "We're not going to be able to go much farther north. Check the map and find us a place to land."

She scanned the aeronautical chart.

"How about Gettysburg, Pennsylvania? It's nearby."

He nodded.

"There won't be a crew to greet us," she mentioned.

"Even better," he said. "If we land quickly, we might have a few hours to walk the battleground before sunset."

The staff at the country airport helped them secure the airplane inside a hangar and tossed them the keys to a courtesy vehicle.

"All we ask is that you bring it back with the same amount of fuel," the lineman said.

"Thank you very much," James told the young man. "We'll be staying the night...at least until this storm blows over. We'll see you in the morning."

James and Betsie cruised over to the battleground as the storm approached from the distance. The sun was setting.

"I love the sky during this part of the day," he said. "When the evening starts to blend with the night."

"Me, too," she agreed.

They tumbled out of the truck and started walking across the grass. The wind gusted, but the rain looked to be about half an hour away.

"I can hear the blasts of cannon fire," he remarked.

"What?"

James inhaled deeply through his nose. "This humid air also whiffs of gunpowder."

"I think I smell it, too," she said. "But that's strange. There's nobody around here."

"Over forty-thousand American soldiers lost their lives in three days of battle," he said. "You can't have that much violent death without leaving behind traces of energy and unrest that will always resonate here."

"It's mind-boggling to think about how many Americans lost their lives fighting each other here," she lamented.

"Brothers fighting brothers," he said. "It was a dark time in our country's history."

"They say this is one of America's most haunted places," she said. "Do you believe in ghosts?"

They continued strolling across the sacred battleground.

"I believe in the afterlife," he said.

"I want to believe, too," she said. "How can you be sure, though?"

"It's difficult for me to explain. It's like television or radio. I don't understand how it all works, but I enjoy its benefits."

"At least you can see and hear television," she said.

"Sometimes I think God is talking to us, but we're not listening."

The once-distant grey clouds rolled in and brought a torrential downpour with them.

"Wanna head back to the truck?" he shouted over the cracking of thunder.

She shrugged her shoulders. "Why bother? We're already soaked."

"Okey-doke," he replied with a smile. He held her hand and they continued walking side-by-side.

# CHAPTER SEVENTY-FOUR

THEY ENJOYED A light breakfast at their B&B before they departed Pennsylvania and flew to New York. A chauffeur drove them to Warwick in Midtown Manhattan for their live appearance on *Today*.

"What's been the best part of the tour so far?" a cohost asked during their on-air interview.

Betsie smiled. "The chance to meet so many marvelous people at every stop," she answered honestly. "Everyone has been so wonderful," she gushed.

The charming cohost returned the smile and turned toward James for his answer.

"Getting to see how diverse our nation is has been the most insightful part to me."

"Please explain," she encouraged him to elaborate.

"The United States is one country, but each state has its own unique culture, and sometimes its own language, as I learned in Louisiana."

"Do you have a favorite state?" she asked.

"Texas!" Betsie blurted out of turn.

James chuckled. "Definitely Texas, but I haven't seen all of them yet. Perhaps I'll have an answer for you when we've finished this grand adventure."

"What's been the worst part of the trip so far?" she asked.

"I can answer that one," Betsie said. "With just five changes of clothes for this entire marathon, we'll have to build a bonfire when we get back home and torch them."

Everyone laughed and the music started playing in the background to indicate the end of the segment.

Betsie shook her cohost's hand and turned to James as they headed toward the exit. "How are you holding up so far? Twenty-four states and we've still got fifty-some days to check off the other half."

James shot her a look of disbelief. "Miss Earhart, have you checked out a map lately? A bunch of the states we've landed in so far are about the size of ping-pong tables compared with the ones out west. Montana alone is about the width of the Soviet Empire."

"Well, then, Mr. Lindberg," she said with a wink, "I guess we better get to bed early tonight and take off early in the morning."

"Now hold on," he said. "We're in the Big Apple."

"Yes, we are."

"So, we gotta hit the town!"

"What did you have in mind?" she asked.

"Top of the Empire State Building, hon."

# CHAPTER SEVENTY-FIVE

THE FLYING DUO continued their trek across America and landed in Oregon for a home-cooked dinner with the Karls.

"I'd be less than honest if I told you I've seen every last one of your TV highlights about this great air adventure of yours," Hans said over a casual dinner at his home. "But I haven't missed many. It seems only appropriate that you two are soaring your way into this exciting new decade, since NASA and the space race are all over the news."

"Maybe JFK will invite you to the White House when you've finished your trip," Anna said and gulped her drink.

James had learned that Anna was the more sarcastic of the two sisters.

"If we get invited, would you like for us to see if you can come along?"

Anna started to cough. Agnes jumped up and patted her on the back.

"Is that a yes, Anna?" James smirked.

Anna nodded vehemently.

"Of course, any invitation to the White House would likely depend first on us having finished the trip and second having done it in the allotted time frame," James said.

Betsie added, "That's the greatest thing about being a reporter. You get to meet interesting and sometimes really powerful people. Granted, I'm just a roving reporter for a TV station, but I'd love to meet the president someday. Meeting Jackie would be such a thrill."

"Hey," James said, "let's not get greedy. After all, the vice president is practically your uncle."

"Is that true?" Anna asked.

James asked Hans, "Sir, would you mind if I made a long-distance call to check on things at the *Herald*?"

"Son, this is your house. Use the telephone as you need."

"Thank you very much," he said.

He dialed the number by memory.

"Anything new, Johnny?"

"I'm so glad you called Mr. James. You and Ms. Betsie's adventure has been making quite the news stir, even more so than Vice President Johnson's visit to South Vietnam."

James turned his attention to Betsie. "Johnny said our cross-country flight is getting more press attention than your pal, LBJ."

Betsie laughed. "Getting upstaged by two television reporters. He's probably having chest pains over it."

"Also Mr. James," Johnny continued, "Mr. Robert Moore was trying to get a hold of you."

"Who?"

"Mr. Robert Moore, the principal of the new Westwood High School. The first senior class of Westwood graduates on May thirty-first, and he wants you to be the commencement speaker."

"May thirty-first?" James quickly tallied the dates in his head. "Please tell him I appreciate the offer, but there's no way in the world we'll be back in time."

Then it hit James like a ton of bricks.

*The 1961 graduating class of Westwood? My little girl will be graduating high school...*

"Mr. James? Are you there, Mr. James?"

"Yes," he answered. "I'm here." He took a deep breath. "Please tell Mr. Moore that I'll be more than happy to do it. No matter what, Betsie and I will be there. If we have to skip meals and fly at night, we'll do it."

# CHAPTER SEVENTY-SIX

GRADUATION DAY TURNED out to be an extraordinarily beautiful day with blooming Texas bluebonnets and a cool breeze that eased the sun's heat.

James held Betsie's hand as the couple walked side-by-side.

"I was hoping the ceremony would be outside."

"I'm sure the principal wants to show off the school's new auditorium," she said.

"It's nicer than anything you and I had as kids," he remarked.

"Yes it is, and that's why he has to show it off after how much it ended up costing the school board. Frankly, I was surprised he asked you to speak to the graduating class, considering the *Herald* published several articles that highlighted the numerous delays and rising costs."

James looked upward into the blue sky.

"It's fate. Sometimes the good Lord smiles on me, even when I don't deserve it."

"Is that one of your examples of God talking to you, and you listening?"

"Yes ma'am," he said.

"I'm not sure if God has ever talked to me," she said. "What's His voice sound like?"

"Southern drawl. He's definitely a Texan."

She giggled. "I'll have to listen for it more carefully now."

"Mr. Karl," Principal Moore said, walking up to him with his hand extended. "It's such a pleasure to meet you in person. I've been following your writings ever since you came to Palestine. Even when you moved to Alaska, I always enjoyed your send-in stories. I especially liked when you contrasted living in Alaska to East Texas. I can't imagine the harsh winters with twenty-four hour darkness and temperatures that dropped to negative seventeen degrees Fahrenheit."

"That was a warm month," James replied, then chuckled.

"Or about eating powdered eggs and milk when you think about all our bountiful farms here in Texas."

"Thanks for reading my work, Mr. Moore. Some days it was like living on a different planet."

"You wrote so well that I felt like I was there," the principal continued his compliments. "I enjoyed the article you wrote a few years ago when the Soviets had successfully launched their rockets, meanwhile our American scientists still couldn't get even the simplest contraption off the launch pads. The success of the Soviet Sputnik led to Americans calling failed U.S. projects as 'Kaputnik.' You suggested every failed American rocket should've been called 'Civil Servant'—because you can't fire it and it won't work."

"Oh, that one," Betsie remarked. "I remember that article very well. We still receive complaints about that article and about Mr. Karl's sense of humor, or lack of it as one reader wrote."

"Well, you can't please everyone," Principal Moore said. "Trust me. As a principal, I know that feeling all too well."

"No doubt, you have a tough job," Betsie said.

"Mrs. Karl, I'm not much into politics, but I did enjoy reading your political commentaries. I liked how you gave it to Vice President Johnson about his comments regarding Vietnam."

James chortled. "Don't let her fool you, Mr. Moore. Betsie and the VP are very close friends."

"Politics at its best," she said and smiled.

Principal Moore forced an uneasy smile.

"If you'll please excuse me," Betsie said, "I see a friend I haven't seen in a while."

"Certainly," the men said.

"Do I need a hall pass?" Betsie joked.

The men chuckled.

"Well, shall I introduce you to the graduating class of 1961? This is Sharon Axum," Principal Moore said. "She was also our representative in the Miss Westwood beauty pageant at the county fair this past fall. She made us all proud when she came in first runner-up."

James was stunned. Hundreds of thoughts flashed in his mind. He wanted to tell her how the draft in 1944 required him to leave her and her mother.

*You were just a baby then. Now you're a young woman graduating from high school. You've grown into such a beautiful and responsible adult. You'll never know how incredibly proud and overjoyed with love I feel right now.*

"That is so fantastic, Sharon," he managed to say. "Your family must be very proud of you. I hope they are here with you today?"

"Yes, sir. My mom, Annie Mae, and my stepfather, Milton, and my husband is somewhere around here."

"Your husband?" he asked incredulously. Though it was not uncommon for 17 and 18-year olds to marry, James still thought of Sharon as a little girl. The fact she was married made him realize how much of her life he had missed. *Birthdays, her first steps, her first day at school, teaching her to ride a bike, everything about being her dad.*

"Yes," she answered and pointed into the crowd of seated people. "That handsome man over there and I married a few months ago. All my family is here, except my biological dad. He was killed in the Second World War. It's weird. I never knew him, but I sure wish he could be here."

James started to choke up. He pulled the handkerchief from his coat pocket.

"Don't you worry, sweetheart. I'm sure your dad is here today watching you. I can feel it right here," James said as he touched his heart. I know how proud he is of you, because I'm proud of you."

"Thank you, Mr. Karl. That means a lot to me. My mom and I enjoyed watching you and Ms. Betsie on the television. She sure is pretty."

"I'll be sure to tell her you said that," James smiled.

"I want to do some traveling of my own someday."

"Anywhere in particular?"

"Europe. My dad was buried at a military cemetery in Belgium. It would mean so much to me to be able to visit his grave."

That somehow he was a presence in his daughter's life overwhelmed James. He did not know what to say.

Hearing the sadness of her story, the principal quickly changed the subject.

"Sharon is the reason our high school is named Westwood. The school district decided last year to consolidate Woodhouse Country School with this one. Since they didn't have a name for the new school, they allowed the senior class to come up with the name and the mascot. Sharon is the student who suggested Westwood."

"Congratulations," James said. "How did you come up with the name and the mascot?"

"Well, another student came up with the panther as our mascot. I think he saw one near the Dogwood trails. But I thought of Westwood since our high school is west of town, and the name still keeps the history of Woodhouse alive. I think history and tradition are important, don't you? It reminds you of where you came from."

James nodded. "That's why I came to Texas. It was my home in a different life."

She gave him a confused look.

"I know I just met you," James said, quickly changing the subject, "but I believe you have a very promising future ahead of you. You should be very excited."

"Oh, I am," she replied.

"If you ever want to come work at the *Herald*, I'd be happy to give you a job."

"That's mighty kind of you Mr. Karl, but I'm not much of a writer."

James chuckled. "That makes two of us."

He fought the urge to tell her everything. He so badly wanted to be a part of her life. There was so much he wanted to do for her.

At that moment, Annie Mae walked up and stood next to her daughter. She extended her hand, and for the first time in 17 years James held it in his.

"It's a pleasure to meet you, Mr. Karl," Annie Mae said.

"The pleasure is all mine," he replied, looking directly into her eyes. "Your daughter is a wonderful young woman. You done good, Annie Mae."

She looked as if she had seen a ghost. Her legs wobbled beneath her and Sharon grabbed her by the elbow to steady her.

"Are you okay, Momma?" Sharon asked.

"Yes, sweetheart. It's just that...well, that is exactly what your daddy told me when he held you for the first time."

"Mr. Karl," the principal said, "we're about to start the ceremony."

James nodded, then looked at Annie Mae and Sharon. "I guess it's showtime." He reached into his coat pocket and clutched a few note cards. "Today's speech is for you," he winked at Sharon before turning and walking toward the stage.

"Graduating class, faculty, friends and family," Principal Moore said from behind the podium, "it brings me great honor to introduce our guest speaker. Mr. James Karl is a World War Two veteran, owner of the *Herald*, and a national reporter. He is most recently known for flying to each of the contiguous forty-eight states in a remarkable seventy-five days. Please join me in giving him a warm Panther welcome."

"Hello and thank you for having me. That's my lovely wife sitting over there. She warned me not to bore you fine folks. She's gripping a large shepherd's hook and waiting to pull me offstage if I do," he said to pleasant laughter from the audience.

"These are truly exciting times we are living in. Fantastic opportunities are available for anyone willing to work hard. Men and women alike. A few days ago, the president promoted the very first woman to be his personal physician. Imagine being the doctor to the president of the United States.

"Back in January, my wonderful wife Betsie and I watched, for the first time ever, a live broadcast of the presidential inauguration. I dare say President Kennedy inspired us all when he said, 'Ask not what your country can do for you, but ask what you can do for your country.'

"Three weeks ago we all sat transfixed in front of our TV sets as we watched the first American launched into outer space. What once seemed impossible was proven to be possible. I can't emphasize enough what amazing times we are living in.

"Our country needs you. You are the future doctors, teachers, scientists, journalists, politicians, and mothers and fathers of what will be a new generation. Today, you are taking ownership of the proverbial torch and you will light the way for all the others who follow you.

"I confess that I was never much of a reader until I became a commercial fisherman after I returned from World War II. Then I read everything I could get my hands on in order to pass the endless hours at sea. One of my favorites was William Shakespeare's Julius Caesar. He said, 'Cowards die many times before their deaths; the valiant never taste of death but once.'

"Please believe me when I tell you that life will challenge you in ways you can't imagine. You're going to have fear. You're going to have failure. You're going to have regrets. It's part of being human. But you will always have two choices. You can hide from fear with your eyes shut and let it make you *bitter*, or you can face the fear with your eyes wide open and let it make you *better*.

"You've earned this epic moment in time. Cherish it. Go forward with your heads held high and your eyes wide open. I don't believe in goodbyes, so I will say good luck, Godspeed, and I'll see you when I see you. Congratulations graduating class of 1961."

The graduates flung their caps into the air to the loud applause of many proud friends, family members, and teachers.

"You say your goodbyes and I'll get the car, James," Betsie said.

"Sounds good," he replied. He said goodbye to the principal and started walking toward the exit when he noticed Annie Mae and Sharon rushing toward him. Their faces beamed and tears streamed down their faces.

"Is everything okay?" James asked.

"My dad said that," Sharon cried.

"Beg your pardon?"

"I'll see you when I see you. My mom always tells me that. She said it was the last thing my father said to her before he left for the war."

James looked at Annie Mae who was dabbing her eyes with a handkerchief.

Suddenly Sharon embraced him and buried her face in his chest.

"Thank you. Thank you so much. Because of you, I feel like my father is here with me today." She began to cry.

Mage held his daughter close to him, never wanting the moment to end.

"I will always be here for you," he whispered.

He eventually made his way outside, where Betsie was waiting in their red and white convertible.

"I'm so glad I came here today. This is one of the greatest days of my life."

"Your speech was good, honey, but don't start thinking you're the next Franklin Delano Roosevelt," she giggled.

"My speech was irrelevant today. For mine eyes have seen the glory."

# CHAPTER SEVENTY-SEVEN

I N THE AFTERMATH of their impressive flying adventure, James and Betsie were resting at their home in Palestine when the phone rang.

"You probably don't remember me," the high-pitched caller said, "but I knew you two once upon a time."

James instantly recognized the voice on the line.

"Champ Albright?"

"The one and only, but I'm going by C.R. Albright now. They've got enough genuine champs in Texas. I hope I didn't catch you at a bad time."

"Betsie and I are about to watch *The Red Skelton Show*."

"Well, I don't want to keep you."

"Nah, I'm glad you called. How is Alaska treating you?"

"Thanks for asking, but I got out of there and worked my way south. I've been in Dallas for a few months, and I think I might stay. I like the weather here a whole lot better. Plus, I'm proud to say that I've been sober for ninety-one days."

"That's great news!"

"I'm working for the *Dallas Times Herald* and they've got me writing general assignments. I'm calling because my editor wants an exclusive about your grand aviation adventure.

I told him that I saved your life in Alaska, and that I could manage an interview since you owe me."

"What?" James started to wonder if Champ really was sober, but he knew the reporter well enough to be familiar with his delusions of grandeur.

"Please, give me a second. It's killing me writing these mundane articles. This would give me a step up. I'm begging you."

James thought for a moment before answering.

"Don't ask me why, but I'll do it."

"Thank you so much," Champ said. "It's nothing too formal, but I'll bring a photographer. You won't regret doing this."

# CHAPTER SEVENTY-EIGHT

CHAMP AND HIS photographer showed up the next day at the Palestine airport. James and Betsie's hangar was the setting for the interview. The sleek twin-engine airplane, a shiny red white and blue American flag, and a wall full of framed pictures filled the backdrop.

"The original photos of Betsie and her father are still hanging," James said and pointed to the wall, "but we've added some new ones over the years."

"Do you have a favorite?" Champ asked, a notepad in one hand and a pen in the other.

"My favorite is that one." He pointed to a photo showing himself looking over his shoulder as Frank Rogers cut off the back of his t-shirt.

"What in the world is happening?" Champ asked.

"That's the day I soloed my first airplane. That's my instructor, and that's Betsie grinning from ear to ear."

"I wouldn't be that happy if someone as diabolical as that man was tearing up my shirt."

"Are you kidding?" James asked. "That was an incredible day."

"It's unique," Champ said. He turned to his photographer. "Make sure to snap a picture of that photo."

James started to point out another favorite picture on the wall when Champ interrupted. He couldn't stand being out of the limelight.

"I think it's worth noting," Champ said as he examined his barely visible scar, "that the eight-ball that took most of the bullet is still on display at the Parallel 60."

*The keyword being "most," if not "all" the bullet,* James thought.

"And the story of what happened," Champ continued, "is getting more and more embellished every year."

"Especially if you have anything to do with it," James teased. "So, where is Tom Bannon nowadays?"

"No idea. He was tried by a lenient judge and only convicted of discharging a firearm in a public place. He was awarded time served and placed on two years of probation. One of the benefits of getting sober was my improved judgment. I cut all ties with that loose cannon."

"Tom Loose Cannon Bannon," James chuckled. "What's the word on the streets? I know you have your ear to the rumor mill."

"The last I heard was that after he got released from jail, he bought a boat and became a fisherman. Rumor had it that he lost his bearings in a bad storm and ended up landing on the Soviet Union coast."

"It would be poetic justice if they charged him for being a spy and sentenced him to the Gulag," James said.

"Justice indeed. Just be careful," Champ cautioned. "Bannon is like a bad penny. You never know when he might turn up again. I can't guarantee I'll be there to help you like I did in Alaska."

"I appreciate your concern, but don't worry about me. If war taught me one thing, it was always to be aware of my surroundings and to expect the unexpected. I'm ready if he ever decides to threaten Betsie or me again."

"You don't want the third time to be a charm," Champ warned.

# CHAPTER SEVENTY-NINE

*New York City*
*October 22, 1962*

J AMES AND BETSIE were at NBC Studios on 30 Rockefeller Plaza on Sixth Avenue to video record an interview with a young man described as a "protest singer."

"Mr. Dylan," Betsie began the interview.

"Call me Bob, please. You and I aren't that different."

"The quality of our singing voices says we're very different," she said.

James laughed.

"You see, even my husband agrees."

Bob Dylan smiled. "You're from a small town in Texas-...I'm from a small town in Minnesota."

"We do have that in common," she said. "You made your debut concert at New York's Carnegie Hall last November, where you introduced to the world a fresh style of lyrics. How do you respond when people say your songs are anti-war or pro-Civil Rights?"

"That's a great question. When people ask me about that, I tell them—"

"I'm sorry to interrupt," Max barged into the room. "The president is addressing the nation."

"I'm in the middle of an interview," Betsie said, irritated at the unprofessionalism.

"It's breaking news," Max replied. "The interview will have to wait."

All three of them huddled around the television screen along with Max, their cameraman Joe, and a few others who helped with sound and lighting. President Kennedy addressed the nation from his desk in the oval office.

"Good evening my fellow citizens. This government, as promised, has maintained closest surveillance of the soviet military buildup on the island of Cuba. Within the past week, unmistakable evidence has established the fact that a series of offensive military sites…"

Everything seemed to go silent. James continued watching the president, but it was like the sound went out.

"The purpose of these bases," the president continued, "can be none other than to provide a nuclear strike capability against the western hemisphere."

"My God," Betsie gasped and turned to James. "The Soviets are provoking us into a nuclear war!"

James eased himself into a nearby chair. He loosened his tie. "I thought I fought in World War Two so that they'd never be World War Three. They'll be no victors in this type of war. A nuclear bomb…even the winner is dead."

"You have to reach out to Vice President Johnson," Max told Betsie. "We have to know what's going on behind the scenes."

"I'm a reporter," she said. "I can't use my personal connection to him to call to get information about national security for NBC!"

"Of course you can. As a matter of fact, you have a duty as a reporter to get this information for the American people. Like James said, we could all be dead tomorrow."

Betsie seemed to be in a daze as Max barked out orders about the threat of a nuclear bomb exploding in Manhattan.

"You can use the telephone in my office," Max said.

James grabbed her hand. "I think Max is right...folks deserve to know what's going on."

The White House operator answered the phone and patched Betsie through to the Vice President, who was in the Situation Room.

"Mr. Vice President, it's Betsie."

"I know it's you, darlin'. That's the only reason I took the call. I'm sure you saw the president's speech."

"That's why I'm calling," she said. "There are a lot of worried people. I'm one of them."

"Me too," he said. "I'm with the Joint Chiefs of Staff right now. We're discussing strategy."

"Anything you could say to reassure the American people would be great about now."

"Your daddy, God rest his soul, would've understood that there are times when it's just not prudent to talk with a journalist, either on or off the record. My advice...you and James should find a reason to get back to Palestine as soon as possible."

"Is Palestine safe from a nuclear bomb? From what I've heard, our entire country would be reduced to ashes."

"Betsie, darlin', we both love the great state of Texas, but I think the red bastards would pick New York City and Washington, D.C. as their targets of choice over Palestine."

"Where's Lady Bird?"

"The Secret Service has taken her to an undisclosed location."

"You won't be with her during this? I can't imagine going through this without James."

"I've sworn an oath. This is my duty." He took an exaggerated breath and let it out. "Please, don't put me in an awkward position. I'll deny ever talking to you if any of this conversation gets out."

"Be safe, Lyndon."

"I love you, darlin'. You and James take care. I've gotta get back to work."

Betsie started to tear up.

"What did he say?" Max said.

"He said 'no comment.' That it wasn't wise to talk to a reporter, even one he trusted."

"Damn politicians!" Max yelled out.

"I'm sorry," Betsie said and began to cry.

James embraced her. "No, no, no, it's alright babe," he whispered. "You made the call."

"It's not that. Lyndon was worried, James. I've never heard his tone like that before."

"We're all worried, honey."

"Well, I'm going to the legendary Ear Inn," Max announced. "It might be my last drink on earth before the Soviets blow me to hell."

*Max makes a convincing argument*, James thought. *I've lived through war, but this is totally different. These two superpowers have the technology to destroy Mother Earth in minutes. If there were ever a time to tell Betsie who I really am, it would be now.*

Though he had rehearsed it so many times before, his stomach churned.

"Betsie, sweetheart, I have something I need to share with you."

# CHAPTER EIGHTY

"COME ON TEAM!" Max shouted. "You too, Mr. Dylan. And of course you, Big Joe! I've got a wallet full of money that might be useless tomorrow. Drinks are on me."

Betsie looked into James's eyes.

"Yes, dear?"

Before he could answer, Max threw his arms around Betsie and James. "What do y'all say...Tom Collins again, like we had in Dallas?"

James sighed as his opportunity disappeared.

Max whistled as he escorted them out of the studio.

New Yorkers lined the sidewalks to buy the latest edition of the paper. The bold headline read: "CRISIS!"

James bought the last copy and skimmed page one.

"Do you think war can be averted?" Betsie asked.

"I don't want to damper your mood any more, but as long as men occupy this world, I reckon there will always be talks of war."

"Peace is possible," she said. "My daddy often reached across the aisle with people he despised to get support to pass a bill to help Americans."

"The Soviets aren't smooth talkers like your father was. Their language is force. You've heard of Leon Trotsky, right?"

"Of course, the Soviet writer."

"He said, 'You may not be interested in war, but war is interested in you.' I've never forgotten that quote. And apparently war was interested in that particular communist because he was assassinated in Mexico."

"It's so sad, but I guess you have a point about the world always being in conflict. When you think about our lifetime, we've lived through World War Two, the Korean War, Vietnam's still going on, and now we have this Cuban Missile Crisis."

"In your lifetime?" Max laughed. "Imagine what I've seen in *my* lifetime!"

"One thing is for sure. Pacifism doesn't work," James said. "We have to confront evil when it manifests. Pacifism is as logical as expecting a grizzly bear not to eat you because you're a vegetarian."

"That's good," Max said as they continued walking several blocks, passing the Hook and Ladder Company Eight Firehouse. "If we survive this crisis, that'll be the headline I use."

"James," Betsie tugged at his arm, "what did you want to tell me back at the studio?"

"We're here, fellas!" Max announced, standing underneath the red neon light that simply stated: "BAR, established 1817 A.D." He gripped the door and held it open for the gang.

"Don't worry about it," James said, noticing that Max either had the best timing or the absolute worst. "We're in New York City. Let's seize the day and enjoy the moment we have together."

"*Carpe diem,*" she said and kissed him.

## CHAPTER EIGHTY-ONE

THE HISTORIC BAR provided a refuge from the nervous energy created by the pedestrians going to-and-fro outside. The establishment's owner was the sole bartender working that Monday evening, and poured the drinks for Max and his friends.

Betsie squeezed the juice from a sliced lemon into her glass and stirred it with a straw. She took a sip, and shook her head.

"Something's not right," she said.

"What is it?" James asked. "Something wrong with your Tom Collins?"

"No, the drink's fine. It doesn't sit well with me that we're in here partying, avoiding our responsibilities. We should be out there doing our jobs," she said as she pointed with her hand. "We don't run away from World War Three, we run toward it and document it. We inform the world. We're national reporters."

James nodded. "You're right."

"Dammit!" Max said. He took two quick swigs of his drink. "Betsie, you would have made one hell of a war correspondent!"

"She already does," James said and faced his beautiful wife. "I'm with you, sweetheart."

She smiled and nodded. "Let's go do our jobs...till the very end."

# CHAPTER EIGHTY-TWO

*JULY 4, 1963*

THE CUBAN MISSILE Crisis thankfully eased within a week after President Kennedy had initially addressed the nation. Betsie's and James's stellar reporting kept many Americans informed. Vice President Johnson had made mention that President Kennedy read their daily articles, but never knew that LBJ was one of their "sources" inside the White House. Lyndon delighted in the notion of pulling strings behind the scenes.

The terror of a possible World War III brought on by the Cuban Missile Crisis reminded James and Betsie about the brevity of life, as well as the independence offered by owning their own private aircraft. James had been lobbying for a bigger and faster airplane for quite some time, and was pleased to find that both of them decided a twin-engine aircraft could haul more of "our" luggage, a married code word for Betsie's stuff.

"I can't believe how fast time has flown," James told Betsie as they cruised around the Texas countryside in their new airplane. "Our thirteen-year anniversary is here."

She feigned surprise. "Has it been thirteen years? Feels like just the other day this good-looking fellow walked into my life and I was smitten. Then a couple of days later, I met you."

"Har-dee-har," he said.

"Good God, James, I'm pushing forty-four but sometimes I feel like fifty."

"Then it's lucky for both of us that you still look twenty-nine, like the first day I met you."

"That's sweet of you," she smiled. "At least neither of us has been shot at in a while."

"There's that," he said. "I was thinking...with the onslaught of the presidential campaign coming up in a few months, how about some relaxing time and sunshine at Playa del Carmen?"

"That would be great."

James abruptly banked the airplane.

"Mexico, here we come."

"Wait! What? Not now, silly!"

"Why not now?"

"Well, for one, I didn't bring any luggage."

"I already packed all the essentials for us. All we need are bathing suits and sandals."

"Um, not exactly," she said. "That's just one of the differences between men and women. I need—"

"Mexico has clothing, darling. We'll buy it there if we need it."

The twin-engine airplane zipped through the skies at a record pace.

After landing at the Mexican airstrip in Cozumel, they endured a bumpy boat ride to the village. As the nightfall approached, they clinked their cold margaritas and went to the veranda of their casita to watch the fireworks display on the beach.

As the waves crashed nearby, and the fireworks lit up the sky, they recalled the great memories of the last thirteen years together.

"Could you have imagined our careers moving along at breakneck pace when they first offered this job?" Betsie said and gestured her glass for yet another toast.

"Nope," James replied. "Thank God Johnny and the excellent professionals have been keeping the *Herald* prospering during our absence."

"I know. Hiring Johnny was one of my best decisions."

"You may have hired him," James said and winked, "but I trained him."

"Don't get jealous. Hiring Johnny was a great decision, but hiring you was by far the best move I ever made at the *Herald*." She paused for a beat. "And marrying you was by far the best decision I ever made in my life."

James finished his margarita and poured himself another and topped off her glass.

"I couldn't have done this without you," he said.

"I *wouldn't* have done this without you," she said.

He smiled and kissed her. "We make one helluva team."

# CHAPTER EIGHTY-THREE

*WASHINGTON, D.C.*
*AUGUST 28, 1963*

RACE RELATIONS IN the United States dominated the headlines. Black leaders continued to preach nonviolence. However, the mounting pushback from Southern whites against integration made it seem inevitable that violence would erupt. NBC dispatched Betsie and James to cover Dr. Martin Luther King's much-anticipated speech.

James and Betsie crammed between more than 250,000 protestors who united at the Lincoln Memorial to advance civil rights.

"One gunshot and this whole thing goes south," James told her. "We'll be trampled like cattle in a stampede."

"I'm sure that's what the networks are secretly hoping for," she said. "It'll increase their viewership and ratings."

"Well, somebody else would have to report it then, because we'd be dead."

"Like Max would say: 'Even bad publicity is good publicity,'" she noted as they continued forcing their way toward the front of the stage.

The hopeful crowd broke into applause as Dr. Martin Luther King approached the podium in a black suit. People from all walks of life gathered to hear the reverend speak. Men in military uniforms, cook's clothing, and business suits surrounded him in a show of solidarity.

"I'm happy to join with you today," Reverend King uttered in a unique cadence typical of a Southern pastor, "in what will go down in history as the greatest demonstration for freedom in the history of our nation."

James furiously jotted down notes as the reverend's poetic words boomed across the Reflecting Pool and crowd of onlookers. Many of them had stood for hours to be present at the speech. The summer weather was 80 degrees, but the enormous crowds contributed to claustrophobia. More than one person fainted, and others dipped their feet into the Reflecting Pool.

"I have a dream that my four little children will one day live in a nation where they will not be judged by the color of their skin but by the content of their character."

Effusive applause often interrupted the speech. James got caught up in the moment—the reverend's heartfelt words, the statue of President Abraham Lincoln towering behind the podium—and he stopped scribbling notes and became a spectator. He felt like another everyday American who came out to witness history. He got goosebumps as the reverend concluded with a crescendo of: "Free at last. Free at last. Thank God Almighty. We are free at last!"

The crowd erupted in deafening applause and celebration.

Betsie looked over at James and asked something, but he couldn't hear over the noise. She leaned closer and yelled by his ear. "What did you think about that?"

"Let's go somewhere quiet to talk," he shouted back.

Her face lit up and she smiled. "I know the perfect place! My daddy's favorite."

# CHAPTER EIGHTY-FOUR

J AMES OPENED THE door for Betsie at Old Ebbitt Grill, a popular restaurant near the White House. Betsie flashed her press badge and the hostess escorted them to the back, where they took the last two stools at the thick wooden bar.

"This place has so much history," Betsie said. "Presidents used to play dominoes while discussing policy. Obviously, they don't come here anymore, but senators do. My father loved bringing lobbyists here."

"Mason was so charismatic he could sell ice to an Eskimo," James said. "I sure do miss him."

"Me too," she said. "He'd be so proud of what we're doing."

The white-haired bartender with bright blue eyes, clad in the issued uniform of suspenders and a bowtie, stood behind the bar cleaning glasses with a rag.

"Max could get a job here, and he wouldn't even have to change his wardrobe," James joked.

Betsie laughed.

The bartender locked eyes with Betsie. "What are you drinking?"

"Two draft beers," she answered. "We don't care what brand as long as they're cold."

"Coming right up," he replied.

"Also, could you please put an order in for oysters?"

He nodded that he heard.

She turned to James. "So, what did you think of the speech?"

"His message of freedom and racial equality stirred something in me. It's like he was born solely to give that speech."

"I know what you mean," she said. "I got caught up in the moment and forgot I was a reporter for a second."

James smiled and his expression became cheery. "Yes, it was that powerful!"

"So, because you liked it so much, does that mean you're going to do some of the typing this time?"

"Maybe," he smirked. "Or how 'bout I come up with the catchy headline?"

"Let's hear your Pulitzer-Prize-winning headline."

"Let…freedom…ring," he cadenced while motioning a closed hand from left to right like a drummer.

"Ah," she nodded. "That's good. We can lead right into: 'I have a dream that my four little children will one day live in a nation where they will not be judged by the color of their skin but by the content of their character.'"

"I wrote that line down, too," he said.

The bartender plopped down pint glasses of golden-colored beers.

James and Betsie clinked their glasses and toasted.

"To writing history."

James bent down to grab his overused leather messenger bag. He pulled out a magazine and tossed it onto the bar. He pointed to the cover with his index finger.

"What do you think this man has in common with Martin Luther King?"

"Um," she thought, looking down at the military officer with three silver stars across his green helmet. "General Patton and Reverend King? You got me."

"General Patton said a man must know his destiny. If he doesn't, then he's lost. Fate will try to steer a man in the right direction only a few times. Though his life was cut short, I believe General Patton knew his fate and fulfilled it."

"I still don't see the connection between these two very different men," she said.

"I believe Dr. King is a man who, when compared to General Patton, also knows his destiny. Fate may rob Dr. King of an otherwise long and prosperous life, but like General Patton, he will not let the fear of death become an obstacle in the fulfillment of his life's purpose."

"What about you, Mr. James Karl? What is your life's purpose?"

"To cater to your every wish," he answered before cracking a smile.

"No," she chuckled. "I'm being serious."

He took another sip and pondered before answering. "I've given that question a lot of thought over the years. I think it's to live life to the fullest. That's why God gave me a second chance at life."

"That's good, and we should all aspire to do that, but you're forgetting the *Grace*. You were given *three* chances at life."

"I won't argue with that." He raised his glass to meet hers. "So what's your life's purpose?"

"To bring truth to people. I'm happiest when I'm writing or narrating a news story. I hope I will be doing this until the day I die."

James smiled. "I'm sure you will. You've got ink running through your veins."

The server brought out a large plate with a dozen oysters atop crushed ice.

"Oh, this looks so delicious," she said. "They're famous for their raw oysters, and you're about to discover why."

They enjoyed the appetizer and had a second round of drinks before Betsie decided to bring it up. It had been on her mind for quite some time.

"Darling, there's one thing I want to do while we're still young and able to do it."

"Name it," he said.

"I would like for you to show me where you were fighting in the war. It's a significant part of your identity, and I would like to experience it, too."

James felt apprehensive about going back to the battle-grounds where he fought and died. He feared the tragic memories might overwhelm him. He also worried that somehow, in such an emotionally low state, he would reveal his true reawakening to her. *How would she respond? It could be devastating.*

"Sweetheart," he finally replied. "I don't think I'm ready to go back there."

"If not now, when?"

"I don't know that I ever will be."

"Honey, but it's not just for you. It's also for me. Wouldn't you like to see if Father Sidney is still alive?"

"If he is, I sure hope that great man found his way back to Rome," he said softly. "It would be a blessing indeed to see him again."

"I would love to meet him before it's too late," she said.

"Do you know something I don't?"

"No, but he must be pushing seventy by now."

James nodded. "That sounds about right."

"President Kennedy and Vice President Johnson are supposed to be campaigning in Texas this November. NBC will want us around to cover that, so now's the best time to go to Europe."

James said nothing. His mind wandered.

"How about it?" she said.

"Whew," he sighed. "It'll be as much an emotional journey as a physical one."

"I understand, but I'll be with you every step of the way."

"Hmm," he thought, his fingers stroked his chin.

She smiled. "You said a few moments ago that your purpose is to live life to the fullest."

His feet nervously tapped the brass foot rail.

"What did that *Queen Mary* captain tell you?"

James scoffed. "You are indeed persistent."

"Well, what did he tell you that was so impactful?"

"He told me to seize the day."

"That's right!" she exclaimed. *"Carpe diem."*

# CHAPTER EIGHTY-FIVE

"WE'RE HERE," JAMES said as they pulled into the parking lot of Ardennes American Military Cemetery. A gatekeeper greeted them as they exited their rental car and walked toward the cemetery.

"Howdy folks. My name is Christopher. I'm the grounds superintendent."

"Pleasure to meet you," James and Betsie said.

"I detect a familiar accent," Christopher said. "Where are you folks from?"

"Texas," they answered in unison.

"Welcome. It's great to have some fellow Southerners visiting."

"Where are you from?" Betsie asked.

"Born and raised in Florida."

"How did you land this job?" James asked.

"A friend told me about it, so I decided to apply. I got lucky and they hired me. I've been overseas almost two years now. You have to be a veteran to work here. I had the honor of serving in the Great War and I'm still working for Uncle Sam. I don't look at this as a job. It's more personal for me. I believe in President Lincoln's promise: 'To care for him who shall have borne the battle and for his widow, and his orphan.'"

"Thank you for your continued service," Betsie said.

He nodded, and a smile spread across his jovial face.

"There are 5,329 American military personnel buried here at Ardennes," Christopher stated.

James thought about the considerable effort required to confirm that the number 5,329 was precise. "It would have been easy for authorities simply to use an estimate and say, 'More than five thousand are buried at Ardennes,' but the specificity of the body count makes being in the presence of so much loss of life more profound."

"Yessir, and each one of them has a story," Christopher said. "Are you looking for any soldier in particular?"

"Mage Axum," James said.

"Was he family?"

James nodded. "Closer than a brother."

"I know what you mean," Christopher said. "The men I served alongside in World War One were like brothers to me, too. When the enemy shoots at you, it doesn't matter if the soldier next to you is black or white or from the North or the South…brothers-in-arms."

He walked to his nearby office and looked up Mage Axum in his directory.

"Plot B, row thirty-four, grave sixteen," Christopher said aloud before grabbing a canteen and small bucket of sand. He handed Betsie and James a small American flag and a Belgian flag. "Please help me carry these flags," he said and escorted them across the cemetery.

"This sand is from the beaches at Normandy," Christopher said as they approached the grave marker. "It'll bring to life the inscription when I fill the gaps with it."

He used the canteen to mix water into the sand, and then spread it across the inscription. He then grabbed the flags and staked them into the ground, at the foot of the marker.

"If you have any questions, I'll do my best to answer them. Otherwise, please enjoy the tranquility." He scanned the entire 90 acres of land and drew a deep breath. "The stillness here is all the more profound, when you consider the contrast between the silence of these grounds and the din of battle that attended the deaths of the soldiers at rest here. These heroes have earned that peace."

James and Betsie nodded.

"Thank you for visiting and keeping the memory of our fallen brothers alive," Christopher said and started walking the ground to tidy anything out of place.

James looked down at the marble stone that marked his grave. *Am I the only soul who has ever come to Ardennes to witness the evidence of his own remains? I imagine not many people can fathom the idea of looking at their own tombstone.*

"What are you thinking?" she asked.

"That I'm still very much alive."

Betsie pulled him close to her. "I'll forever be thankful for that," she said. "Mage Axum was the man from Palestine. He was the soldier whose death was not confirmed for a while. The not knowing was terribly difficult for the family."

James said nothing. He stared blankly at the three dozen letters and numbers on the burial cross:

MAGE AXUM
PVT 115 INF 29 DIV
TEXAS OCT 18 1944

"The deceased dispatched in thirty-six characters," he said. "I guess that's the extent of it."

"No, darling. That's not the extent of it. His life meant something. His courageous actions caused ripples throughout eternity. Europe is not the same. The world is not the same. The good men eternally resting in this peaceful garden of tranquility never had to ask themselves if their actions helped extinguish the spread of evil. Their tombstones serve silently as permanent testimonies to their successful efforts."

James reached into his pocket to retrieve a handkerchief.

Minutes passed in silence.

"Mage was lucky to have you for a friend. I'll bet he would have been glad to know that you survived. Pop once told me that we honor the dead the most when we do our best to live the good, productive lives that they no longer can have."

*The time has come. I have to tell her.*

# CHAPTER EIGHTY-SIX

HIS STOMACH CHURNED and he thought he might vomit. "Betsie, I have something I need to share with you. It's been a great burden on my soul. It would be so much easier to bear if I were able to explain it, but I simply can't."

She looked into his brown eyes.

"You can tell me anything. You know that."

"I know," he said and nodded. "But this is different."

She grabbed his hand.

"The truth is," he began, "despite all evidence to the contrary, I'm not James Karl."

She listened without judgment.

"When I awakened in a military hospital, I had no recollection of anything pertaining to James Karl. Everything I knew had to do with the life of Mage Axum. The physical remains of Mage have been reduced to dust. They will forever remain buried here, but *my* life goes on. I know of nothing more profound than contemplating where life comes from or what happens after death. All I know is that I have been reawakened. I have been given another chance at life, and I will do whatever it takes to make the most of it. Your father was right. I will honor the dead by living this life to the fullest. If I were a stronger man, I would have told you long ago. But I was afraid of what would happen to the life I had built as James Karl. The thought of losing you terrified me. I love you so much. Please forgive me."

Betsie let go of his hand. She turned to gaze at the sea of marble white crosses in front of them.

After a few moments, she turned back to face him.

She cradled his face with her hands. "My darling James. It is not the man on the outside that I love so much. It is the man on the inside. There is not a single word you said today that will ever change that. It actually helps explain some things I've noticed over the years...your relationship with the Karls and your familiarity with Texas. Your secret is safe with me. I will love you in this life and in the next. I will love you forever."

He wept as the weight of guilt lifted off his shoulders and immense relief washed over him. He had shared the truth with the person he loved the most. She had accepted him for who he was. She was the most wonderful person in the world.

# CHAPTER EIGHTY-SEVEN

JAMES TOSSED THEIR luggage into their convertible Mercedes-Benz 220 rental, and headed south to Italy. Neither of them had been to Rome, but he regaled Betsie with Father Sidney's fond recollections of life in Rome.

They arrived at night and checked into a quaint hotel with a balcony room that overlooked the Campo de' Fiori. They sat at a table on the perimeter of the Campo, nursing glasses of chianti and watching the tourists stroll by. A procession of street performers sang, danced, played instruments, and accepted donations from the café patrons.

"Bravo!" Betsie clapped as James gave a pocket full of lire to the performers.

James woke at sunrise. Careful not to wake Betsie, he tiptoed onto the balcony. *It's as Father Sidney had described it,* he thought as he watched the farmers from Rome's outlying areas arrive with trucks full of produce, spices, flowers, and other wares. They hastily assembled broad folding tables, and customers—natives and tourists—soon arrived to shop.

James left Betsie to sleep as he walked the Campo and thought about his reunion with Father Sidney.

*It's been almost twenty years. What am I going to say? Will he even recognize me after all these years?*

He returned to the hotel an hour later with a bouquet of flowers.

"Oh, they're as beautiful as this city," Betsie said and smelled them.

"Father Sidney once told me that *fiori* is the Italian word for flowers."

"*Fiori*," she repeated slowly with an Italian accent. "I'll hurry and get ready so we can begin our search for Father Sidney."

They walked hand in hand on ancient cobblestone streets and through small alleys. After passing several pizzerias and gelato shops, James stopped at the edge of the alley. Betsie gasped when she saw what had stopped James in his tracks.

"It's unbelievable!" she said.

"Have you ever seen a fountain this exceptional in your life?" he asked.

"No, and I could never get tired of looking at this."

They walked down the Trevi Fountain center steps, and sat on the edge of the fountain, under one of the giant marble horses. They took in the sites of the bustling piazza until an amateur street-photographer approached them.

"A polaroid for the beautiful couple?"

James put his arm around Betsie and the two snugged closely as the photographer captured the moment.

"*Grazie*," James said and paid the merchant. He then gestured to a small café at the edge of the alley. "Betsie, how about we start our search there? Father Sidney told me it was near the Trevi Fountain and that his friend was Vincenzo."

They entered the first cafe and greeted the barista.

"*Buon giorno*," James said.

"*Buon giorno*," the barista replied.

"We are looking for a man named Vincenzo, who is friends with a priest."

The lady giggled. "*Signore*, this is Italy. Everyone is named Vincenzo, or Luigi, or Angelo. And everyone is friends with at least three priests."

James started laughing. He thanked the barista, and then looked at Betsie. "This is going to be much harder than I had imagined."

They walked back outside, where James took a deep breath and slowly exhaled.

"We'll find him," Betsie asserted. "I don't know if it's all the coffee and pastries, but it is so magical here. I've never been to a place that is as marvelous in person as it is in books and movies. It's so romantic. Before we continue to look for Father Sidney, let's throw a coin in the fountain for good luck."

James reached into his pocket and retrieved a shiny Italian coin. He was about to toss it into the fountain when she quickly stopped him.

"Not like that! You have to use your right hand and throw it over your left shoulder. Like in the movie."

"If you insist," he smiled.

"We came all this way. We gotta do it right."

"I'll be wishing for luck," he said.

"Don't tell me! It's supposed to be a secret."

"Well, we need luck. I've seen hundreds of priests and nuns filing back and forth through the alleys on their way to the Vatican."

Four hours had passed as they opened the door to yet another café near the Piazza di Trevi. Betsie pulled out her phrase book.

*"Due cappuccinos per favore,"* she asked the Italian lady behind the counter.

"No," the barista replied.

"No?" Betsie asked surprised.

"No *cappuccini* after eleven," the barista asserted. "The milk is not good for digestive," she said as she circled her stomach.

Betsie looked at James.

"Let's not get too fancy then," he said. "We'll have two coffees, please."

*"Due espressi,"* the barista suggested. "Much better choice." She brewed the espresso into two tiny, white ceramic mugs that looked like they were for a toddler. She placed the miniature mugs in front of James and Betsie.

James's finger wouldn't fit into the looped handle. He used his thumb and index like tweezers and gripped the mug. He took a sip.

"How is it?" Betsie asked.

"It looks like motor oil, and I think I know why. It'll kick-start your engine."

Betsie poured some sugar in hers to sweeten it.

After a few more sips, James said, "Father Sidney once told me that espresso was one of God's many gifts. Personally, I'll stick to American coffee."

James gazed around the café while they took a much-needed pause in their search for Father Sidney. Gelato and pastries filled a large glass display. Bottles of fancy sodas and carbonated San Pellegrino adorned the colorful bar shelves behind the barista. Framed black and white photos adorned the walls. James almost fell to the floor when he saw one in particular.

"There! Betsie, look at that picture. It's Father Sidney!"

Betsie and James rushed to the wall and stood in front of the picture.

"That is my father," the barista said.

"Your father?" James asked. "He's a priest."

"Not the *padre*. The man next to him is Vincenzo. He owns this café."

"Who's the priest?"

"My godfather, Sidney."

"Where are they?"

"Sidney has been sick," she answered. "He is with my father at the apartment."

"Please, can you call Vincenzo? Father Sidney and I are friends. My wife and I came all the way from America to see him."

"I understand, but we have no phone."

She yelled something in Italian at a teenager who was stocking items in the back room. The boy yelled back in Italian. James thought they were arguing but he had a smile on his face the whole time. He straddled a scooter and sped off.

"Don't worry," the barista told James. "Enzo will go and come back."

James and Betsie nibbled on a pastry while they waited impatiently for the news. About thirty minutes later, Enzo screeched to a halt outside the café and a grey-haired man with a purple sweater and black slacks swung his leg and hopped off the back of the scooter.

*"Buon giorno,"* the man with glasses said. "My name is Vincenzo."

"It's a pleasure to finally meet you," James said. "I feel like I know you. I knew Father Sidney eighteen years ago, and he spoke often of you and your café."

Vincenzo smiled. "You must be the American soldier."

"One of many."

"Yes, he spoke of many of the soldiers he cared for, but I believe you are the one he speaks of every day"

"It's so important for us to see Father Sidney."

"He is restricted to bed rest, but if you are who I think you are, Father Sidney will be overjoyed to see you. Please, I insist you both come to my apartment."

## CHAPTER EIGHTY-EIGHT

"*P*ADRE," VINCENZO ANNOUNCED as they entered the tidy apartment. "*Alcuni amici americani sono qui per vederti.* Some American friends are here to see you."

Vincenzo escorted them to a bedroom, where Father Sidney rested in a twin bed with a simple wooden headboard and footboard. A crucifix hung on the wall, over the bed.

Father Sidney's poor health shocked James. He turned to Betsie and whispered in her ear. "I would have never recognized him," he said sadly. "The man I remember was vibrant and full of energy. This man is pale and exhausted."

Father Sidney had a blanket pulled up to his chest. His eyes twinkled as a smile formed on his colorless lips as he recognized the man at the foot of his bed. "James Karl," he said under his breath.

"You remember me," James said as he fought back tears and approached the priest.

"I have been thinking about you every day since you left the hospital, my son."

"I've never stopped thinking about you either, Father Sidney. You're the reason I'm alive."

The priest shook his head. "No. God is the reason you're alive."

Vincenzo made the sign of the cross and bowed his head.

"Or maybe, possibly this beautiful woman is the reason you're still here," he said with a smile.

"Oh, I'm sorry. Let me introduce you. This is Betsie, the love of my life. We've been married for thirteen years."

"It's a pleasure to meet you, Father. James has told me so much about you, and also about your stories of Rome. We wanted to come and see everything ourselves."

"How was your journey here?"

"Who would have ever thought an American veteran would rent a German automobile? But I did, and it was a thrill to put the top down and race here to see you!"

Father Sidney smiled. "Don't drive faster than your guardian angel can fly. The Good Lord knows you need a lot of angels if you are going to drive in Italy."

They all laughed.

"You're right," Betsie said. "The driving here is like nowhere else. We started our trip in Belgium. We visited an old war buddy of James's at Ardennes American cemetery."

"War buddy indeed," Father Sidney replied. He motioned James to lean in closer. His frail arms pulled James's head mere inches from his, and whispered in his ear. "My dear Mage. Why do you seek the living among the dead?" His eyes twinkled like he had known about the unique situation the whole time.

James shot back, almost against the wall.

"James," he now said louder so Betsie could hear him. "Your recovery was one of the greatest miracles in my lifetime. I am so thankful God gave you a second chance at life." His eyes glistened with tears. "Please tell me all about what you and Betsie have been doing?"

James and Betsie stood at his bedside and told stories of their adventures.

"I've always wanted to see Alaska," he said. "I cannot imagine a place where the sun never leaves the sky."

His eyelids fluttered and then closed.

"Is he okay?" James asked.

"He's fine," Vincenzo said. "Father Sidney falls asleep many times during the day. We should expect him to sleep for several hours."

James put his hand on top of the priest's and gently squeezed. He bent over and softly kissed Father Sidney's forehead.

"Sweet dreams, my friend," he whispered. "Even if you won't remember them."

# CHAPTER EIGHTY-NINE

NBC EXECUTIVES SUMMONED James and Betsie to New York as soon as they returned from their European trip.

"Despite the government intelligence about Dallas residents vehemently opposed to President Kennedy and his policies, his staff appears ready to continue with plans to have the president make several appearances in Houston, San Antonio, Fort Worth, and Dallas," the senior-level executive said. "Both of you know Texas better than anyone else on our team, and you always do excellent work. That's why we want you two covering this important event."

"And because the people love her," James complimented Betsie.

"And yes, because the people love her," the executive agreed.

"You've named four cities and the president's day is scheduled to the minute," James mentioned. "Exactly which part of that schedule do you want us to cover?"

"The president will be in Dallas on the twenty-second. We want you there on the twenty-first. You and Betsie will be our eyes and ears. Get video footage of people talking about their thoughts on the president visiting, what fashion Jackie's wearing, and cover the motorcade as it snakes downtown. The White House publicized it will be an open-air limousine occupied by President Kennedy, First Lady Jackie, and the Texas governor."

Betsie looked at James and grinned. "We'll be there. What about Joey—our camera operator?" she asked, still excited how just one year prior a Japanese company introduced a practical hand-held TV camera that was less cumbersome and heavy than the previous models.

"Big Joe will be there too, but since we want maximum coverage for this event, you'll each have your own camera operator that day."

"That's interesting," James noted. "We've always worked as a team, though."

"I know, but this time is different."

"Why is this time so different that you want me to have my own camera operator?" James asked.

"This is such an important election that all the networks will be out there competing with us for the best coverage. We're sending two reporters," he pointed to James and Betsie, "so we'll want two different stories. You'll have to split up this one time."

"You wouldn't separate us, would you?" James said. "We're like Bogie and Bacall."

The executive chuckled. "It's only one day, love birds. You'll survive."

## CHAPTER NINETY

*DALLAS, TEXAS*
*NOVEMBER 21, 1963*

JAMES AND BETSIE checked into the Omni Hotel the day before the president's arrival. They conducted a walk-through of the anticipated parade route. They scouted the best vantage points to get live reactions from the crowds that would be lining the streets. Dealey Plaza would be the epicenter of activity.

"My focus," Betsie told James, "will be to create a story about everyday Americans wanting to come out and see their president in person. I guess everything a president does is interpreted as a political event, but he's in Texas only because Lyndon insisted. Beyond all the politics, most women will only wanna see what Jackie is wearing."

"The leader of the free world comes to town and most of our viewers want to see what Jackie is wearing?" James asked.

"Yep," she replied. "I have spies out there who happen to know a lot about fashion. They promise to contact our producer when the entourage leaves in the motorcade. They'll tell him what Jackie is wearing, so he can tell me whose designer name is on it. Then I can tell everybody else."

James nodded. "I think we've done more than enough preparation today. Let's head over to the Fort Worth Press Club to enjoy cocktails with our peers."

"No more than two, though," she warned. "We have an important day tomorrow. Our most important by far."

The place teemed with more patrons than normal because of President Kennedy's visit. Betsie and James socialized with some colleagues at the bar and met a few Secret Service agents.

"We've flown in from Houston," one special agent said. "We need a bit of liquid nourishment at this late hour."

"I know how difficult our schedules are trying to cover this campaign," Betsie said, "I don't know how you guys do it. And Kennedy is much more active than Eisenhower ever was."

"We're used to living out of a suitcase. It's part of the job," the agent replied, "and campaign years only come around once every four years, thankfully."

"What's Jackie like?" Betsie asked with a smile.

"Mrs. Kennedy is very pleasant. She's very kind to her agents."

"Is it true about the football? Does the president have the nuclear codes in a briefcase by him at all times?"

The athletic agent cracked a smile. "I can't discuss national security issues—"

"Or you'd have to kill me, right?" she said. "I've been told that before."

The agent chuckled. "Let's just say…the Cuban Missile Crisis reminded us why we must always be prepared to present the president with all options."

"I'm thankful that blew over peacefully," Betsie said.

"You and me both," the agent replied.

James spotted Champ Albright at a back table with a group of other journalists.

"It was great talking with you," she said. "Thank you for your service and for keeping our leaders safe."

"Happy to do it," he said and bid them farewell with a raised glass.

Champ stopped his story as soon as he saw the lovely couple walking toward him.

"I was hoping to see you guys here. Come join us. I was telling my favorite joke."

"Please don't stop on our account," James said. "We'd love to hear it."

"So, a journalist assigned to the Jerusalem bureau rents an apartment overlooking the Wailing Wall. Every day when he looks out, he sees an old Jewish man praying. So the journalist goes down and introduces himself, and asks why the man goes to the Wailing Wall each day."

"I have come here to pray every day for twenty-five years, the old Jewish man says. In the morning, I pray for world peace and then I go home and enjoy a cup of tea. I then come back and pray for the eradication of illness and disease from the world."

"The journalist is amazed, and asks, 'How does it make you feel to come here every day for twenty-five years and pray for these things?'"

"The old man says, 'Like I'm talking to a wall.'"

They all laughed at the punch line, and James offered a toast.

"It's an imperfect world, but I for one am happy to be here with you fine ladies and gents. May the wings of friendship never lose a feather. Cheers!"

Champ took a sip of his soda water as a man approached the group.

Uninvited, he sat down at their table.

An uneasy expression washed over Betsie's face.

"Who are you?" James asked.

"Henry used to be my assistant," she said. "Before he got hired as a reporter in Dallas. His departure from the *Herald* actually created the vacancy for me to hire you in 1949."

"I should thank the guy then," James quipped.

"Assistant?" Henry repeated sarcastically. "Well, that was almost fourteen years ago. I've since moved on from Palestine and the small-town *Herald*. I've gotta say though, that this was quite the *Herald* reunion. Too bad we missed Tom Bannon. I heard he was drinking in here for several hours."

Champ experienced a sudden bout of indigestion.

"Tom Bannon? Nobody has seen him since he got out of jail in Alaska."

"I didn't say I saw him," Henry deflected. "I said I *heard* he was here enjoying a few drinks. That giant is hard to miss."

"Tom Bannon in Dallas the night before the president's visit is bad news," Champ said.

"No," James replied. "Tom Bannon anywhere near the vicinity of Betsie and me is bad news. Really bad news."

# CHAPTER NINETY-ONE

*NOVEMBER 22, 1963*

"RISE AND SHINE," Betsie said cheerfully. "The president's visiting us today." She drew the curtains and the daylight poured into the room.

He shut his eyes and groaned. "Close it! My head's pounding...like someone's hitting it with a hammer. It came out of nowhere."

"I'll go downstairs and get you some coffee and an aspirin." She poured him a glass of water before she left and flipped on the television.

"Despite the light rain," the television anchor said, "President Kennedy addressed a crowd of supporters outside his Fort Worth hotel."

James tossed on a pair of sunglasses and sat up in bed to watch the television.

"There are no faint hearts in Fort Worth," the president began, "and I appreciate your being here this morning. Mrs. Kennedy is organizing herself. It takes longer, but, of course, she looks better than we do when she does it."

The screen returned to the lone anchor in a suit and tie, sitting behind a desk.

"After breakfast with members of the Chamber of Commerce, the president's entourage will depart Carswell Air Force Base for Love Field in Dallas. The parade will start along its route through Dallas at 11:30 this morning."

Betsie returned to their room with coffee and two aspirin.

"Thank you, sweetheart," he said and swallowed the medicine and took a sip of his coffee.

"We have to meet our cameramen at the restaurant downstairs in thirty minutes," she said.

"I know." He took two more sips of his coffee and got out of bed. "I need to take a shower first."

"Make it quick, though," she said. "I'll lay out your suit and see you downstairs."

Shortly thereafter James walked downstairs and joined Betsie and their camera crew at the hotel restaurant.

"Are you okay James?" their usual cameraman asked. "Betsie told us you have a headache."

"Good morning Big Joe," he replied. "Yeah, I'll survive. Of all days to get a headache, right?"

"I'm sorry to hear that. I'm such a baby when it comes to headaches. There's no way I could even be doing what you're doing. I'd have to be in absolute darkness."

"It's not a migraine…just a real pain in the rear. That's why I don't want to be running around out there. Let's find a spot to set up and stay there."

"Nothing personal," Big Joe said, "but I'm with Betsie today."

James cracked a smile. "Of course. Who do I have today?" He looked at the other man sitting at the table. "You?"

"Yes sir. I'll be your cameraman today. My name is Doug."

James shook his hand. "Nice to meet you. I'm thinking about us covering the overpass. We'll be able to see the crowds, the motorcade as it comes straight to us, and we can interview a few folks near us."

"That sounds perfect," he said and turned to Big Joe. "Where are you going today?"

"I'm with her," he said and nodded to Betsie. "So there's no telling."

"The president is passing through and won't be here for long," Betsie said. "So, we're going to talk to as many people as possible and then find the best place to cover the motorcade."

James looked at Big Joe. The overweight cameraman was already perspiring. "The rain's gone away, but it's still very humid. Make sure to drink plenty of water. She's going to make you earn your pay and then some. She won't give you any breaks."

"Hey!" she fired back. "We can all take a break when this is over. And if I can do this in heels, you fellas should be able to keep up with me."

They laughed.

She turned to her cameraman. "Joey, our plan is to capture the much better footage for NBC to broadcast tonight than whatever it is *they* get." She pointed to James and his cameraman.

"Good luck," James said sarcastically.

"When you're good, you don't need luck," she said and kissed him. "I'll see you when I see you."

"Hey, you stole my line," he said.

"Didn't know it was trademarked. Sue me," she said and winked.

## CHAPTER NINETY-TWO

J AMES AND HIS cameraman began their hike toward
the overpass. They saw a parade spectator holding a Bell
and Howell home-movie camera.

"My job's already hard enough," James told the man who
appeared to be in his late fifties. "You aren't trying to make my
position obsolete are you?" he joked, feeling better since his
headache had started to fade.

"I almost didn't bring it because of the rain," the man
said. "But my assistant," he turned to the lady behind him
who was about half his age, "insisted I bring it."

James smiled. "My cameraman Doug and I are going to
be located on that overpass there. Please don't outshine us
today. NBC might fire us and hire you."

The man and woman smiled.

"Don't worry sir," the assistant said. "Mr. Zapruder is not
a professional like you gentlemen. This is to show the family
who wanted terribly to be here today, but couldn't make it."

James nodded and smiled. "Have a great day folks. Hope
you enjoy this special occasion."

Betsie and her cameraman positioned themselves along
Elm Street, not far from the Texas School Book Depository.

The street crowds grew greater in size than police officials had predicted.

"We've shot a lot of film," Big Joe told Betsie. "I'm not sure how much we have left, and I only have one extra battery."

"Then let's take what we've got," she said, having to shout to be heard, "and we'll try to find a better vantage point."

Mayhem erupted when they crossed Elm Street.

"That means the presidential motorcade is nearby," she shouted. "There's too many people down here. Look! Up there." She pointed toward the top floors of the seven-story Texas School Book Depository. "Bird's-eye view," she hollered. "And the windows are open. Let's go up there for the best view."

"Dang it!" Big Joe balked. "I've been lugging this equipment all morning. I barely have the strength left to haul it up a stairwell."

"Come on Joey! Let's go," she demanded. "That's where the better footage is. Hurry up. The president is just around the corner."

She and her cameraman ran into the redbrick building. They took the stairs and climbed step after step.

"I can't go anymore!" Big Joe exclaimed through labored breaths. "This is the fifth floor. It's high enough."

"Okay," she sighed. She looked down the long stretch of closed doors in the hallway. She tried the first three doors, but they were locked. "Dang it! We're going to miss the president!" The stress in her voice could be heard. "Let's go up one more flight!"

She dashed up the stairs to the sixth floor. The open-bay room was filthy. "Dang it! There's nobody up here. It's just a warehouse with boxes stacked everywhere. Wait, there's gotta be a window over there. I can see light and hear the people cheering outside."

She navigated through the labyrinth of cardboard boxes and found a gap at the end. She rounded the box and froze.

"Oh my God! What the hell are you doing?"

## CHAPTER NINETY-THREE

"T URNED OUT TO be a gorgeous day," James commented to his cameraman. "Make sure you're rolling and get some video of the president waving at us up here."

POP!

"Whoa," the cameraman said. "Was that a backfire from one of the police motorcycles?"

"It's a firecracker," a bystander noted and returned to waving and cheering at Mr. and Mrs. Kennedy.

POP!

"No! Oh my God. The president has been shot!" James exclaimed as the commander-in-chief clutched his throat and slumped forward in the backseat of the limousine. Everything seemed to happen in slow motion.

POP!

James watched in horror as the back of the president's head exploded. Thousands in the crowds at Dealey Plaza shrieked when they saw the First Lady crawl in her pink dress onto the trunk of the convertible limousine. A Secret Service agent jumped onto the back and used his body to shield the president and Mrs. Kennedy. The Lincoln Continental's engine roared as the driver floored the accelerator to escape the deadly ambush.

Witnesses scrambled to see what was going on and legions of pedestrians scattered in every direction. Some people dropped to the grass to protect themselves from gunfire while others stood and wept. The police seemed to have no idea where the shots originated. James saw several people pointing toward the grassy knoll while others pointed up at the book depository.

Chaos reigned.

"I gotta find Betsie!" James shouted at seeing the mayhem. He scanned the crowds below but couldn't see her or her cameraman. He sprinted toward Dealey Plaza and saw a familiar face in the crowd.

He grabbed Champ by both shoulders and yelled over the din.

"Where's Betsie?"

"I don't know! I last saw her heading toward the depository," he replied and pointed to the redbrick building.

James turned and saw a squad of police officers running into the seven-story building. He bolted in that direction but was stopped when two uniformed officers forcefully escorted Betsie's cameraman outside.

"James," the cameraman said with tears in his eyes.

"Big Joe! Where's Betsie?" James asked.

"They're taking me to the police station. They want to interview me and get my film."

"Where's Betsie?" he repeated.

"She thought it would enhance our reporting," Big Joe said, appearing to be in shock. "I couldn't muster the energy to climb all the stairs with all this damn equipment! I'm so sorry, James." His voice cracked. "I'm so sorry. Betsie was shot."

James pushed through the doorway and into the building when several police officers and Secret Service agents with shotguns pinned him against a wall.

"Nobody's allowed in," one of the agents barked.

"That's my wife in there!" he shouted and continued trying to break free.

"It's a crime scene now," the agent announced.

His knees buckled and he slid down the wall until he collapsed onto the floor.

"BETSIE!" He buried his face into his hands and sobbed uncontrollably.

# CHAPTER NINETY-FOUR

SNOW FLURRIES BLEW gently in the wind, but James didn't feel the cold as he stood under a tent at St. Joseph's Cemetery. Betsie's funeral had concluded half an hour earlier, but he remained behind. He had left her side in Dallas, and he wouldn't do it here. He stared at a bouquet of beautiful purple and gold flowers resting atop her wooden casket.

"She always loved Texas bluebonnets," he told Champ. "But it's not the season. So, I figured she'd like petunias and marigold. I hope she's happy with my choice."

"Betsie would be happy with whatever you chose," Champ replied and paused for a moment. "I want you to know something before I go back to Dallas."

James listened to Champ, but kept his eyes on Betsie's casket.

"Everyone in the world is talking about how the president was assassinated," Champ continued. "And while that is tragic, there are lesser known stories of sorrow that have been drowned out by the shock and horror of seeing the American president murdered as his motorcade drove through downtown Dallas. Betsie, the Texas governor, and the Dallas police officer have become secondary stories. I need you to know that I admired Betsie. I acted like a pompous jerk the first time we met up in Alaska, but she was always kind.

"The press is blaming Lee Harvey Oswald, but there are a lot of people saying that the facts don't line up. If that's true, I promise you that I'll get to the bottom of it. If Oswald had help, or if it weren't him, I will make it my life's mission to find out the truth."

James nodded.

"Champ, I believe you will. Now if you don't mind, I'd like to be alone with my wife."

Champ shook James's hand and walked away.

James stepped closer to Betsie's casket. He thought of their visit to Ardennes Cemetery. *"I will love you in this life and in the next,"* she had told him. "I'll be waiting for you in the next lifetime," he whispered and kissed her casket.

"Pardon me, Mr. Karl."

James turned to see John Robert and Tucker Axum.

"It's been thirteen years," the old farmer said with his hat in his hand. "You probably don't remember me."

"Of course I do," James said. "I could never forget you."

"This is my oldest son, Tucker."

"It's a pleasure to finally meet you, Mr. Karl," Tucker said and extended his hand.

The emotion of Betsie's funeral and seeing his brother for the first time in almost twenty years proved more than James could bear. His legs wobbled and he staggered.

Still holding James's hand, Tucker pulled his brother closer and helped steady him.

"Thank you," James said. "It's been an emotional day for me."

"We understand," John Robert began. "I don't wanna keep you, but I just wanted you to know that I've kept track of you ever since you *landed* that plane in my field. Remember you gave me a copy of the *Herald*?"

James smiled at the memory. "Yessir, I do."

"You'll be happy to know I'm still a subscriber," he proudly said. "Anyway, I just came over to tell you I sure am sorry for your loss. We watched Ms. Betsie on the television about every night and she seemed like a wonderful lady."

"That she was," James said with a smile. "That she was."

"Yes," Tucker added. "She was Palestine's voice of reason. We could always count on her to hold the politicians and county officials accountable. Even when she left and went to Dallas she never forgot about Palestine. No matter how high she seemed to climb, she was always one of us."

"James, I imagine many people at the funeral today probably told you, 'I know how you feel.' They mean well, but most of them have no idea," John Robert offered. "I do. I've also lost someone who meant the world to me."

He put his calloused hand on James's shoulder.

"I reckon this might seem odd to you, but you feel like family. *Son*, I want you to know that if you need anything,

anything at all, please reach out to us. The Axums are your family and we will always be here for you."

James could not control his emotions and he began to cry. "No sir. Doesn't seem odd at all. You are family."

# CHAPTER NINETY-FIVE

*LAFAYETTE, LOUISIANA*
*JULY 4, 2001*

THE TABLE UMBRELLA shielded James from the sun as he sat at the airport's outside patio café. He sipped from a tall glass of sweet tea and perused the day's edition of *The Daily Advertiser*, which had been left on the wrought-iron table. He took frequent breaks from reading and gazed at the tarmac. He smiled as he watched private airplanes and passenger jets arrive and depart the municipal airport.

*It's a gorgeous day to be flying,* he thought. *Florida's white-sand beaches are only two hours away.*

A young man with short blond hair, clutching an aviation headset in one hand, walked across the ramp toward the café. He used the crook of his elbow to wipe sweat off his forehead and he grinned from ear to ear as though he'd just won the lottery.

"Son," James said, feeling emboldened to make an unsolicited observation the way old-timers like him feel they're entitled to do. "Was that you who greased that landing in that pretty blue and white Cessna?"

The young man smiled wider. "Yes sir. Thank you for noticing."

"I had an instructor a long time ago who would have said: 'Amigo, you landed like a duck with hemorrhoids.'"

They shared a laugh.

"I can't tell you how pleasurable it is to see such a wonderful look on a young man's face on our nation's birthday."

"Nothing could erase this smile, sir. I just earned my pilot's license, and I can't think of a better day to have done so than on July fourth."

"Well, well," James marveled and reached out to firmly shake the fellow with short blond hair. "You're to be heartily congratulated! That's quite an accomplishment."

"Thank you sir. I can't wait to take my friends flying. I take it you're also a pilot."

"You better believe it."

"What do you fly?"

James leaned back in his chair and smiled.

"I've flown all kinds of planes over the last fifty-one years, but now I stick to the simpler ones. They're a bit slower than I prefer, but now that I'm retired I've got nowhere to rush off to."

"That's awesome that you're still flying. I hope to still be flying when I'm your age."

"I didn't say I'm ancient. I said I was retired," James cracked.

The young man's face reddened. "I'm sorry sir. I didn't mean to off—"

"Easy partner, I'm messin' with you." James smiled. "I'm sure you will be. Flying keeps you young. I was about to order some food. Have a seat. It would be my pleasure to treat the new licensed pilot."

The young pilot smiled. "I'm paying my way through college and flight training. So, I've learned to never say 'no' to a free meal. And it would be *my* pleasure to sit with you and talk about flying."

James stood out of courtesy.

"I like your boots," the young pilot said.

"Thank you. Lyndon Johnson gave these to me."

"As in the president?"

"He was just a senator then," James chuckled.

The two took their seats.

"By the way, my name is Tucker Axum."

James gulped his tea and started coughing.

"Are you okay, sir?"

James nodded and raised his hand. He coughed a few more times to clear his throat.

"I'm fine. The old ticker can't take too many surprises anymore. You said Tucker Axum?"

"Yes sir. Tucker Axum the Third."

"That's not a name a person could easily forget. I once knew a Tucker Axum. As a matter of fact, he had a brother named Mage. They lived in an East Texas town called Palestine."

"They were my kin, but unfortunately I never had the opportunity to meet either one. My great grandfather, Pa Tuck…"

James smiled at the thought of his brother being a grandfather and having some little ones calling him Pa Tuck.

"...died before I was born, and my great grandmother told me that her brother-in-law, Mage, was killed in Germany during World War Two. She remembered him well, though. She said he liked music and loved to make people laugh. She has a picture of him at her house in Palestine. A military photographer took it and sent it to the family. Mage was hunched under a tent—"

"To stay dry from the rain," James interjected.

Tucker tilted his head as a look of surprise washed over him. "How did you know that?" he asked with a raised eyebrow.

James gazed into the cloudless blue sky as he thought back to that day in October 1944.

"It rained cats and dogs over there, but writing home was important. It kept us connected to our loved ones and reminded us why it was so important to sacrifice and win the war. So, Mage did exactly what we all did and used the tent to stay dry."

Tucker nodded. "We think it was the last picture of him, and his last letter for that matter. My great-grandmother treasures both the picture and his letter."

James fought to hold back the tears. He dabbed at his eyes with a napkin.

"Pardon me. That tea went down the wrong pipe and it's making my eyes water."

"I hate when that happens. I don't believe I caught your name."

"James. James Karl," he answered and grabbed the single-page laminated menu. "What do you recommend?"

"Since you're in the heart of Cajun country, I recommend the fried shrimp po'boy on a baguette."

"Mmm, that does sound delicious, but I'm not sure my cardiologist would approve."

Tucker gave him an affable smile. "You only live once."

James chuckled. "If you say so."

An elegant lady wearing a periwinkle scarf approached their table. James stood to greet her.

"Hi sweetheart." He kissed her on the cheek before turning to Tucker. "This is my lovely wife, Amelia."

Tucker stood and said, "Pleasure to meet you, ma'am."

She smiled. "Is he boring you with a bunch of our old flying stories?"

"Not at all. Your husband is very interesting. Apparently, he knew one of my kin."

"It wouldn't surprise me. James knows a lot of people."

"Sweetheart, this here is Mr. Tucker Axum the Third."

"Oh my," she said. "It is a small world after all."

"You knew my family, too?" Tucker asked.

"Not as well as James, but yes."

"I invited Mr. Tucker to join us for lunch. Is that okay with you, honey?"

"Of course," she answered and turned to Tucker. "That's one of the benefits of owning our own plane. Our Piper doesn't leave without us. We can take all the time we need. After all, it's our anniversary."

"Happy Anniversary!" Tucker said. "How many years are you celebrating?"

James smiled as he reached over the table and squeezed her hand.

"Thirty-four, but it feels like fifty-one." He took a deep breath and slowly exhaled. "Tucker, I tell ya, fate sure is a funny thing. We had stopped in Lafayette to gas up and have some lunch before we continued our journey. But this is way too coincidental to cross your path like this. If you'll humor me, I've got one helluva story to tell you."

# AFTERWORD

THANK YOU FOR reading my novel. I'd love to hear your feedback. You can send me an email with your thoughts at tucker@tuckeraxum.com. If you enjoyed the book, I would be grateful if you left a review on Amazon. *Carpe diem!*

# ABOUT THE AUTHOR

TUCKER AXUM is a special agent for the U.S. Government, world traveler, and adventure pilot. He co-authored the international thriller *Cajun Justice* with best-selling author James Patterson.

For more information,
please visit www.tuckeraxum.com.

Made in the USA
Coppell, TX
31 July 2020